Death in a White Coat

Larry Kirshbaum

First edition May, 2024

For Barbara,

Over nearly sixty years, you have made almost every day an adventure and a joy. As the matriarch of our family, you have risen to every occasion and provided the love and direction for all of us.

Table of Contents

The Major Characters in This Novel i

Prologue: Hillside Hospital, Manhattan, Friday, 4:30 a.m. iii

Early Friday, Day One, 4:30 a.m. 1

1. Barney Kazinski 1

2. Barney Kazinski 6

3. Dr. Ashley Dillon 16

4. Barney Kazinski 19

5. Barney Kazinski 27

Flashback: 90 Days Earlier 35

6. Dr. Ashley Dillon 35

7. Dr. Wendy Jamison 42

8. Ms. Rosemarie Li 44

9. Prince Geoffrey 46

10. Barney Kazinski 49

Saturday, Day Two 53

11. Barney Kazinski & Dr. Alfred Post 53

12. Barney Kazinski 59

13. Dr. Wendy Jamison 66

14. Barney Kazinski 70

15. Barney Kazinski 73

Sunday, Day Three 85

16. Barney Kazinski 85

17. Barney Kazinski 92

18. Ross Parker 104

19. Barney Kazinski 107

20. Barney Kazinski 111

21. Barney Kazinski 117

Flashback: 60 Days Ago 122

22. Dr. Ashley Dillon 122

23. Dr. Ashley Dillon 132

24. Dr. Wendy Jamison 138

25. Ralph Gruber 140

Monday, Day Four 142

26. Barney Kazinski 142

27. Dr. Ashley Dillon 150

28. Barney Kazinski 152

29. Rosemarie Li 165

Flashback: 12 Days Before Death 167

30. Dr. Ashley Dillon 167

ay, Day Five 176

rney Kazinski 176

y Kazinski 182

Kazinski 191

34. Rosemarie Li ... 197
Wednesday, Day Six ... 199
35. Barney Kazinski ... 199
36. Barney Kazinski ... 208
Thursday, Day Seven ... 216
37. Barney Kazinski ... 216
38. Barney Kazinski ... 222
Flashback: Weekend before Death ... 225
39. Dr. Ashley Dillon ... 225
40. Dr. Wendy Jamison ... 230
41. Prince Jeff (Geoffrey) Laird ... 233
42. Dr. Ashley Dillon ... 235
43. Dr. Ashley Dillon ... 240
Friday, Eighth Day ... 245
44. Barney Kazinski ... 245
45. Barney Kazinski ... 251
46. Barney Kazinski ... 260
47. Barney Kazinski ... 267
48. Dr. Ashley Dillon ... 274
49. Barney ... 278
Saturday, Day Nine ... 281
50. Barney Kazinski ... 281
51. Barney Kazinski ... 289

Sunday, the Tenth Day 300
52. Dr. Ashley Dillon 300
Monday, the Eleventh Day 305
53. Barney Kazinski 305
54. Dr. Ashley Dillon 314
A few months later 318
55. Rebecca (Becky) Muller 318
The Final Piece 324
56. Barney Kazinski & Becky Muller 324
Conclusion 327
57. Barney Kazinski 327
Barney Kazinski: Epilogue 329
Acknowledgements 331
About the Author 339

The Major Characters in This Novel

Inside Hillside Hospital

Sherman or Sandy Wainwright – A wealthy golden-boy who was destined to be a superstar doctor.

Dr. Ashley (Dillon) – Known by her first name, she's an alluring resident physician in her first year at the Hillside Hospital.

Dr. Alfred Post/Jennette Park/Peter McClain – The NYC Medical Examiner and his top aides who are seeking truth from a corpse.

Rosemarie Li – Sandy's current lover who grew up on a dairy farm in Iowa.

Dr. Wendy Jamison – A pediatrician and close friend of Dr. Ashley

Nurse Geoffrey Laird – Known as Prince Jeff or simply "The Prince," he's a British import from Liverpool.

Dr. Maura Davis – The head of surgery at Hillside.

Ross Parker – One of Sandy's roommates

Ralph Gruber – A med student who keeps turning up in annoying ways.

Inside New York Police Department

Detective Barney Kazinski – A NYPD veteran of 27 years takes on a crucial case where a "person of interest" becomes too personal.

Detective Charles Oliver Gunderson – Known as Gundy, he is the 4th generation to wear the shield, and an expert in cracking the knottiest cases.

Detective Becky Muller – A lawyer by training, she has joined the NYPD because she likes the nitty-gritty of law enforcement.

Captain La-Tanya Lawson – The head of the NYPD Special Detectives Bureau, known as The Command, she is pressured to get results.

Miss Shannon – An outsider who runs a favorite salon for older women and their young consorts, a place of interest always for the cops.

Prologue: Hillside Hospital, Manhattan, Friday, 4:30 a.m.

Sirens blared as police officers draped yellow crime scene tape around the street in their harried choreography of crowd control. From a staging area in the lobby of the medical student dorm, two paramedics from the Medical Examiner's transport team were bearing an HRP, a human remains pouch, on a stretcher. The body was being conveyed to the M.E.'s mortuary downtown.

The bulging tarp appeared to contain a large, bulky body, most likely a male. The paramedics were struggling to move the stretcher through the police maze into their ambulance. The commotion had escalated as police cars provided a frenzied sound and light backdrop of squawking sirens and revolving turret lights.

The resident on the night shift, Dr. Ashley Dillon, pushed through a wind-resistant side door of the E.R. and into the street. In stained, surgical scrubs and a billowing white lab coat, her hair bunched like a mop, she was an unwelcome intruder to the phalanx of cops securing the perimeter.

Half in a daze, she confronted the frenetic scene that she had witnessed before as the overnight physician on duty. The nighttime death scenario in the hospital occurred as regularly as the moon. Yet even in her exhausted state, Dr. Ashley, as she liked to be known, could sense that this time, the elements were more personal and threatening than usual.

A death taking place in the student dorm was highly irregular. Her mind was whirling amidst the waves of neighborhood thrill-seekers piling into the street. If Ashley's instincts were correct, she knew the victim only too well. She feared her romantic fantasies might be crushed while her career was hanging in the balance.

Amidst the chaos, Dr. Ashley recognized a familiar face preparing to accompany the body. It was Jennette Park, the NYC Medical Examiner's primary Medico-Legal Death Investigator. As always, her tall, soothing presence and sleek M.E. jacket might have passed muster at the Met Museum's Costume Ball.

"What happened?" Ashley shouted above the tumult.

"We gotta tough one here," Jen yelled back, "a young male med student, possibly a suicide. This case is not going down lightly."

"A medical student? Are you sure?"

Jen Park gave a somber nod.

Suddenly, Ashley felt her blood pressure spiking into panic mode. As a first-year resident, she was very familiar with the clinical third-year med students. She had calmed their anxieties, fist-pumped their successes, and gently nurtured them along the path to becoming doctors. She prided herself on being rated one of the most capable and accessible supervisors monitoring the students' progress as they rotated through the surgical wing.

Now she dreaded confirmation of the student lying in that body bag.

She dashed toward the medics' stretcher like a last-minute savior who could crack open the man's chest and reignite the heartbeat.

"Tell me what happened here? Who's the victim?" Ashley was now verging on hysteria, abandoning any pretext of her usual, unruffled demeanor.

"I'm sorry, Ma'am," one of the body bearers said. "We have strict orders from the M.E.'s office to bring the deceased immediately downtown and prepare for autopsy as soon as possible. The young man is long gone."

"He can't be. I won't let him be gone. We'll bring him back." She flashed her badge to the transport team. In the swirling light, their innocent faces looked like high school grads coming from their senior prom.

"I'm Dr. Ashley Dillon, the resident on call here. Please let me see the body…"

"Sorry, Ma'am, the first responders already tried everything. Almost ninety minutes worth of CPR—defibs, compressions, shocks—the whole bit, and nothing. No pulse. He was dead, probably back to midnight or so. None of us got the call until shortly after midnight. He might well have been dead already."

"Why didn't someone get to him sooner? You lost the 'golden hour' when you could have saved him. This might have been a borderline case, warm and dead, yet still capable of resuscitation!"

Jen Park tried to intervene and calm Ashley's rattled state. Hearing the raised voices, several officers approached and formed a protective phalanx in front of the ambulance.

Jen was a tough, experienced investigator, and she was not thrilled to be tasked with this assignment. The death of a prominent medical student would be all over the NY Post and the Times. She didn't relish having to recall and note each dirty little detail of this night.

She had spent over two hours at the death scene inside the dorm, snapping photos and performing a standard checklist of on-site tasks. Among them were taking the rectal temperature to determine the time of death (between eleven and midnight), along with scraping and swabbing trace evidence while rolling the body for photo purposes from numerous angles. She had also managed to briefly interview the victim's roommates, who were the only available witnesses at this point.

In addition to eyeballing the body generally, part of Jen's protocol was to apply a portable ultraviolet light focusing on exogenous details. These included latent prints, rogue fluids, or DNA that might later provide a clue to who was with the deceased in the final hours.

Even a suicide might have enablers.

The NYPD's Crime Scene Unit was now fully activated. It would finish up collecting all the ambient data, ranging from vacuuming every mote of dust or toothbrushing every surface that might yield new details of the death. Given that many students would have access to the roommates' suite, Jen knew this would be a complicated investigation to sort out.

She was happy to stay in the background, leaving it to the Chief Medical Examiner to field the inquisition from the media that would come full force within several hours. Already, her cell phone was spitting out inquiries from the press, tracking rumors courtesy of social media. Jen wanted to get the ambulance moving before the TV and tabloid reporters arrived and further corrupted the scene.

Medical students expected to work until they dropped from fatigue, but they weren't supposed to drop dead in their dormitory. Jen knew this young man, Sandy Wainwright, was of particular interest since his parents had privileged connections to the city's medical and political hierarchy. Among other acts of civic generosity, they had donated the surgical wing less than 50 yards from where their son's body now rested. Jen was impatient to move this show along when she caught a glimpse of Ashley pacing around the ambulance as if she were preparing to throw herself under its wheels.

"Hey, Jen…" Ashley tried to control her emotions, now assuming the stoic posture of a detached observation. "Could I get one last look…I have a feeling he was one of my favorite little soldiers."

Jen reluctantly began to unzip the bag and confirmed Ashley's devastating hunch. She repressed a deep-throated retching sound while adjusting her mask to hide a thin flow of tears trickling down her face. She removed a glove and placed her hand on the decedent's cheek. He was ice cold and stone dead, the fatal state of CNR—Can Not Resuscitate. The early signs of rigor were already evident in the staccato light. Lividity, the thick pooling of post-mortem blood, had started to bruise his backside. The profusion of blood might indicate he was on a blood thinner. That would be unusual for such a young man in athletic condition.

Jen found herself a bit shaken. In the amplified light, even as the tattoos of death made their mark, Ashley could tell Sandy still resembled a muscular specimen. His athletic body was resisting the inevitable decay into a formless, fleshy mound. His wit, his humor, his intelligence—all had disappeared inside a brain whose neurons still fired aftershocks, running on empty.

The more conclusive flesh and bone work would come later. Ashley imagined the M. E., preparing his sternal saw at the autopsy, ready to tear through muscle and bone as methodically as a hobbyist building a back deck.

She could tell the M.E. a lot about that body, Ashley thought. What if she had been the last person to see him alive? Her practiced eye noted a puncture mark in his right thigh that might have been caused by the injection of drugs. She pointed the lesion out to Jen, who said simply, "Yes, I noted it, we'll review it at autopsy. Please don't touch any evidence."

Jennette completed zipping up the bag and waved at her associates, making final preparations for moving the body. "Very unfortunate, Ash, this guy's death is a loss. He was born with a big surgical ego, but his roommates said he was a very competent physician in training. With a name like Sandy Wainwright, he had a lot to live for. The parents are a force in this city. All he had to do was hang out his shingle and rake in the patients."

"No! No, it can't be. Not this one, anyone but him." Ashley wanted to scream into the fetid air while her free hand clenched into a fist, knuckle white. The transport team finished loading their cargo, including Jennette, and started threading their way through the police matrix of vehicles.

Ashley stood there, a forlorn figure in the middle of the street. The scrum of cops was still glaring and wary as if she were a mental ward patient on the loose. She made her way back to her office, numb and exhausted, overcome by a feeling of finality. Sandy now belonged to God and the Medical Examiner. Somehow, she would have to find a way to let him go.

Walking back upstairs, a burst of guilt flashed through her mind.

A few hours ago, I thought that I wanted to murder him, but I didn't mean it.

Or did I?

Early Friday, Day One, 4:30 a.m.

1. Barney Kazinski

Upper West Side of Manhattan

The cell phone flared to life and triggered the ringtone of Fleetwood Mac, recalling the stillness of lost happier days. I emerged slowly out of a deep sleep and groped for the phone. At age 53, with 27 years on the force, my body could never get used to these frequent emergencies. I had crawled up the ladder to detective first grade, and yet it still felt as if I was being treated like a rookie on the midnight shift.

I clicked off the alarm and focused on the acerbic voice of Captain Sam Harrad, a veteran officer who was covering the overnight wheel for the NYPD Chief of Detectives at One Police Plaza. As usual, there were no pleasantries. "The Chief would like you to get your butt moving on this case," he said, offering no further details.

"I know; the Chief appreciates my help," I groused. "Whatta, we got this time? Drugs, DUI, Domestic spat?

Someone prominent, no doubt, make sure to keep their name out of the papers."

There was silence on the other end as the captain waited for my rant to subside.

I kept complaining even though I knew it was like responding to a "no reply" email. "Can't the night shift handle this until morning?"

Captain Harrad perked up. "Afraid not, Detective. He's been pronounced D.O.A, we got a wealthy kid on our hands. It looks like a possible overdose or suicide, and the press will be smelling foul play."

"Is there an I.D.?"

"Oh yeah, this is a beauty. Sherman "Sandy" Wainwright III, whose parents built the damn wing where he was currently a med student on a surgery rotation."

I knew this must be a big deal; a V.I.P. donor always resonated with the Mayor and the NYPD brass. Where was the Chief of Detectives himself? Too busy to make crime scene calls. Oh, that's right, I had forgotten the memo. He was taking care of more important business on his honeymoon, officially breaking in his newly anointed third wife. He'd be reluctantly rushing home for this investigation.

"One last thing," Captain Harrad said, and I cringed at what might be coming next. "Your partner, Detective Gundy has the crime scene covered, so get dressed and head down to the M.E.'s mortuary. Young Mr. Wainwright will be happy to greet you there."

A little humor, maybe the captain had a pulse after all.

"Okay, got it, appreciate the call." We hung up. I needed to calm down for the benefit of the transcript being recorded at headquarters, thus protecting my overtime pay for this emergency. I gingerly pushed my expansive frame upward and outward from the bed, propelled by a tiny toot from the backside.

The front wasn't performing much better. "You're just a rusty old pipe," I muttered into the bathroom mirror above the toilet.

Ah, the private joys of living alone.

With almost unconscious speed, I was showered, dressed, and seated within less than 30 minutes at an all-night greasy spoon. I was accustomed to the post-midnight ambiance, where everyone and everything performed a zombie waltz in slow motion. I knew this drill: no one was rushing behind the counter.

"Hey Gladys, where's my stale Danish?"

She walked over and thrust a lump of burnt dough down in front of me. It bounced on the plate like a rubber ball. She had slathered on a couple of melting pats of butter, which had barely seeped into the pastry's outer layer.

I was in no hurry. The forensics team would be filling garbage bags with possible biological evidence. The M.E. criminal investigator would be scraping the body for clues along with my sidekick, Detective Gundy, who was a human vacuum cleaner in absorbing shreds of evidence.

The M.E. himself, the theatrical Dr. Alfred Post, would handle the full autopsy downtown after daylight. Right now, the corpse was headed into an anonymous cold freezer, and I wanted to be there while it was still fresh.

The case didn't seem to bear the usual taint of murder. I hated overdoses involving celebrities or the over-privileged who had always felt innocent of any charges due to their strong sense of entitlement. Here, most likely, was a medical student who partied too hard and took some substances that choked off his vital functions. The parents "urgently" expected the NYPD to find the killer…who might logically be their chemically unbalanced son, but that is not what they wanted to hear.

And yet, my presumptive diagnosis of the case felt too fast and too harsh. The boy's parents deserved some sympathy. I had a daughter; I understood the pain. All the money in the world wouldn't bring their kid back. They must be asking themselves, "We gave him every opportunity; what makes a young man with all the benefits give up like this?"

I understood why I'd been summoned. At police headquarters, the brass was always playing hot potato with sensitive cases. They enjoyed throwing me into medically related situations since I'd been pre-med once and understood a little biology. Plus, I'd graduated John Jay with Honors. They seemed to ignore the fact I had flunked organic chemistry. Of course, I had delicately upgraded my transcript, and no one checked in those days.

At least this case should be relatively safe; no Kevlar vest or taser required, and for right now, I could also leave the video camera in my car. In just a few more years, I would collect my pension and float away to a beach somewhere, or nowhere, without leaving a trace.

Except, full confession, I knew I'd miss this crazy life: the front-row seat for the greatest show on earth. I'd miss the tumult in the streets, the occasional glory of recognition by

One Police Plaza, the camaraderie, even the tedious construction of a digital trail to nail a deserving perp.

Sitting in the diner, I dredged up a moment of satisfaction as I heard the early garbage collectors banging and cranking outside. Like me, they hoped to clear the human debris off the streets, even if it would be back again tomorrow.

Sleep didn't matter all that much when no one occupied the other side of the bed. My ex-wife Jill and our daughter Sarah lived in Los Angeles, and I'd remained single for almost three decades after they vamoosed.

I guess you would call me a guy's guy or a cop's cop. I loved pure testosterone. My motto was 'give me a good cold case'—either of stout lager or a long-buried, unsolved crime. I preferred enjoying the former with the guys in my squad. We would sit in a sports bar and indulge ourselves in regretful memories after we'd pounded some cold ones.

Screw the world; we wanted to get off unless the Knicks or the Yanks were winning championships. That placated our sorrows.

Everyone in Manhattan liked to complain; noise, traffic, subways, dog poop, weather, spouses, kids, in-laws. In short, our life was a pity party all the way. I enjoyed walking around incognito on weekends in a t-shirt that said, "Don't give me your attitude. I got plenty of my own."

Enough philosophy for the moment. Thanks, Socrates. Now time to get my lazy butt over to the morgue. Don't book a gurney reservation there for me quite yet.

2. Barney Kazinski

Friday, 6 a.m.

I arrived at the M.E. building, on the Lower East Side, sleep still coiling in my eyes, with a coffee mug and a small notebook in hand. I managed to find an unlocked side door and entered the dark stairwell that led to the basement morgue lab.

It was creepy, frigid, and very murky. Not very fragrant either. The rumor persisted that Dr. Post, in a foul mood, would sometimes open up all the vents in the autopsy theater and let the odors permeate the building.

"Hello, anybody down here?" I expected to see a ghost replying.

"Yeah, who's asking?" a female voice answered.

"Detective Barney Kazinski, Special Investigations, NYPD."

A tall, young Asian woman appeared from the haze. She looked damn good, considering the fact she'd probably spent a sleepless night with the corpse. Small talk would not be appreciated right now.

"Can we start with your name?" I inquired, flashing my shield.

"Well, Detective Kazinski, yes, we've met before. The name's Jen for Jennette Park, the chief legal-medical investigator for the Medical Examiner of the City of New York. I was present at the death scene, all the way through the staging of the decedent Mr. Wainwright for his transportation to this morgue. Rode with him down here."

"Okay, good, I'll write that down; we got the chain of custody going already—smart girl, nice to meet you again. The Chief of Detectives' office has sent me over. Mind if I run some routine questions by you as part of an investigation, high-profile death and all?"

I dug out a pen and prepared to record all of the gory details. I would transfer them to a formal DD5 and our digital Case Management System later. Paperwork had never been my strong suit. Our balky computers seemed to favor the perps. The transfer of data to our new A.I. Chatbot would make things worse.

Jennette brought me back to the moment. I could feel her reluctant energy pulsing against fatigue. "Doesn't Special Investigations mostly do major crimes of violence?" she asked. "Go ahead, knock yourself out. Although I'm no expert, this has the feel of suicide. The young man may have had some heart problems, so I can't be sure. His roomies said he'd been seeing a specialist for an issue in his lungs."

I piped up, "perhaps we should call ourselves Investigators of Nasty but Unlikely Homicide. That's a sure budget-winner downtown. Not that a suicide investigation is a walk in the park."

She pursed her lips into a semi-smile, sharing some quick gallows humor.

"Well, you sure got here fast," she said, quickly back to business. "I just arrived here a few minutes ago. I already spoke to your man Detective Gundy at the death scene. Couldn't this wait until daylight?"

"I love watching the sunrise like you do," I said, "while the news of a prominent student's death travels fast." *Good grief, are we going to have a little sparring match at this ungodly hour?*

"Alright, I get it," she recovered. My boss, the M.E. has instructed me to avoid the press and, frankly, dodge you detectives as well, pending a formal autopsy."

"Let's give it a try and start from the beginning."

"You're a very typical male, hearing what you want to hear."

"It's a genetic problem, we don't hear so good. I've been learning a lot about our inherent failings from DNA profile training."

"There are many mysteries to the why of genetics, detective. All I know is your suspects have introduced a lot of boorish males into my life. But as you request, I'll do my best to be helpful, as long as you don't quote me publicly. The good Dr. Post likes to control the media. He is a born showman. He's a great favorite with the corpses.

She smiled devilishly, showing a touch of annoyance in her voice. I liked this plucky broad, in a fatherly sort of way.

"Okay, Ms. Jen. The first question is, time of death?"

"The rectal temperature was a couple degrees less than normal, ninety-six and a fraction, which by general formula means 3 hours after death. It was taken about two-thirty a.m., so that puts death, best guess, in the eleven to midnight category, give or take a few either way. There was limited rigor, so the guess is good enough for your purposes, but again, we'll know better after autopsy."

"Remember, off the record." She gave me a stern, warning look that meant no further discussion of that subject.

“Okay, next question. You seem convinced that the death of Sandy Wainwright was a suicide. Pretty fast conclusion for a preliminary.”

“I gather you didn’t see the boy’s suite, where he was discovered? I’m not here to tell you how to do your job, but Detective Gundy and I did a quick, initial survey of his room. They found the deceased surrounded by bottles of amphetamines like Adderall, plus a bong, lines of coke, a bottle of Glenlivet, and a packet of lovely little Molly. It all sounds like a toxic assortment that could promote wild behavioral swings and an overdose. Dr. Post will have the emergency serology and toxicology reports within 48 hours.”

“All right, moving on. Give me your chronology of the past few hours, please.”

“The call to 911 came from one of the roommates, named Ross Parker, shortly after midnight. It took a while to alert me, and I live downtown, so I arrived at Hillside a bit before 1:30 a.m. Your crime scene unit had already arrived since a prominent death gets top priority. The first responders tried to resuscitate without response. They kept at it for close to ninety minutes and finally gave up.

“I appreciate the estimates. I won’t hold you to it. Next question: was Sandy alone when he died?”

“Not sure. There was a definite odor of Chinese food and one carton of leftover sesame noodles in the kitchen trash can, but that could have come much earlier at some point. Taking out the trash is not a priority for med students. Sandy’s roommates said he often had a late-night craving to balance his extreme reactions to stimulants. I realize that doesn’t answer the question of whether he had company. The roommates said they were bowling downtown last night and claimed to have gone to bed."

"How did Ross Parker find the body?"

"Good question. He was the only roommate who had wandered downstairs since he was curious why Sandy's door was closed, which was rare when he was alone. Not sure how reliable some of this information is. My experience is that med students can reach a stage of exhaustion where they tend to walk around in a stupor and get their facts jumbled. Lots of pressure, all-nighters on call, not much sleep."

She seemed to be feeling a lack of sleep herself. Then a look of panic crossed her face. "I'm speaking out of turn. Please keep these comments out of the database."

I put down the pen and made a mental note. A suicide enabler or a killer could have quickly taken advantage of the wee small hours, even in a dorm suite with multiple roommates.

I continued. "Were you acquainted with the deceased?"

"Well, detective, the world of surgery at Hillside Hospital is a narrow one. I've been up there quite a few times lecturing to the students on aspects of forensics. The students seem to rotate through the pathology lectures like ants marching across a sandlot searching for greener pastures. I do recall meeting Sandy once. I noticed him when I was doing some work in one of the labs. The pathogens get boring after a while. He was more interesting."

"And what made him stand out?"

"Hmm, well, he was very recognizable. Reddish-brown hair, sandy complexion, wide shoulders. A big guy. I'm sure I've seen him a few times surrounded by an entourage of his ‘posse’ in route to one of their athletic outings or flirting with some doctors or nurses in the hall.”

“Very recognizable? Flirting? That is an interesting choice of words, Ms. Park. More specifically, how did he stand out? Let’s be blunt, would you say he was attractive to women in a physical way?”

A thin coating of crimson crept up her cheek, which she quickly managed to drain back into her poker face. “Detective, please excuse the political incorrectness; we like to classify the male medical students in training as what you might call geeks. They’re known for their social ineptitude, nerdy in fact. Someone like the deceased would not take much to stand out.”

“Okay, let’s leave it that female physicians and nurses and possibly the male staff found him enjoyable to be around. Maybe it was his precocious medical knowledge?”

“Detective, you’re trying my patience, and I barely got one ounce of shut eye after midnight. The young man was appealing because, in our world of diseased tissue, a clear sparkle of intelligence and, yes, charisma has appeal.”

She knew this was a sensitive terrain, so she picked her next words carefully. “He was cocky, what I’d call a pretty boy. Not my type. We do not know these med students well, and we certainly don’t keep track of them when they’re off-duty. This isn’t the rectory.”

“I apologize for this line of questioning. Just bear with me a moment,” I said. “I’m trying to establish a pattern of this young man’s behavior. It might have relevance.”

“Very well, I don’t have a lot of time. I probably shouldn’t be speaking to you at all.”

"Got a hot date tonight? This guy's pretty cold?" I couldn't resist, although a red warning signal flared in her eyes. We were both getting tired, and I didn't want to trigger an angry blow-up that would be reported downtown.

"Ms. Park, can you briefly run through what you found in your examination? Any more specific conclusions as to cause of death?"

"Well, I've already told you too much. We were looking at his fresh body when we noticed a punctate hole in his right thigh, a likely injection site. Heroin, maybe, although none was present on a cursory glance in his room. Perhaps he had already finished the bag. Very likely there were a lot of drugs in that body, but I would be hesitant to draw any conclusions until we get the full analysis from toxicology and serology plus the M.E's formal autopsy."

"What do you mean when you said, 'we' noticed a puncture wound."

"Come again?"

"You said 'we' were looking at his body. When I arrived, you were alone here in the Morgue. Someone was with you earlier?"

"Oh yeah. Dr. Ashley Dillon, the surgery resident, was on call overnight at the hospital. We call her "Dr. Ashley," she's very involved with the med students. She raced into the street to see what was happening and created a scene wanting to examine the body. Sandy was considered one of her best students. She seemed a bit broken up, although who knows how to read a resident surgeon's mind—they're masters of the art of sublimation. She pointed out what seemed to be an injection site in his right thigh. This was while the transport guys were anxiously waiting to get going.

"Wait a sec. Just to be clear: what are you saying about her relationship to the deceased?"

"No idea about personal stuff. The students are known to get deeply involved in their surgery rotations. They eat, sleep, and shit surgery. Their big egos love tearing into flesh."

I paused for effect. "Okay, I get it. Theirs was professional intimacy. Mr. Wainwright, Sandy, loved surgery, and maybe he loved his mentor too? Is it typical for a surgical resident like Dr. Ashley to want to examine a fresh body?"

"Not that frequent. Ashley seemed convinced she could resuscitate him, but there was no hope at that point. Occasionally, when a surgeon is curious about how a patient died, they might ask an in-house pathologist if they could come down and watch the preparation for the post-mortem conference. Her attitude was more immediate, desperate."

"Anything else that you think would be helpful?"

"Well, when I flipped over the body, I noticed some excess postmortem lividity, the reddish-purple marks that come from blood accumulation in his lower body, most likely from taking blood thinner. Even a strong young athlete can have some heart or lung issues if it runs in the family. Yet, overall his was a very muscular body. He apparently was a rugby and hockey star in college."

"Could these bruises represent some type of struggle? A blunt instrument, perhaps?"

I doubt it. I looked under his eyelids, which are a good indicator if there's been brain trauma. Nothing abnormal there."

"Did your surgeon friend Dr. Ashley react to the sight of these bruises?"

"Ashley? Not exactly my friend. Surgical residents have few friends. She was long gone by then. She had probably been up all night, dealing with the living patients in distress, the usual lot. She looked like she needed a warm bath and some sleep. That's how I feel now. Sandy's going into the freezer, and we'll take him out when Dr. Post arrives later this morning. He's a stickler for not mucking up potential evidence."

"Any last thoughts?"

"The only other interesting note was I did a quick check with a portable ultra-violet light. There was a good deal of viscous fluid in the abdominal and genital region. That will be a good source of DNA cells, but my guess—not to be repeated, detective—is there might have been an overflow of some sexual fluids from another male or female. The roommates said Sandy had a wandering eye, and there were plenty of women who hoped it would wander over their way."

I would have followed up that statement when suddenly my cell phone chimed.

The boss lady, the head of our unit, Captain La-Tanya Lawson, was stirring things up at the office. La-T was a formidable force, and attention must be paid at any hour.

“Where have you been?” she queried. “We are gonna have an early staff briefing. Ten a.m., prompt. So, try for a bit more shut-eye and then get your ass over here.”

“I’ll be bright and shiny darlin,’ though I’ve been partying all night.”

“It’s lucky I don’t believe you. I’ll put up a pot of your favorite brew. Black, tastes like crap, extra strong. Good morning, detective, we’ve got lots of fun in store.”

I had lost the moment for a follow-up with Jen on the DNA possibilities, but I’d get to that later. Time to race home for a nap.

3. Dr. Ashley Dillon

Friday 7 a.m.

I had thrashed fully dressed on a couch for a few hours before sunrise, popping Xanax tablets as if they were M&Ms. Finally, I gave up. There was no point in trying to get a decent night's sleep. The memories of Sandy were seeping out of me in bursts of tears. I was in no condition to go to work, so I left a message for my superior, Dr. Maura Davis, that I was taking an emergency weekend off. They could call my cell if they needed me. I dragged myself into an Uber to Penn Station and boarded a train up to my parents' residence in Westport, CT.

I had nowhere else to go for sympathy, except my childhood home, and yet I hated to go there. Mockingly dubbed Taj Two by our neighbors, the gargantuan brick-and-stone edifice always felt like a gilded mausoleum. Presiding over and pruning every inch, my mother Beverly had directed her passion into the house at the expense of the love I craved. Hugs and praise were an inconvenience, like an insubordinate speck of dust.

This morning, I called ahead, and my dad picked me up at the station. We were both silent on the short drive to the house while I continued to press tissues to my face, trying to stem the tears. Arriving at the house, amidst acres of flawless greenery, dampened my already deflated spirit.

All our luxury had left painful scars. Childhood felt like a tower in which I awaited execution by my regal mother. My legs felt woozy now as I trudged robotically up to my small upstairs bedroom. It was sterile and tidy, shorn of the trinkets and posters where I had drudged through my early studies and daydreamed of breaking out.

Reality finally drained all tears. Sandy, the man who represented everything I'd fantasized about, was now dead. Hopefully, my home and family would console me.

As dad had wandered off and my mother was tending her garden, I realized they were silently punishing me for taking up with a rebellious boy and faltering from the rigid, emotionless life they had scripted for me.

A burst of dread sliced through my body. Sandy was gone, and it would be my job to comfort my parents, not the other way around. My dream was shattered, but theirs was still intact. Somehow, I had sullied the highest calling, the priesthood of the physician, to which my father had dedicated his life.

Here I was, a gushing fountain of sorrow, and dad said nothing, only shrugged in a quizzical attempt to understand why Sandy's death could evoke such an emotional reaction. Of course, sourcing sympathy from my father had always been like dislodging a thick clot from a thin vein.

My mother suddenly appeared in the bedroom doorway, and for a moment, I longed to throw myself into her arms. Not a chance. The implacable parental face was locked into default mode. Mother was keeping the options open for the fulfillment of her worst fears.

I had come back home in a broken condition, and there was no inclination to help put me back together. Everything was my fault, and I must pay the price. No one said another word. Mother walked out and shut the door as if she didn't want to disturb a corpse. I sat and brooded; my nerves were deadened by the pain.

I reflected sadly that this was no longer a place that felt like home.

I could not get comfortable rummaging through the house all day. Shortly before midnight, I crawled out of bed quietly, grabbed my overnight bag, and ordered an Uber. I was headed back to New York before my parents realized that I was gone.

4. Barney Kazinski

Friday, 8:30 a.m.

In cases involving death that originate after midnight (a frequent occurrence), I have a well-worn instinct for slowing down and taking my time. After a severe crime with emotional public reaction, there is pressure from the police bosses for arrests and a rush to judgment. Without conclusive evidence, the lead detective must recognize the need for restraint. From long experience, I have learned that my instinctive reactions come from the gut and frequently misfire. The wiser, more reflective theories need time to develop amidst a public frenzy for action.

Better to think nothing and say nothing. Let the evidence speak.

In this case, my gut seemed to be sending up more imperative signals than usual. Despite a few drowsy hours on this case, I had to repress my inclination to start questioning whether this was suicide.

More importantly, I wondered if this case could be my last hurrah. Had I hit the tipping point within middle age, the start down the path where you spend most of your time reeling backward rather than looking forward?

New York always made me feel like I was outside the glass looking in, a natural-born cynic. In adolescence, I had usually been the wise guy and the ringleader of skirmishes in the schoolyard. I'd bloodied a few noses, ripped a few tendons, even broken a few bones, and never let anyone fuck with my desperate craving for self-respect.

The family had settled in the Bronx, which further incited rebellious behavior. My parents could barely control me even though they tried to provide a decent, "traditional" family upbringing. My dad was in public construction, the down and dirty kind. Sewers, tunnels, subways, he was game for anything with lots of mud and rats and a few squadrons of kamikaze mosquitoes. There was never a night when dad could thoroughly scrub away the muck or the rank body fumes that permeated the house.

My mom was a dedicated homemaker. She would pray for just about anyone on earth, even her wayward son. Her hands were raised to Jesus, and she expected her only child to behave like a son of God too.

From birth, she'd been a devout Catholic, dashing to mass almost every day. She had poured her expectations into me since I was the only kid available. Later, it hit me: they must be practicing the rhythm method, not that they were generally in sync. They seemed to endure an outwardly pleasant relationship set to a "low bickering flame," with spurts of anger quickly repressed in my presence.

At night, dad would mostly retreat to the television or the local bar while mom fluttered around her religious relics, often alighting on the Book of Mark that featured the battle between Satan and Jesus. She was very black and white, which was where a lot of mother-son conflicts started. Somehow, she always seemed to assume she would be my savior since I needed to be rescued by her prayers.

Give my parents credit: they were dutiful and hoarded every penny, so their boy could graduate from junior college and join a wealthier (if not happier) rat race. I became a good student in the humanities, with a sprinkling of science courses, and then applied to medical school.

Would you believe I got 15 rejections and one waiting list response that never panned out? My transcript, even in an altered state, had made rejection easy for admissions directors who favored Ivy credentials.

So, off I went to John Jay College of Criminal Justice and found my vocation, a graduate education in reality. Field training consisted of patrolling the housing projects and hidden corners in New York City, where innocence morphed into street cred. I gravitated toward psych and sociology courses in the classroom because I was trying to find my permanent niche in the world, somewhere between Jesus and the Devil.

Part of the training required us to have behavioral therapy, most likely to plumb any hidden rage, a dangerous commodity when you have a gun in your hand. I recalled saying to my therapist, "You're a shrink. How do we shrink the bad stuff and leave my good stuff alone?"

"Doesn't work that way," she protested. "You're human, meaning you're an intricate fabric of good stuff and bad stuff, all intertwined. You can't pluck out the faulty strands without it all falling apart. Just remember: if you're going to be a street cop, treat the suspects and friends with respect, understand the painful context of their lives. Those of us who haven't grown up with a silver spoon need respect and empathy. Your job is to de-escalate a situation, don't inflame it. Don't be a jerk and don't bully minor arrests into dangerous situations that you'll regret later."

Maybe I should have tried a little harder to be a doctor. Yet somehow, deep down, I knew I was best suited for the life of a cop. Less corporate restraint, more daily freedom, an occasional sense of some higher purpose (thanks mom), and, in a distrusting world, a core pride in the integrity and camaraderie among the good guys in blue, hanging out in the urban foxholes. Of course, as I quickly learned, you can never trust anyone one hundred percent. No therapy or experience can prepare you for every contingency. I was guilty of some hasty decisions and wound up at one point on the downtown shit list. But there was never any complete loss of control or violence that might have torpedoed my career.

Recently, I had thrown myself into flipping a stack of hopeless cold cases into DNA convictions and one acquittal of an innocent suspect. That had been a turning point. Now I was considered a modern, new age, "sensitive" detective, or at least I hoped so. The gang in my squad called me "Big Brain," sort of like "Big Bird," sticking out awkwardly from the fray. Somehow, I had earned respect, although having brains was always a barrier to being fully trusted by those who put more stock in their lessons from the street.

Captain La-Tanya had demanded my early presence back at our Command Center. But there was time to take a quick look at Sandy's final residence.

I passed through a special police security desk at the entrance to the Hillside student dorm. The morning shift of med students was already clogging the lobby and emptying into the street. I felt a quick jolt of reality. I hoped this didn't turn into a murder case because there were a lot of potential killers living amidst this throng.

The elevator groaned up to the fourth floor, with apartment 4G a few yards away. Sandy had shared these quarters with his two roommates. The floor held an eerie silence as if his ghost had taken over.

The first police responders, including my partner Detective Gundy, had moved all the residents off the floor to create an undisturbed crime scene. Yellow tape was billowing in endless waves.

A faint clicking of footsteps sounded down the hall, along with a door slamming. Who was still on this floor? Guarding the 4G apartment, a patrolman had the dazed look of a sleepwalker. He was clearly in a sour mood, having been designated to sit on the crime scene and repel the morbid visitors who buzz around it like insects around festering fruit.

At my suggestion, the cop went to canvass the nearby apartments along the hall for possible witnesses who might still be illegally on the premises. The outer door to 4G was closed and overlaid with strips of yellow tape. There were no signs of forcible entry. A small white poster board swung loosely next to the door with the welcoming letters 4G-ORGY scrawled in a red marker, courtesy of an intoxicated roomie. No one had seen a need to take it down.

I put on nitrile gloves and carefully peeled away enough tape to open the apartment door. Having forgotten disposable shoe covers, I didn't want to tread into the apartment for fear of upsetting any footwear evidence. A group of techies was hopping around the floor, looking for latent scuff marks like a party of adolescents playing Twister.

If there were any accomplices to suicide, they could have walked in while the roommates slept. A drug dealer, familiar with the apartment, might have made a fast hit and split, with the credit card on file for payment. Worst case (or nightmare case?), some jealous friend might have half-drunkenly aided and abetted Sandy's last trip.

The vantage point from the open entrance looked directly into the large living room that served as the pad's central gathering place. A large television screen hung on a far wall. In front of it were some sectional sofas strewn around in a helter-skelter arrangement. The whole space indicated a scenario of disheveled lives patched together by a modest attempt at IKEA civility,

Med students are traditionally poor housekeepers due to their workloads and irregular hours. Burrowing into the muck of the suite, the forensics team was still hard at work. Even without seeing the apartment's upstairs portion, I sensed death had begun to spread its tentacles and aromas. A faint, unpleasant odor of fecal residue competed with the whiff of forensic solvents. Maybe the Chinese meal was the last supper, perhaps a Judas had come offering Moo Shu Pork wrapped in a poisonous pancake.

I should have brought a mask. The food residues in my gut were looking for an exit ramp. There was no immediate place to find relief. The forensics team downstairs was sifting through the bathrooms. Likewise, a whole crew upstairs could be heard hauling out their sacks of evidence from upstairs as well.

My cell phone buzzed with an important message. A high-priority text appeared from one of my long-standing colleagues in forensics. "FYI. Plenty of drugs but no evidence yet found of any injectables." In other words, the deceased might have overdosed on an oral cocktail, but that didn't explain the puncture mark on his thigh.

The raw police sentinel returned and indicated the adjacent apartment was still currently occupied. With my ear up against the door to 4F, a boisterous masculine voice could be heard inside. Someone, and possibly other inhabitants of the floor, had managed to avoid the evacuation order. Our impatient captain, La-T, had buzzed me twice, so it was time to get to our Command Center. I asked the young rookie to obtain the necessary info from whoever inhabited 4F and make sure to kick them off the floor. They could be essential witnesses later.

In the lobby, I examined a security ledger that suffered from the same handwriting inscrutability that plagues doctors. There were a handful of entries, several with Chinese characters. The entries ended shortly after midnight when security closed for the night. We would have to check if the dorm's outer door had been locked and assign priority to investigate the nearby Mandarin restaurant and other popular late-night take-out establishments.

There was no security camera in its holder. Standard repairs or a missing clue?

We employed a select branch of forensics to analyze the handwriting and review the security log in general. My colleague, the unstoppable Detective Rebecca "Becky" Muller, would be voracious in tracking down and following up those kinds of details.

I quickly dictated a Siri message for La-Tanya: "On my way, get the coffee going…things may be a bit more complicated than expected. We'll need more bodies to investigate."

I knew La-Tanya would not be happy. She expected egg-timer resolutions to cases, as did her downtown bosses. The word "complicated" did not win favor in their tool kit of expectations.

This was not going to be an easy day, and I was already running on fumes.

5. Barney Kazinski

Friday, 9 a.m.

I drove my unmarked vehicle to our gloomy Command in the shadow of George Washington Bridge. The building had been originally a classic red brick firehouse, but now it had turned ashen gray from neglect and the savagery of New York winters. A remnant slab of the firepole still stood amid the first floor.

Captain Lawson was in her office having a quick breakfast, which provided time before our meeting for me to pick up the 911 report, transmitted overnight from police headquarters. An audio app re-played the frantic voice of Sandy's roommate, Ross Parker. He'd called for help at 12:10 a.m. The horror in his voice sounded genuine. He reported that he'd made a quick check of Sandy's body, partly covered by a white coat, and found no functioning vital signs. Ross had feared correctly that the first responders would not be able to resuscitate that body.

My open-office space on the first floor consisted of a battered metal desk, a file cabinet, a propped-up window with prison bars, and a restricted view of the street. The space made our holding cells underground seem luxurious. After a quick database search of the National Crime Information Center for Sherman or Sandy Wainwright, I found one minor drunken incident reported by the local Palo Alto newspaper. It sounded like a typical adolescent prank without further consequences. Nothing else in miscellaneous online bios of him seemed unusual or worth pursuing.

Sandy Wainwright might have been a playboy, yet no "Me Too" allegations showed up in his record, pending further research. Several local news articles alluded to his family's wealth and its naming grant to Hillside's surgical wing a decade earlier.

The gift had been controversial as it displaced some popular local shops and a small housing project. No specific violence had surfaced that would indicate a call for revenge or make Sandy a target for murder.

My colleagues were already working on the phones. Our Special Investigations Division had been the brainchild of the NYPD Chief of Detectives, to be activated when a critical case, usually murder, required a rapid response of investigation and resolution. While "rapid" in our world often meant going from a snail's pace to a tortoise crawl, our group had built a reputation for a reasonably fast accumulation of evidence and virtually 100% convictions in court cases.

"We've got enough yellow tape around here. Let's try to cut the red tape," the detective chief liked to warn us. Translation: if a case was high-level, get it resolved while the body was still warm to avoid public hysteria and the inflammatory media. The best chance of finding the perp was in the first 24-48 hours before the "X" and Facebook mills started spewing out wild speculation.

No question, we'd need help on this one, suicide or not. His family and the police brass would not be patient.

Our unit had been squeezed out from an over-committed city budget; hence we were a tight-knit group of half a dozen dedicated detectives and an overworked Police Admin Assistant, all under the auspices of Captain Lawson. She was a robust black woman whose take-no-prisoners attitude applied to her staff as much as the possible perps.

During her career, she'd been burned by the political heat from the NYPD leadership. The constant pressure had generated an uncanny cynicism regarding human foibles, white or black. Yet underneath it all, La-T maintained a true leader's decisive inclination to make the right decisions under duress. She was as hard knuckled as they come while frequently proving her common sense was vastly superior to that of her flintier male colleagues.

Our crew had been assembling in the main squad conference room. The additional hands from neighboring precincts did not appreciate the extra workload. The hour was now beyond 10 a.m., later than La-T wanted, but expedited considering the recent time of death.

The most sizable chair around the table sagged under the weight of Charles Oliver Gunderson, known as "Gundy," a large barrel of a man who used his bulk presence to intimidate any "person of interest" in a case. He had been our first detective on the scene in Sandy's room.

Gundy was the foremost master of interrogation, using his mercurial personality as a truth-seeking missile. Like a child arranging the facial parts of a plastic toy, he could activate his rubbery features by arching an eyebrow or venting his pugnacious jaw to summon a vast range of expressions from indifferent or owlish to shocked and enraged.

Due to his facial mechanics, he was privately known as Mr. Potato Head, a nickname that might suggest his existence had sprung from a basket of toys. Quite the opposite. No detective could assemble his demeanor faster for assuming the "bad" cop role than Gundy.

He was a steadfast cop who ardently believed the shield stood for uncompromising integrity since three generations of Gundersons had worn it. Gundy also liked to say his ancestors arrived in a hay wagon, which is why he could find the needle in any haystack when the other clues didn't add up.

Our other crucial colleague, Detective Becky Muller, was a former lawyer who had worked in the Manhattan DA's office. Among other specialties, she had pioneered the prosecution of assaults against women. Thus, she showed little tolerance for the "idiocy and perversity" of the male beast, an attitude that applied to both law violators and law enforcers. "We're lucky the 'bad guys' are usually male," she liked to observe. "They are dumber and greasier, and they tend to leave plenty of DNA at the crime scene."

Becky was no typical courthouse lawyer. Her intuition and practical counsel kept our investigations from going off target. She reveled in the rhythm of the street and had earned grudging respect from the most hard-wired patrolmen. As an experienced prosecutor and a self-trained forensics specialist, she was skilled in taking wads of incoming digital reports and synthesizing the essential evidence that would hold up in court. Facts mattered. Inadmissible raw speculation was filtered out by her legal eye.

Becky prided herself on being reserved and professional. "We should be all business at all times when we're here," she'd warn, "leave the gossip at home." That went for lengthy coffee breaks and other distractions, such as sports-talk. "Why do men find it so fascinating to watch someone throwing or kicking a ball?" she'd query as she pretended to throw a football with a very sour look plastered on her face.

The other female staff-members (who were a brazen minority) appreciated Becky's independence and her alertness to laziness or excuses. Out of earshot, she might be subject to resentment for her meticulous standards. We appreciated she was always thinking ahead like a prosecutor in the courtroom: how would the defense try to puncture the chain of logic?

Call her modest in appearance, yet, when necessary, she could turn on the feminine charm while barring anyone who tried to get too personal. "The lady likes her privacy, so leave her be," La-Tanya warned when her acute antenna sensed a surplus of male testosterone flooding into our discussions.

This morning, despite the broader support, I knew Gundy, Becky and I would be the core team responsible in the trenches.

My reverie was interrupted when Captain Lawson suddenly appeared and called everyone to order. Gundy and I outlined the basic facts known at this juncture. We emphasized that downtown had a "special interest" in a quick resolution of the "situation." Every other case would be thrown on the back burner in our triage of priorities. A couple of neighboring precincts had contributed some staff investigators to help us cover more ground.

La-T issued the new assignments quickly. My task with Gundy was to take the friends and hospital staff who were closest to the deceased. The others would canvass the neighborhood to look for leads from outside Sandy's immediate circle. Becky would co-ordinate the field reports, or DD5s, that came in digitally (the preferred method) or physically from the techno numb nuts. She had set up a special Case Management File (called "Rich Kid") to systematize the data.

La-T added one last warning. "We believe this is a drug overdose, but let's not rule out homicide. The family is from California, they own a large piece of our city, and they're trying to snatch the body and take it back home for burial. The M.E., Dr. Post, will not let that happen because he's driven by law and personal pride. He won't sign off until he does his full autopsy, or virtopsy as he calls it due to all the digital input involved. The social media wonks are already stirring up trouble, so I don't want any leaks out of this group. Got it?"

Gundy wisely remained silent, but his eyes gave him away. He saw the case as another instance of bureaucratic hysteria over an apparent suicide, in other words, a waste of NYPD time and resources.

I wasn't so sure.

La-T gave us one last piece of instruction. "Get out there and get this one done quickly," she advised. "You're dismissed, except Detective Kazinski, my office, please."

I followed her down the corridor, not sure what to expect. Walking into her office was like arriving in the future citadel of crime enforcement. Her outer glass wall was a spotless, bulletproof U.L., Level III. Her desk was a sparse NYPD model, with gray metal legs supporting a faux mahogany top. There was not even a paper clip out of place on the desk's surface because there was no paper in evidence.

Also absent: a writing implement or a speck of dust. It looked like a Silicon Valley wet dream.

La-T sat down and slid out a computer tablet from a side drawer. Obsessed with crime statistics, she maintained a whole range of spreadsheets to monitor the M.O.

I sat across from the desk, and she started airing her concerns.

"I think we got ourselves a lot more trouble than we expected," she fretted. "There's a huge probability of overdose, so I hope you can get to the boy's pre-death state of mind quickly and we can move on."

Then she flashed the implacable look that said, 'Don't bother arguing with me.'

Naturally, I had to respond since she always anticipated my insolence. "I'm glad you're open-minded about our investigation," I offered gently, trying to smooth out the pebbly edge of a contrarian. "Overdose in any form, frankly, including suicide, can be a tough diagnosis when there's no note left behind."

"That's my man Barney, you old dog. Never jump to conclusions unless they're your own."

"Right now, my dear, I'm jumping through hoops. Conclusions to follow shortly." I gave her my sanitized, polite, fuck-you smile.

La-T tilted her head back and chuckled, her smile gleaming brightly and reflecting off the polished desktop.

"That's good and righteous, my man. I appreciate this recent concern for proper procedure. Let's see ***you*** play this one by the books, a new strategy for a change. You and Gundy know the routine. I've been up for hours myself, and I have a few friends over at Hillside. This boy was a medical phenom, a real brain inside an athletic body. He was getting quite a bit of action from the ladies."

She paused for effect, a small twinkle animating her face. "Maybe that was his problem, a little too much of the unzipped life will catch up with you."

Then she started to stand up, the signal for me to get going. I jumped up as she swung around the desk and put a hand on each shoulder like some kind of holy sanctification.

"Good luck, soldier," she said, now directly eye-to-eye. "I know you'll find the right answer. You're still my guy. You're calling the plays. The case depends on you."

Flashback: 90 Days Earlier

6. Dr. Ashley Dillon

Hot & Sweaty

It was August, the heart of the New York City summer, with one sweaty, sweltering day melting into another. As I trudged through my chores at Hillside, every patient's problem seemed to multiply in the fetid air. After only a month of indentured servitude as a resident physician, my dream of becoming a surgeon felt less glorious.

Everything was about to change.

I had been hearing about Sandy Wainwright, the boy wonder who had been making women sweat buckets, well beyond the thermostat's impact. He was said to be a born medical star, and his appealing persona was just the icing on the cake.

When he walked in our physicians' lounge, I knew this was going to be trouble with a capital 'Holy Shit.' His reputation had been an understatement. He was the hunk of hunks: over 6 feet tall, with a smooth complexion and soulful bedroom eyes. I first estimated him to be in his 30s, most likely a resident that I had somehow missed. His muscular build reminded me of our steady stream of athletes arriving for their ACLs.

But wait—I'd forgotten all that I'd heard. His white coat was cut off at the hip. Damn! That meant he was a med student wearing the uniform for those at the bottom of our medical pyramid. Maybe the scuttlebutt was wrong, and he was older. Perhaps he hadn't gotten the memo that residents, fellows, and attendings wore long white coats.

Maybe, just maybe… my fantasy trip began churning out pangs of possibilities, most of them involving a ring. I tried to compose myself. *Ashley, put this man OUT of your mind,* I warned myself. *Take your common sense back. Recite your vow: no interactions with doctors-in-training outside this building.*

"What's your name?" I asked him brusquely. Like so many supervisors before me, I had followed the protocol of being a mad dog, keeping him at a distance.

"Sherman or Sandy," he replied gently, in a cultured voice. I knew his family name represented the Wainwright dynasty that was plastered everywhere in the surgical wing.

No doubt, Sandy was to the manner born.

I abruptly cut him off with a drill sergeant sneer. Who was this younger, masculine alpha dog? I looked down at his shiny, un-scuffed clogs. These were the mark of an older doctor, yet Sandy was still a student starting his clinical work.

Just then, Dr. Maura Davis, Director of Surgery, entered the picture. It was 7 a.m., already late for her usual routine to start our daily rounds. We had 40 patients to see and a couple of precious hours to see them. Dr. Davis usually had an early morning surgery. She would lead us to the first case, and then we'd split up into smaller teams.

We passed into our first patient's room. An intern presented Mr. Joseph Hart, a 45-year-old male who had developed a painful obstruction in his colon. He had undergone surgery as a child to correct a congenital intestinal defect. Over 40 years later, he had developed a blockage due to a buildup of scar tissue.

Dr. Davis turned to Sandy.

"Who are you?" She asked in a strident, don't-waste-my-time voice.

"Dr. Davis, I'm Sandy or Sherman Wainwright if you prefer."

"Sherman, did you say? That sounds like a more adult name. Would you be so kind as to describe for us the relevance of the Duhamel Procedure here?"

Dr. Davis was tossing him a clinical question for a year or so down the road. She intended to make him look foolish. It was doubtful a rookie clinical student would recall the answer from his textbook training, yet I sensed this cocky neophyte might be up to the challenge.

He ignored Dr. Davis's condescension, a budding smirk on his face. The boy was confident, almost dismissive. His arrogance was the quality so many women love to hate and hate to love. No wonder he already had so many followers—plus quite a few jealous nay-sayers.

He nailed her question. The patient had been born with a defect called Hirschsprung's Disease, in which nerve cells were missing where scar tissue had obstructed the bowel.

Unable to propel waste properly out of the rectum, the infant's disposal mechanism basically 'backed up and clogged up.'

"The corrective operation, called the Duhamel Procedure," Sandy explained patiently, "would involve pulling down healthy bowel tissue over the diseased segment to allow for normal function. In this patient's case, although his condition was corrected as a child, over the years, the scar tissue had returned to obstruct the exit passageway and impeded a clean discharge. Surgery would correct it."

I felt like applauding. The boy had called Dr. Davis's bluff. She offered a sickly smile, and I knew she was seething inside. He'd thrown a bucket of water on the wicked witch.

Meanwhile, what spell had he cast over me? I felt dizzy, almost intoxicated. Our wedding flashed before my eyes, both of us dressed in white as we exchanged rings on a secluded beach at sunset.

Wait! Careful girl. A wedding fantasy? This was out of control. At least a few years my junior, this young man was verboten for personal hook-ups. A warning bell clanged in my head, sounding like a death knell. I was still vulnerable from breaking up a year earlier with an older married doctor. My physician father had used his influence to bail me out of that scrape.

I snapped back to the heat of this initial moment, watching Sandy in action. Everyone waited for Dr. Davis's reaction to his audacity.

"Nice job, medical student," she said gamely. Her off-key tone carried a hint of future repercussions.

"Sandy or Sherman," he corrected her, a sly grin sprouting from his unkempt stubble. For an instant, his deep, dark, electric eyes probed mine. It felt like brain surgery and heart surgery all at one glance. My whole body shuddered with agitation… or was it anticipation?

We awaited assignments from Dr. Davis. I couldn't help myself. I silently prayed: "please put us together…"

"Sherman, go with Dr. Dillon," she said as if she'd read my lips. Ah, the beauty of synchronicity.

"Follow me," I told him. She had sealed our fate. I should have realized that Dr. Davis knew exactly what she was doing.

We moved to a vacant desk and did some perfunctory paperwork, then completed my rounds.

My pulse quickened when he came into view the next morning. He seemed to relish the collision course he had set with Dr. Davis, the arrogant bastard.

There would be no harm in giving him some advice. I pulled him off to the side before we started our rounds.

"Mr. Wainwright, we need to talk privately."

"Ah, a private consult with the boss already," he said.

"Well, I'm looking ahead in your training, and I have some basic advice."

"I'm all ears…and eyes," he said, launching an obvious assessment of me, head-to-toe.

I should have sent him, right there to H.R., for harassment. Instead, I suggested a cup of coffee during a break.

"This sounds like an important discussion, Dr. Ashley. It calls for a more formal conclave. There's a dive bar on

Amsterdam and 95th a mile or so south of here. Shall we say 10 p.m.?"

"Good plan," I conceded quickly. Was I totally crazy? Going off the rails already?

We had an uneventful morning, and he needed to study in the afternoon. "See you later," he said, slipping away before I could change my mind.

At the appointed hour, I was already waiting at the bar in a leggy sundress, sipping a glass of Pinot Grigio, and questioning whether he would show up. Maybe he didn't have the guts? That might be a blessing. At about half-past ten, I glanced at my phone, preparing to order one more for the road and call it a night. The bartender excelled in refilling my glass before the wine reached the bottom.

Suddenly, I felt a warm hand on my upper back. The boy had done a bit of prep on his own. His hair was still damp from a shower. He had slapped on an enticing fragrance and wore the requisite costume: a polo shirt with ragged shorts, and delicate dragon tats on his arms, curling down to torn sneakers.

It was obvious. Business be damned, this was dating mode for us both.

He sat down next to me as we dropped into the conversation, lubricated by his red and my white wine. What began as idle hospital gossip morphed quickly into witty, semi-drunken banter. I could feel a blurry boldness and loss of inhibition as a couple of hours flew by. His fingers periodically grazed the hem of my skirt and lightly scratched an unshaven thigh.

Somewhere in a waning hour near closing time, sobriety tried to enter the conversation. I lectured him with a burst of drunken rectitude that we must respect the medical school rules restricting off-campus socializing. My words came off choppy and foolish as my breathing had become constricted.

We shared the check and left the bar, walking side by side, his arm casually draped over my shoulders. We faced an awkward moment. Should I just say goodnight? Perhaps a hug? Could I now go back to being a senior advisor the next morning?

My thought processing was too late. At the entrance to my apartment complex, he spun me around quickly and kissed me hard. I could taste our red and white wine residues dissolving together.

"I don't know if we should do this." He stopped and pulled away.

"Do what?" I was sober enough to pretend nothing had happened.

"Dr. Ashley let's take a break and think about it. We're screwed if we get caught."

"This was your idea, all I wanted was a cup of coffee."

"But will you love me tomorrow?" he observed in a playful yet declarative way.

"It is tomorrow, my dear."

In the enveloping darkness, I could feel him suddenly struck by the same reality that had hit me and could affect our careers.

He put his hands up defensively and started walking away as I lurched through my apartment door…thankfully alone for now.

7. Dr. Wendy Jamison

Flashback: 90 days earlier

The arrival of "Sherman" Wainwright into our clinical world reverberated like an electric shock through the whole campus. Usually, life is more relaxed during the summer semester, and the informal Sandy seemed to fit right in. He had been a classic nerd in hibernation through his first two years of med school. Suddenly, he became more visible in the student dorm and hung out with friends in Riverside Park, where his athletic skills (and body) could be appreciated.

We all knew his parents were significant donors, yet that was only a minor consideration. From the start, Sandy appeared larger than life. His reputation quickly attracted mixed reviews. He managed to be loved, admired, revered by those who had gotten to know him, and resented by those who found solace in dismissing his attributes.

Talk about a Renaissance man. At the hospital, our coinage was flesh, and he delivered a big payoff in that specimen department. But believe it or not, I was to discover he had an authentic and sensitive side, especially for the sick kids I was treating,

I first saw him one sunny day while taking a bike ride through the park down by the Hudson River. He was tossing a football around, and you might have thought Patrick Mahomes had arrived for the growing crowd of dog walkers and joggers who had stopped to admire him.

I was mesmerized and nearly ran my bike into a park bench. I jumped off as if preparing for an athletic intervention.

Fortunately, I had anticipated he might be in the park that day, and I wore short-shorts and a tight t-shirt. We sparked into an instant connection. He threw the ball with zip in my direction. By God, I jumped up and snared that sucker. I walked it back over and introduced myself. We talked for a couple of minutes, and he responded to my being a resident in pediatrics. "I love kids. I'll come to check it out when the semester starts."

I'd been moping about having to babysit a bunch of sick children, and now it seemed like I'd wound up in the best specialty of all. I hated having to wait a month. I'm an itchy girl from the Tinder generation. My philosophy is simple: if the chemistry is right, "get it on now," and do the moonlight walks on the beach later. I surmised Sandy might be a wild child who defied convention and felt the same attraction that I did.

The only impediment to an instant hook-up involved my best pal from med school, Dr. Ashley Dillon. I fretted she had managed to get in the queue ahead of me.

That might be a problem.

8. Ms. Rosemarie Li

Flashback: 90 days earlier

I was born on a large dairy farm in rural Iowa. As the only Asian family in an all-white community, we were isolated and self-sufficient. My parents had emigrated from China in the early '90s and raised me as an only child. Given the numerous duties in maintaining a farm, I grew into a caretaker role almost from the crib. During my pre-adolescent years, my parents home-schooled me so that I could help with the farming chores that began early in the morning.

While I was limited in my dealings with the neighboring children, working under the perilous weather conditions over the winters gave me a fundamental understanding of what raw survival means. Forget the concern about the frills of life. Milking the cattle, birthing their calves, or playing veterinarian when they became ill; all these roles were lessons in human behavior as well. When the boys started taking an interest, my mother warned me about the human male ideas of romance.

I managed a few feverish sessions in high school with a neighboring boy, but we never went beyond second base. My sexual knowledge was derived from the farm. Dairy cows need to be impregnated and regularly calved to continue producing milk. Having watched a single bull inseminate dozens of cows on an annual basis, I wasn't anxious to let the boorish male adolescents in the neighborhood imitate the natural world on my behalf.

When I began advanced schooling, I was still immature and staying local. I went to a community college and then finished as a biology major at a nearby state university.

I was used to hard work and discipline, the essential prerequisites for success as a grad student. My parents, God love them, encouraged me to go into medicine. Rural doctors were in short supply, and almost before I knew it, I was accepted and enrolled at the Hillside Medical School in New York City. The female gossip mill was turning out reams of publicity about a third-year student named Sandy Wainwright. He sounded like a bit too sure of himself for a naïve farm girl like me.

Maybe I should have stayed on the farm.

9. Prince Geoffrey

Flashback: 90 days earlier

I was out of sorts about a lot of things when I first travelled across the pond. I grew up in Liverpool, and the only clue that Americans had about my town was based on the Beatles' music. I didn't give a sod about their fame, never had. But the American girls, they all practically popped their cherries every time they heard a Beatles song. Who wouldn't fancy that opportunity?

My birth name was Geoffrey Laird, and since I'd come via London, I quickly acquired the nickname Prince Geoffrey or Prince Jeff from my new friend Sandy Wainwright. No, thank you, I didn't ride across the ocean in a Yellow Submarine, although me old Paz was a sailor at heart. He was proud of being called a "scouser," named after a mutton or lamb stew that had nourished local Liverpudlian seafarers for centuries. Paz had grown up in the docks and had shipbuilding in his bones, going back to his grandfather, who had designed some of the Titanic machinery.

Growing up, I had some summer jobs at the Cunard-White Star Line headquarters in my hometown, but I never felt the same glory on the sea that radiated through the family DNA. There's an old Liverpudlian expression: "I wanted to go out and come back so I could see how far it was to go someplace else."

I liked that refrain, and I knew the going out part was my destiny. There would be no coming back. The old man tried hard as he moved us to a respectable suburb and put aside a unit trust fund for me that had accumulated some nice bits of cash annually.

My dream was to make use of it across the ocean.

I was never a great student. I barely made it through secondary and then took a bit of a nursing apprenticeship to avoid the A-levels pressures. I had a natural bent for science and maths, plus a blimey patience for detail, a quality often lacking in the younger American workforce.

A few years in London with the British Health Service helped fortify my medical skills and create a more refined British accent and vocabulary. I then managed to swing over the Atlantic to the States as a scrub nurse or surgical tech to utilize my practical training.

I applied to Hillside, where Dr. Maura Davis showed immediate appreciation and assumed some of a parental role given that I was far from home. She had directed me into a more serious med school career. I resisted initially as I preferred spending time with the younger, wilder birds who flocked round Sandy, so I joined in that worship, basically like an extra roommate.

Along came his friend Pil, who was a dodgy chap and as witless as his name with a missing letter. However, he provided a full-service medical source for the uppers and downers that medical students required to regulate lack of sleep. Pil's pharmacological skills proved invaluable for Sandy and me since, with our escapades, we could sometimes burn out like an overloaded socket.

Sandy and I hit it off and loved to bum around together. Everything came so easily to him that he didn't need much study time, and we were both fair game for the nightlife.

Prince Jeff, hinting at a heritage of royalty, turned out to be an instant success in wooing consorts for our wild times.

In the end, I think Sandy fancied me because he was bored with the medical crap and needed someone to spice up his life so that he could live out on the edge.

I was happy to oblige. Occasionally, I felt overshadowed by his engagement with the ladies, but I was managing to develop my own bits for romance.

Perhaps Sandy and I could share Doctor Ashley!

10. Barney Kazinski

Flashback: The single life

The early weekend mornings provided me with time for a nostalgic rewind of what might have been. After a restless night, I would lie in bed when it felt as if I were facing 1000 days of solitary confinement. I considered making tiny scratches on a wall calendar like a prisoner.

The essential dilemma always perplexed me: I accommodated the single life, and yet it seemed unfulfilling without a partner. At that moment, my only true love, Jill Bennett, would enter stage left into my reverie. I pondered: what possessed the human-animal to linger endlessly on its earliest passion? Women seemed more realistic in moving on and finding a better lifelong mate. They understood that the ticks of time did not flip the coin in their favor.

But I, Barney Kazinski, had never moved on as if I secretly craved being a self-pitying, discarded male.

I flashed back to my early 20s and the first sight of Jill when she was sitting near a pool table, her beige dress and flaming red hair lending a streak of glamour to a tawdry bar. What was she doing there? And what was I doing trying so hard to impress her with my mediocre bar-room gaming skills? Yet there was an instant connection: We were like two pieces of driftwood washing up on the shore of seven-and-sevens.

I was finishing my last year at John Jay College of Criminal Justice, and she was starting her senior year upstate, innocent and single, dropping down to Manhattan for weekends. While she soaked up life biting into the Big Apple, I was dithering about whether to follow the police career path. We enjoyed two years of on-and-off bliss, then plunged ahead into a City Hall marriage.

At first, we copied what many young couples do in Manhattan, highlighted by the weekends. We started with a jolt of temptation as we struggled out of bed. "Save him for later," she'd scold my bulging briefs with a gentle squeeze. Then came our standard routine: a quick brunch at the nearby diner, some shopping at discount stores, a movie, a quick pizza dinner, then back to the apartment to settle down for the night.

Once we were resting in bed, the furious attraction sparked into explosive lovemaking. I always felt frantic with lust. So was she in the early days. My sex drive tore down her inhibitions and guided us through long nights of pleasure.

Naturally, that led to the unexpected pregnancy bringing us our daughter Sarah. We'd tried a sporadic rhythm method that ignored Jill's fertility cycle in the heat of our encounters. As a nice Catholic girl, she wasn't giving up her baby.

Of course, I acquiesced, and that changed everything. I'd always considered it a miracle that Jill chose to go out with me in the first place. She had movie star attributes, a divine presence with a passion for the earthly objects in life. Unfortunately, I was still learning the ropes as an entry-level patrolman on a tight budget.

She was brand-addicted, accumulating Jil Sanders pantsuits, Chanel handbags, and Louboutin red-soled shoes. I was proud to go into debt to fortify my fashion-plate wife and her already well-stocked closet.

"Just a lot of gifts that have accumulated from previous boyfriends," she would assure me. "None of them were sweet like you, Barney."

I should have realized that sweetness in our relationship would last about as long as consuming a Snickers bar.

I was in my twenties, with all my adolescent hormones still roaring off the charts. I wanted her so badly; I needed her like crazy. After a few months, I imagined life without her would be like trying to survive without water or sunlight.

Initially, she'd applauded my limited means as an acceptable price for taking on the bad guys. Our baby Sarah's arrival was accompanied by Jill's fierce migraines and underlying depression. She started thinking seriously about her long-term plans, in which a future detective's life suddenly didn't seem so attractive.

We broke apart very fast.

With little fanfare and a peck on the cheek, the love of my life and our daughter moved out across town and left me in a lifeless walk-up in Hell's Kitchen.

I pulled myself together and ascended through the police ranks quickly. Granted, I wasn't the most attentive father; I couldn't help resenting Sarah for being an interloper in our halcyon days, although I did try to visit her on weekends. Those visits became every other weekend, or eventually, once a month. There were so many urgent cases piling up. Jill got tired of being a single mother, and she became obsessed that I would be killed on duty.

Our daughter started having nightmares. Jill remarried quickly, and hoping for Hollywood glory, she decided to move with Sarah to California. That spelled the end of our direct connection. Jill's new career faltered in minor roles on soap operas. Her memories soured and cast me as a former biological convenience that was no longer necessary in their lives.

Since that time, nearly three decades, no female had inhabited my pad for more than one half-sleepless night, with morning tea and shower included, plus a bounty of scrambled eggs and a bagel on Sundays.

After these brief encounters, I felt relieved to be alone.

Saturday, Day Two

11. Barney Kazinski & Dr. Alfred Post

Back to the present

There was only one way to start finding concrete answers for this case. I turned to the one man who always liked to brag, "the buck stops here."

Or, as his police cronies liked to needle him, "the body stops here."

Dr. Alfred Post was the highly respected and often controversial Chief Medical Examiner of the City of New York. Balding and short in stature, he compensated by being an accessible public figure who could turn the most complex science into a simple winning argument for juries.

However, with his dramatically timed diagnoses for the benefit of the tabloid headlines, he frequently inflamed my police colleagues. No one denied he was a pioneer who had brought forensics and technology to the forefront in criminal cases. During his 35 years as an ME, he had witnessed and elucidated virtually every perversion that humanity could reap upon its unlucky victims.

The doctor's methods won plaudits from the bereaved because he always kept in mind the family dynamics operating on both sides of a crime.

While his first duty compelled inspecting the victim, he recognized there were relatives and friends who depended on him for closure. His philosophy was simple. He liked to tell his students that "in our world, there is rarely a purely innocent victim, or a purely pre-ordained criminal, only a two-sided combustion of bad judgment, bad intent and bad timing."

The doctor's portly stature revealed a propensity for caloric take-out that never wavered amidst the daily gore. His reputation and girth had expanded together. "Some angels have their halo over their heads. Mine settled around the midriff," he liked to observe with a self-satisfied smirk.

Yet he prided himself on being a latter-day Sherlock Holmes who could deduce more clues from a dead body than the detectives could glean from live witnesses. "We're both pathology hunters," he confided to me in one of our congenial moments. "My evidence is mostly drawn from the silent tissues and organs of corpses. Yours is provided by witnesses who are very self-serving and untrustworthy at best. My subjects lie on the table. Yours lie, period."

In recent years, the chorus of complaints had grown louder, with the media attacking his self-aggrandizing style and lumbering investigations. Nonetheless, I needed the benefit of his intuition and skill, so I raced over to the ME building on the East side and prepared to be a supplicant in his medical domain.

One thing that I had learned over the years was that the coroner hated interruptions during the workday. He was best cornered in the morgue theater before sunrise while sharing his customary bagel and salmon with a gruesome 'beauty' lying just a few yards away from his tiny office.

I was already a bit late for breakfast and too early for any weekend security guard, so I walked down a flight of stairs and entered his domain. I glanced over to find Sandy's body on the autopsy table, still intact. The doctor was preparing his equipment, aided by a young resident who appeared to be in his late 20s and a bit jumpy.

"Not-so-good morning, Barney."

The doctor didn't look up as he played his usual welcoming theme. "Detective, you keep turning up like an impacted kidney stone. Very painful for us all. Don't they give you some more lively cases?" He half-turned and flashed a smug smile. His attempts at humor made me cringe. Best to refrain from telling him that fact.

We began our combative routine. "This could be more exciting than you realize, Alfred," I observed, "although I see you're a bit late in starting the autopsy. What's the boy still doing in one piece?"

"You mean this waste of taxpayer's dollars on some self-entitled hellion? Yeah, there's a hold-up. The family of Mr. Wainwright has sought an injunction to ship the body untouched back to California. They don't want their boy mussed up any further and demand he be returned in pristine condition. Maybe they'd like to avoid the publicity of an autopsy report citing substance abuse as a cause of death?"

He glared at me, and I shrugged in sympathy. He continued: "I finally got clearance early today from the

Judge to proceed. They can't throw me out of the body parts business so fast."

I wondered if Dr. Post was weighing any serious doubts about the cause of Sandy's demise, but I held my fire. When he started full autopsy mode, it was best to observe and remain silent.

"Barney," he stopped and looked up. "I want you to meet our latest hotshot intern from one of those elite medical schools where they teach you how to run everything rather than learn anything. His name is Peter McClain. He'll be getting the Nobel Prize before he's 30."

"Peter, nice to meet you," I responded. "Good to see that this cranky old guy has some competent young blood helping the boss. He's been overworked for a long time."

"Nice to meet you, detective; I'm flattered that you think I could be helpful," Peter said. I had a hunch we were going to be co-conspirators against the boss in this morning's exercise.

"Okay, you two," Dr. Post intruded. "No side conversations. Peter, please help with the grown-ups doing our work. Kazinski, you're here to observe without comment. These are the photos from Jen at the crime scene in case you didn't receive copies of them already." He handed them to me.

"Thank you, Alfred. I only saw a few preliminary photos, not these in 'full color,' so to speak."

"Barney, yes, it's going to get gruesome now as I use my expertise from eighth-grade shop class. Time for you to step back away from the table while we get you the proper apparel for this bloody procedure."

He suddenly paused. “Oh my God, what is it now, Julie?”

An over-eager, young blonde rushed in, looking frazzled. The M.E. always had some vigorous live specimens on hand to help him balance out the dead ones.

“Dr. Post! Stop the autopsy. We just received this Fax. It says ‘Urgent, Read Immediately.’” Julie struggled to catch her breath and handed him the Fax.

“Here we go again. Check this out, Kazinski. The damn judge has reversed course and is giving further injunctive relief to the deceased’s family. They’re delaying any tampering with the body, including an autopsy. Good grief, what garbage. Doesn’t Hizzoner understand that this body’s evidence is perishable and might spoil by delay?”

“So, what are you going to do next, Alfred?”

“We’ve got no choice,” Dr. Post said. “We’ll put him back in his ice-cold drawer and hope he doesn’t decomp too fast. Peter, make sure this body stays preserved. Kazinski, no point in your sticking around here. Check back with me tomorrow when we’ll be working on Sunday per usual in a case like this one. Peter will show you out, and you should be grateful to get out of here.”

He looked sternly at his associate. “Peter, please don’t engage the detective in a long-winded conversation about your fascinating life in the morgue. We’ve got a few other impatient bodies to work on, so get your ass back here quickly.”

Peter quickly responded. “I’ll be right back. Just need to make a quick pit stop,” he said.

As he escorted me out, Peter gently nudged me into a visitor's lounge. He continued to seem a bit jittery. When we were out of earshot, I could sense he wanted to convey a private message.

"What's up, Peter? I don't want you to get the old guy upset. He has a nasty temper that's unforgiving."

"We don't have time now, Detective Kazinski, but there are some additional details that might interest you. I'll call you later when I have some privacy."

"What's the big mystery?"

"You'll know soon enough. I'm on duty tonight. No one alive is around on Saturday night. That might be the best time so that I can show you a few things in private."

I gave him my card with a cell number and eagerly departed. The side conversation with Peter McClain had increased my suspicion that this might not be the typical drug overdose after all. The M.E. could be hiding something. I'd known his subtle machinations for years. When he so desired, he could keep communication tighter than a gnat's ass.

I stopped and called Captain La-T with the bad news. We'd have to wait on the autopsy. She was not appreciative of the message. I clicked off swiftly to salvage my eardrums.

12. Barney Kazinski

Later Saturday

I decided the day's next quarry would be Dr. Maura Davis, the Hillside Surgery Program Director, a vascular surgeon by training. Budget cuts had forced her to assume a dual role as Chief of Residents. She occupied one of a depressing maze of glass-fronted offices scattered in an aging brownstone across the street from the surgical wing.

I was showing up on a Saturday without an appointment to catch her off guard. Fortunately, Dr. Davis was working alone, her door half-ajar, so she was trapped.

She was a middle-aged woman who probably felt being called drab would be a compliment. Her short hair was clipped in a boyish style and bleached out into a lackluster gray. A white lab coat had not lost its crisp creases while draped over a thick frame that managed indications of a human profile.

The office was simple and functional. If hell froze over, it would look and feel like this space. I pictured icicles sprouting from her ears. Behind her stood a small bookcase, some filing cabinets, and diplomas prominently displayed. She might have been renting the office temporarily; there were no family mementos of sentimental value indicating a human touch.

No photos. No plants. No artwork.

I approached her desk cautiously, like a petitioner approaching the bench. Still no reaction. I sat down in the one stiff wooden chair facing her desk. She leaned over as if her laptop was a wall protecting any interaction with a visitor. She looked up periodically but did not acknowledge my intrusion.

A nasty thought pervaded my mind: An Operating Room must be her idea of a playground.

"Dr. Davis, I'm Detective Kazinski."

"Yes," she responded in a low-pitched growl. "I've heard the name. Do you have an appointment?" She knew why I was here. *We'll both play dumb for a while.*

"Dr. Davis, as you may know," I finally ventured, "a valued member of your community died before dawn yesterday morning. I'm heading up the police investigation into his death. I need to ask you a few questions."

"Very well, I'll hold you to that few minutes," she said, eyes still engrossed on her screen. "The OR is being prepared, and my patient will be on the table shortly."

I knew how doctors hated to keep patients waiting, so I flashed a synthetic smile and ignored her rebuff. I was seated between her and the door, and I had borrowed a small taser that could melt her polar kneecaps.

I thought with private amusement: *She ain't going anywhere right now, except on crutches.*

"Doctor, then let's dig in quickly. What was your relationship to the deceased student?"

"Relationship? I'm the Director of Surgery. I'm temporarily in charge of the residents as well. Doubled my workload. The students are generally not my immediate problem, which belongs to the Med School Dean in this building." She clicked off and powered down her computer as if our meeting was already ending.

"You did know the deceased?"

She turned momentarily flustered, a tincture of scarlet popping into her cheeks like a small chip in the ice.

"Yes, I knew Mr. Wainwright, you couldn't miss him," she said. "Frankly, detective, I would never wish anyone dead, but this fellow could be a handful."

"You disliked him? And others disliked him, presumably?"

She thought for a moment and retreated into her management role.

"Detective, you must understand that we have rules which allow us to maintain decorum during training. Our newer students know very little, and yet they're thrown into life-and-death situations, supervised of course, and they have to be very careful not to distract us when we're in the midst of a delicate procedure."

"Makes sense." I sat bravely, trying to encourage her to continue. Maybe she would emerge from the spotless white shield and be human. *Or worst case, I could get dispensation to sell her a ticket to the Police Benevolence Ball.*

"Here's the rule," she explained almost gleefully. "Medical students remain silent unless specifically addressed. When I speak, it's teaching; when they speak, it's static and noise."

"Like children," I said brightly, "who are to be seen and not heard."

She stiffened and gave me a look that said, "Don't push it.*" Or maybe: "don't try to be a bigger asshole than I am."*

Her lecture continued. "Detective, we don't have time for your smart remarks. This kid, officially named Sherman, didn't know how to respect the wisdom of his elders. He was a bright young man, and although considered winsome by some of the female students, he never knew his place. Maybe it was entitlement because his family's money built much of the surgery facility."

"Fair enough, doctor. Let's switch gears. I have not obtained the deceased's current schedule. I presume you met with him frequently in a teaching capacity."

Dr. Davis opened her computer, pretending to search through the calendar. I suspected this was an alibi excursion. She ignored the patient in the OR for the moment.

"Yes, that is correct. I met with the young man you call Sandy last Wednesday. His name is in my calendar."

"Do you recall the nature of the meeting?"

"I'm a surgeon, Detective. I'm expected to pay attention to details. Sandy dared to seek a letter of recommendation for a summer residency program. He had been on a few of my rotations and assumed his clinical brilliance electrified the rest of us."

"Then you did have close contact with the deceased. You said earlier..."

She interrupted and started to stand up, a little less friendly now. "I really must wind this up. Patient care comes first. As I told you, I don't generally get involved with medical students. I'm sitting in for the dean while he's on a brief sabbatical. In this case, the boy's performance thus far had been so outlandish, so arrogant, so lacking in respect that I refused his request for a recommendation to the outside residency. It was a no-brainer."

"What did this mean for him?"

"His failure to receive a recommendation would make it unlikely that he could get into a decent residency even if his parents promised to donate a whole medical campus. Merit and quality of performance, along with respect for experience, still mean something in our world. He'd have to be just fine sticking with our program."

Her frame ballooned into a bursting posture of pride.

Dr. Davis reached into a drawer and handed me a beautifully reproduced CV with bold cursive lettering in gold. I was clearly not the first individual to have witnessed her lifelong progression from one outstanding achievement to another.

"Now, detective, I really must go. I just realized that I also saw Mr. Wainwright on Thursday afternoon. He was assisting, not significantly, in a vascular procedure. This was my first of two surgeries that day.

"You didn't even have to check your calendar, so this must have registered."

She ignored the sarcasm. "When someone dies a few hours after he scrubs in with you, it tends to stick in your memory."

"You said there were two surgeries that afternoon. What time was the second, later surgery, and who else was in the OR with you?"

"It started at dinner hour, a cold-foot emergency, a blood circulation failure. I recall those participating included a circulating nurse, Eve Flores, from the Philippines. Also present was my best scrub tech, Geoffrey Laird. He's a Brit. They call him Prince Geoffrey. Able chap with a bit of an upturned nose if you get my drift. I'd have to check any others. I don't believe Sandy was there. I'm pretty sure he wasn't."

"Anyone else in the room?"

"Come to think of it, Dr. Ashley Dillon made a rare but brief appearance. She was on-call overnight. Another one of those residents who believes 'everything revolves around her.' I don't have to try very hard to keep her out of my surgeries, which suits me just fine. She doesn't like my garden-variety cases. Prefers surgical oncology, the big-time stuff with big-time fees."

Dr. Davis was getting a bit worked up, and her composure was melting around the edges. She continued her rant: "Mr. Wainwright always appreciated being around her, and she liked having him in her surgeries. It was obvious. He seemed to enjoy Dr. Ashley flaunting herself. As an aside, she could stand to tone it down on the push-up bras, maybe stop making a spectacle of herself in front of the male doctors, married or otherwise."

A little female rivalry here. Maybe a touch of jealousy. Just wondering, how deep is her rancor?

"Dr. Davis, one final question. Can you think of anybody who would have wanted the boy dead?"

I looked down at my notes, and she somehow managed to slip by. I was afraid to try and stop her. There would be a harassment suit coming in a New York second.

From the doorway, she looked back, very pleased with herself to be escaping. "Take care, Detective Kazinski. I hope for your sake it's an accidental overdose. If you'd like to know who might have disliked Sandy, get a copy of our phone directory. That would provide about a thousand possible names for you to track down."

She marched out and called back over her shoulder: "If you have any further questions, please call the Dean. He'll be back next week He's *our* bad ass. You'll be buddies in no time."

13. Dr. Wendy Jamison

Saturday afternoon

The death of Sandy Wainwright was a serious blow to our campus community. As the word spread over the weekend, everyone was wandering around in a daze. Classes were cancelled. The cops were swarming like spiders spinning webs of yellow tape as they searched for witnesses. Students and teachers stumbled around, hugging each other. Even strangers were sobbing into each other's arms.

I, of course, admired this young man's reputation for rebellion. Medical school can be a tight-assed place, and Sandy didn't particularly like being robotic in his studies. He craved excitement and action, like a boiling pot that was always ready to spill over the top.

I heard the rumors about his all-night escapades and his posse of mixed genders going to strip joints and blowing their wads in champagne orgies. Or his playing hockey down at the pier and killing it on the ice after working a shift all night. Sleep represented a mindless necessity.

I knew that one of his friends, a wacko named Pil, was a drug purveyor who kept him and his roomies living on chemical fuels. I had recently heard from a friend in electrocardiology that they were tinkering with Sandy's heartbeat rhythm. The problem ran in the family, according to social media gossip. His father's athletic career had been cut short by serious clotting in the deep tissues of his circulatory system.

We all knew Sandy had abused his body with drugs and late-night partying. Somehow, we always thought he'd pull through because he seemed so indestructible.

Naturally, a woman like Maura Davis would be resentful of his attitude. She played life according to the rulebook, and Sandy was a born rule-breaker. His various girlfriends could be resentful also, as they wanted him all for themselves, and that just wasn't in the cards. I realized that my friend Dr. Ashley was smitten with him, so I avoided the subject when we were together.

Full confession: Ashley didn't know that I was also pursuing a relationship with Sandy, albeit a chaste one. If she found out that I was involved in any way, it would have killed our friendship. Ashley and I had been inseparable in med school. Thus, I was torn by twin loyalties, starting with my old friend with whom we had joked our way through the anatomy labs together, (putting the male skulls in some embarrassing positions). I was also, responding to my inner craving for the out-of-bounds excitement where Sandy and I could engage more intimately.

My personal erogenous zones were itching for that boy. As Dr. Ashley always warned, I never obeyed the rules of the road, especially the speed limit. If there was a stop sign in front of a potential playmate, I preferred to push my foot down on the accelerator,

After our summer encounter in the park, when school started, Sandy had come down to see my work as promised. I was running a clinic for young children with severe birth defects. Their prospects were often heartbreaking. How could you play Risk with a ten-year-old and tell him the game was not that important, his life was much more tenuous than three on two in Kamchatka?

Then Sandy Wainwright showed up as promised. He had a younger brother with a serious birth issue. That forged a connection between us. His love for kids was sincere, and they instantly loved him back, the Pied Piper in scrubs. What a performer! He did magic card tricks; he played songs on an old beat-up guitar; he had them laughing with infantile riddles ("What do you get if you cross an elephant with a dolphin? … Swimming trunks.")

And yes, there were the inevitable fart jokes. What's wrong with an overgrown adolescent bringing hope and affection to needy kids? The girls laughed right along with the boys.

I was hooked.

Best of all, when a child or parent confronted him with a medical question, he would sit down and patiently review their situation. It was not his obligation as a medical student. Yet, he had a marvelous gift for explaining things clearly with the underlying inspiration of a pep talk, like a football coach telling his team they could go out on the field and beat a hated rival.

The whole place vibrated to the charisma of his personality.

I must admit he gave me a great kind of guilty pleasure. He was building relationships with the kids and their parents as if we were a community or even a family. I had never been close to my parents. Having to deal with the most painful child-rearing circumstances at the hospital, it was natural that I'd be resentful. But as a friend Sandy showed me how to bring the best out of everyone who was admitted to our sector.

Nor was he the hit-and-run kind of guy where the kids were concerned. Damned if he didn't memorize all their names and keep track of them on a mental spreadsheet. When one of the sick ones lost the last throw of the dice and was suddenly missing, Sandy somehow managed to call the parents or show up at a wake or shiva.

For the lucky ones who went home, he'd get their address from the billing office and arrive with balloons and chocolate cake. Sometimes I'd tag along and break down in tears at the look of joy on their families' faces. The experience of being around him generated a revived purpose in the humanity of medicine.

I'd be lying if I didn't say I was attracted to Sandy, very much so. I sensed we were both soulmates and body-mates. It killed me that Dr. Ashley had somehow beaten me to it. With each of his visits, I could feel the personal attraction growing between us.

Out of respect for my friendship with Ashley, the question rattled between us: how long could we stay professionally engaged and repress our desire to consummate the dirty deed? I had been celibate since I saw Sandy in the park, a world record for my lusty bones. I felt a spurt of betrayal that he wasn't directing himself to my needs.

Sandy's death ended my romantic strategy and opened a whole bag of unintended consequences. The thought resonated: was I in some way guilty of causing his death?

14. Barney Kazinski

Saturday, late evening

When I was a younger man, drifting from pre-med into criminal studies, I became obsessed with the murky space between good versus bad behavior. Despite my mother's frequent outbursts of biblical citations, I was never a moralist, seeing myself as a maverick with a compass that tended to waver away from due north.

That approach didn't work out so well. My path into adulthood was too awkward and self-conscious to be the odd man out when I desperately craved acceptance. After becoming a cop, I honed my awareness of the thin line between innocence and guilt, as if it were a porous membrane allowing normalcy and pathology to bleed together.

Some of us managed to walk right up to the edge of trouble and averted it. Others started timidly with mundane lies and deceits, the minor treacheries that can bloom and engulf us until we've crossed a line of self-deception and there is no turning back.

Over the years, a career of pursuing bad dudes had pushed me into a cop's ambivalence. Warning: be on guard because evil lurked in us all at various times.

Lately, I'd been having recurring nightmares of standing on a cliff and feeling the ground skidding away under foot until I toppled into the abyss. By day, I struggled to recapture a firm toehold on my life. This case was already slipping into a void that corresponded with my darkening mood. I was almost identifying with the victim and his possible enablers of suicide.

Peter McClain called in the late afternoon to confirm our meeting. Dr. Post had not come to the morgue; he'd been tying up some loose ends with the district attorney to expedite getting Sandy back on the autopsy table.

The ME had no tolerance for gray areas in his role. He stubbornly upheld his belief in the law that this body belonged to him after it took its last breath in what might have been a serious crime including suicide.

Sandy Wainwright's story played out a scenario that the M.E. had seen so often: a young man with all the outer trappings of success had lost his way and paid the price by his own hand or from the hands of others.

I was admittedly confused by an unexpected flare-up of insecurity and jealousy. I could not understand how a brilliant young medical student would throw his life away. I'd abused so much of my own life because I was a plodder, a follower, an underachiever with big dreams. After my beloved Jill, the Dr. Ashleys of this world never looked at me twice.

I would have given anything to be like Sandy prior to two evenings ago. Now we were bound together in sharing unfulfilled lives. I was fortunate to be on the legal side of that bargain, at least for now.

One thing was evident on this night: I was cruising the murkier back roads of deceit. Here I was in my 27th year on the force, sneaking into alien territory like a burglar. This clandestine meeting with Peter McClain, the M.E.'s underling, violated all NYPD protocols.

It's not clear why I took such risks when I should have stayed home watching a streaming comedy film. Instead, a half-digested burger rumbled in my belly like a freight train passing through my intestines. Maybe I was losing it—the dark side had won after all as I parked down a side street offering little illumination.

Peter represented a throw of the dice. He was a complete unknown, a rookie forensic investigator. I was assuming a great deal of inherent risk just by showing up. Only criminals chose to meet in this clandestine fashion to do their business.

While we could trust the dead bodies in the freezer not to talk, any bystander witnessing a detective walking into the morgue near midnight on a Saturday might be suspicious.

I knew that Dr. Post would not tolerate Peter's kind of disloyalty. Thus, a career risk loomed for both of us. The driving force, in this case, was desperation. I had a hunch that Peter had turned up a piece of forensic evidence that could help unravel the strands in our case.

At least if he could prove this wasn't a suicidal overdose, then my unspoken suspicion was correct.

We might be starting to begin a search for a killer.

15. Barney Kazinski

Saturday, late evening

I stood outside the morgue on First Avenue near a clump of bushes and called Peter's cell as instructed. A few moments later, I heard a side door opening, and my partner in stealth beckoned me inside. He was wearing a white lab coat bearing the stains and wrinkles of his long day. We walked down a flight of stairs as quietly as possible back into the main exam chamber where Sandy Wainwright's body had been pulled out and unsheathed on a metal dolly.

Peter got right down to it.

"Detective, let me give you a two-minute course on the circulatory issues in this case.'

"Okay, I was pre-med, but a little review won't hurt."

Peter pointed to a large wall chart that emphasized the links between the heart and the lungs.

"Let's simplify things this way: The human circulatory system is a huge distributor of oxygen-bearing blood to the body, using the heart as the central pumping station and the body's 60,000 miles of veins and arteries and capillaries for distribution."

I nodded and he continued. "The heart itself is a durable machine that has been compared to an automotive engine. In bodily terms, there are chambers for blood which are like an automotive gas tank. Both the car engine and the human heart have valves that guide the "fuel" going in the proper direction without backing up."

"Can we stick to the heart," I suggested. "My car is doing just fine."

"Here is the miracle of perpetuating human life," Peter said, his eyes glowing at this late hour like a young scientist who was entranced spiritually by the miracle of creation.

"What I'm about to explain," he said, "is the basic cycle of how blood distributes oxygen throughout the body, and then collects the cells that have become oxygen-depleted for waste disposal. This whole process is renewed repeatedly."

"So far so good," I urged him on.

"The starting point is a healthy heart that's a muscle pumping blood to the lungs and brain and kidneys 100,000 times a day, or 35 million times in a year. Imagine that durability."

"So why does it break down?" I queried, starting to feel fatigued and making me wonder how my tired ticker was doing.

"Follow this logic. The heart has two major functions. First, it absorbs the oxygen-depleted blood from the billions of thin-walled specks of capillaries that flood into the veins and arteries which will deliver the tired blood to the right side of the heart. Secondly, this blood will be guided through valves into the pulmonary artery which pumps the blood into the lungs for an oxygen rejuvenation.

Peter added: "The next cycle occurs in the lungs where we breathe in oxygen from the air and exhale carbon dioxide. This so-called 'gas exchange' also involves the kidneys which remove waste products from the blood and produce urine. Back in the lungs, once the blood has been filled with oxygen, it is driven back into the left side of the heart by pulmonary veins and then dispersed back through the body via the circulatory system of arteries, veins and capillaries."

"To summarize: the left side of the heart pumps out blood to the body with oxygen and nutrients. The right side takes back the oxygen-depleted blood, then pumps that blood through the pulmonary artery into the lungs to receive a fresh oxygen supply. From there, the capillaries take charge of distributing the blood to all the remote areas of the body.

"Good description from 7th-grade science," I said, with my weariness gathering strength. "Now why are you telling me this?"

"Hang in there," Peter said. He was as fresh as if he'd been chugging five-hour energy shots. "Here is the ballgame."

"I'm all ears," I muttered.

Peter was ready. "If the blood headed for the lungs becomes obstructed by a huge clot; the body will starve for lack of oxygen. It's like a massive stroke or heart attack, and death can come very quickly. As the primary carrier of blood between heart and lungs, the pulmonary artery plays a critical role in keeping the system operating smoothly."

"Okay, got it. When do we get to something that resembles a felony?"

"Detective, you met Jennette, the investigator who collected evidence while the corpse was still fresh. In Sandy's room, the forensics team took extensive photographs of a drug called Ecstasy or Molly. It's a strong stimulant that brings pleasure and loss of control."

I nodded, and he continued.

"This drug could have been countered by a sedative. From what we know, uppers and downers were standard parts of Sandy's repertoire. But their presence at the time of death was ruled out by toxicology as the main factor in his death. That is true as you'll see when I get to the cause of death. Sandy had apparently functioned well on his rounds earlier that day, but he declined to go bowling with his roomies, which was unusual for him. He complained about being tired, an irregular concern."

Peter kept going while I tried to avoid spacing out. "Let's simply say we're left with a big question mark on the role of addictive drugs leading up to the death of a healthy young man—in combination with the traces of alcohol recorded in the blood samples."

"Okay, makes sense. But if not drugs, what would have caused his body to collapse?"

"There's an important factor to consider here. Sandy was very athletic; we know that from his undergraduate hockey career. He might have needed some mild sedatives or stimulants, but he wasn't a habitual drug user."

"Yes, Peter, you might be right. But let's get specific. What about heroin, for example? That can be a pretty good killer in and of itself. Sandy certainly knew how to give himself an injection. Jen's report from the hospital took note of a fresh nodule in the right thigh."

"That's precisely the point, Detective. No heroin was found at the scene. None. While heroin can be administered through various routes, there were no injectables found after a thorough search. No bags of liquid, no needles, no intravenous tubing, and insufficient evidence in the bloodstream of a toxic overdose from pills."

"Are you sure, Peter? Maybe you didn't see the entire forensic report from the CSU…."

"No, I'm quite sure. Dr. Post is meticulous; he pores over all the collected data before picking up an instrument. Sandy was a precocious med student. He knew how to find and sterilize intravenous tubing if he wanted it."

"Let's try a hypothetical," I suggested, sounding like he was my expert witness in a trial. "You seem to be leading to the conclusion that a drug overdose wasn't the main cause of death."

"That's right, detective, although the first lesson of a Dr. Post autopsy is 'never say never.' We try to rule out the most unlikely diagnoses since the body has many ways to fool us. This body showed no track marks or other signs of chronic intravenous injection, only one acute puncture."

I asked, "How do you explain it?"

Peter jumped gleefully into his response. "The upper thigh wouldn't be a preferred site of injection for someone who was an experienced IV drug user. The femoral vein, where the puncture started, is hard to access on one's own body. There are other vessels that would be easier to use, with much less effort or pain. Sandy would know this."

I had to concede these were logical deductions.

Peter continued with a natural earnestness that would play well with a jury. He wasn't stopping. "A medically savvy murderer would know that most fatal embolisms (or deep vein clots) often start within veins in the lower body, often formed during surgery. The pathway from the femoral vein up from the thigh to the pulmonary artery is one of the most common routes for serious embolisms. But here's the key take-away. An air embolism has the same capability of causing a blockage as a more visual clot, since the air clot can bubble away and be overlooked in autopsy. That is frequently the case. A deep clot from the thigh or ankle traveling and combining to form a pulmonary embolism is one of the leading causes of death, right up there with Altheimer's or serious Strokes.

"Not sure I'm grasping the last point." I felt dizzy, ready to pull up a gurney for the night.

Peter was getting over-excited. Instinct told me that this is where he might veer off into emotional miscalculation.

His eyes were blazing with show-and-tell fervor, the hallmark of a young scientist on the trail of a breakthrough discovery.

"Let me repeat myself," he said. "None of the drugs found in Sandy's room were injectable. The drugs that were present are generally taken up the nose or orally. The blood tests showed only tiny residuals of some opiates, as we just discussed. Not enough to kill him, but possibly enough to allow someone else to take advantage with a syringe…"

"Okay, let's do this again," I grumbled. "Were there any needles and other paraphernalia? Maybe they got thrown out in the trash. They must have been somewhere if an injection occurred into his thigh?"

"No question on the injection," Peter said. "Its sole purpose in my opinion was to create a clot. There was also the factor that the victim had been having some heart irregularity and was on a blood thinner. His father was a professional athlete who dealt with clots all his life and had to retire at an early age. Hereditary factors can be significant.

"All right, Peter. You seem to be leading somewhere at last. I'm feeling bushed."

"Detective, the logic is right in front of us." Peter had slowed down, drawing me gradually into his theory. "When we reviewed the evidence to date, I conjectured that the puncture wound in the thigh was administered by someone other than Sandy So, I started thinking, who could have assisted in giving that injection?"

"Peter, you're making quite a leap here. Maybe the injection was administered a day earlier and took time to activate. I'm not a doctor. You would know better."

"Sure, detective, there are always other possibilities. I checked again with Jen, and she was sure the puncture in the thigh was fresh."

"Okay, I'll go along with you for another few minutes. Is there a coffee machine operating in this frigging establishment? You've been here over 12 hours, and you don't seem a whit tired."

Peter disappeared and returned a couple of minutes later with a plastic cup of a toxic mud brew that might well have been responsible for poisoning a few of the stiffs lying in the fridges. I kept sipping in the hope that the caffeine would overtake my desire for death or sleep, whichever came first.

"Normally, we don't allow food for visitors in here, but I guess it doesn't matter," Peter noted with grave seriousness.

"Peter, what do you say we move on and finish up before some of these dudes in here wake up for breakfast?"

"Okay, got it." Peter didn't smile. He was rolling into the grand finale. "I wanted to figure out how the death occurred and then try to see who could have assisted in an injection. Of course, that's where you come in."

"Appreciate it. Keep going."

"I narrowed the possibilities down in my mind. I first considered potassium chloride, the drug they use for assisted suicide, as in Dr. Kevorkian's euthanasia protocol. And there are other poisons that could have been used."

Peter paused; I was suddenly wide awake. "Come on, out with it."

"Then I finally came to the cheapest and most convenient method, by using the one free and most available substance on the planet."

"Let me guess: free love?"

Peter tried a half-smile. He looked goofy. Better for the jury when he stayed somber. "You're a funny guy, detective. "The correct answer is air, the gaseous composition that we breathe all day long. That's why doctors always do a quick finger flick and squirt when they're administering a drug by a syringe. They're getting rid of potential air bubbles."

"Isn't death by embolism very rare?"

"No, to the contrary, when traveling from what we call 'a deep vein thrombosis or clot', and combining with a pulmonary embolism, it's one of the four or five major diseases that kill annually, right up there with cancer and heart attacks and strokes and recently Covid.

"Keep going, buster; you seem to have been formulating a creative theory for the cause of death."

"Detective, if someone were to inject, say fifty to a hundred CCs of air into the femoral vein and it traveled up to the pulmonary vessels, it's an instant showstopper. That could blow up a lot of blood circulation, but it might not be detectable unless you're looking closely at an X-ray or CT scan. Perhaps the murderer didn't realize that Dr. Post always looks at a scan in major cases before we start cutting."

"The good news," I chimed in, "is that rarely do criminals perfectly execute their intentions. They always blow it. Why is this clot procedure so brilliant?"

"Because when a full autopsy here is conducted on a body, if no one suspects air as the culprit, the heart and lung connection is cut open, the air bubbles dissipate, and it's as if there was possibly a small, more natural blockage. The crime goes cold."

Peter tugged at my arm. Detective, follow me over here to the computer images downloaded from my portable X-ray."

I dutifully followed him into an alcove where there was a large console for viewing by patients' families and doctors. Peter loved being in full demo mode. "You recall yesterday how a judge delayed Sandy's autopsy by an injunction. Pursuing my hunch, I had already X-rayed Sandy's head, neck, and chest since it's been intact and untouched this whole time. Dr. Post would likely fire me, maybe even kill me, if he found out."

"I may kill you now if you don't get to the point. There seems to be plenty of room here tonight at the inn."

Peter was not going to be rushed. He pulled a chest X-ray up on the screen and had his pointer ready to direct my attention. "This is what we call a posterior to anterior view, taken from the back with the front-facing us. You can see the rib cage that protects the lungs."

"Okay, got it."

"There are several black spots which are evidence of air that is outside the normal pulmonary airspaces. On the left side of the image (which is the right lung facing us), you can see the faint outline of the pulmonary artery's lower lobe. A black smudge has replaced the normal white outline you should see. On the right side of the image (the left lung), other black streaks represent unhinged air also. Again, this is abnormal and indicates there's a circulatory breakdown, meaning an air embolism has lodged between the heart and the lungs."

"Can't it also be due to a faulty seam in the negative?" The kid might be on to something. I wasn't buying it so fast.

"Okay, Peter. Stop right there," I said." Can you prove the air bubbles have explicitly appeared in this case?"

"Well, we haven't cut him open yet to prove it definitively. Dr. Post will want to order a CT scan to give us a better view inside the vessels that are feeding and leaving the heart. A good radiologist will be able to see the problem in about 10 seconds. When we open the actual pulmonary artery, the bubbles should look like a disorderly string of pearls. Right now, the bubbles show up on X-ray as darker spots. The profusion of these dark images is a good indication of an air embolism that's as efficient as any stroke.

"Okay, Peter, an 'indication' doesn't quite nail it coming from an intern. So, here's what you must do, even at risk to your job. You must show these X-rays to Dr. Post and ask him to confirm your suspicion."

Peter turned a shade of color that resembled a corpse. "I know you're right, detective, but I need this job."

"Believe me, I understand; you knew the diagnosis when you called me. If it helps, you'll have the support of our NYPD detective bureau. Dr. Post and I go way back, and hopefully, I can talk him into giving you a fair hearing, especially considering that you may have uncovered a murder. He'll be happy to take all the credit."

"I'm young and inexperienced, but you'll see I'm right when we do the autopsy," Peter said with dogged certainty. "I'd bet on my diagnosis."

"If you're right, you can always be the first to say your autopsy was a success, but the patient had died." I wondered if Stephen Colbert could use me for a little boost in the nightly ratings. Peter made a snorting sound and gave me a wimpy fist pump.

Our session was finished.

It was now after midnight, and I considered lying down on a gurney for a sweet long-awaited sleep. No, I decided, not here. The other bodies were not embalmed; they wouldn't be very fetching in the morning.

I gave Peter a firm pat on the back.

"Good work, young man. Don't give up on your dreams. The world of forensics needs more doctors like you. Maybe Dr. Post is right about that Nobel Prize."

I crept out softly and headed home. Were we dealing with a murder? There went our theory of a conclusive overdose. La-Tanya would be less than thrilled.

We had to rewind our thinking. I began to percolate with Ms. Li's logical hunch that the most likely suspect of murder might be a woman scorned.

I sure hoped not. As Maura Davis, the surgical chair had warned, there were plenty of candidates for revenge.

And I knew a possible one in particular.

Sunday, Day Three

16. Barney Kazinski

Morning, 8:30 a.m.

The phone call came much too early. It was Peter McClain. He was slurring his words as if he had a hangover. Perhaps he'd slept in that lovely chamber?

"We're cleared to take off, detective," he said. "Better come get on board right now. We'll have masks and gloves and all the necessary garb for the autopsy at the security desk."

I managed to shower and grab a quick cup of coffee, and off I went once again to the emporium of Dr. Post. Seeing the aging building by daylight was like noticing a one-night stand after a sleepless night. Not so pretty. I decided to drop in through the front door this time and use my shield to disrupt whatever the old man was doing.

His other cadavers could wait, although the morgue was buzzing with activity. The receptionist handed me a small, battered metal tool kit packed with three pairs of gloves, two layers of body-length scrubs, duplicate full-face goggles, plastic shoe covers, and an airplane vomit bag. (The latter may have been Dr. Post's idea of humor or a standard precaution.)

I glanced above and behind the receptionist's desk, where it read, "This morgue is the place where death delights in helping the living." That was the philosophy of Dr. Post in a nutshell. I squeezed into my armor in a dingy closet-sized room designed for anorexic visiting firemen.

I now looked like a reject from a Star Wars film, but I was prepared for battle. I arrived at the anteroom outside "the pit" or main autopsy chamber, ready for the worst. The good doctor was not happy to be interrupted during his probing and sawing. He came out to reception with spatters of blood and flesh clinging to his scrubs.

"What's the emergency here?" he growled. "Who pissed in your Cheerios, Kazinski?"

"Good morning to you, Dr. Post. I take it you haven't spoken to your intern, Peter McClain, yet?"

"No, we've been in the middle of an autopsy. We haven't been sitting around waiting for you to show up."

"So, Peter McClain is here already?"

"Yes, he is, downstairs. We started about a half-hour ago. We're doing a body that you're not involved in, thankfully. At least I pray you're not."

"You haven't spoken to your young associate?"

"That's correct; I haven't had a chance yet to find out what he wants for Christmas. We've been a bit busy on a three-bullet job. What's McClain done now? I know he got a parking ticket last week. He looked a bit ghostly this morning. Maybe burning the candle, a bit too much?"

"Well, the kid may be out exercising his hormones, but his instincts are solid."

"What does that mean?"

I knew that Dr. Post hated more than anything to learn about his group's work from an outsider. I pressed ahead, ignoring the impact this might have on Peter's job security, or mine.

"Let's start this way," I cautioned as gently as possible. "He called me last night after taking X-rays of Sandy Wainwright."

"He did WHAT?" Dr. Post looked like he was about to burst a few arteries of his own. I took a step backward.

"You heard me," I continued bravely. "Peter had a suspicion that someone might have injected an enormous bolus of air into our Golden Boy. As you know, there was a puncture wound on his right upper thigh near the groin area. The clean-up crew found no injectable substance anywhere at the crime scene, and the preliminary toxicology and serology tests came up empty also.

"Oh, good grief, let me call down and get his butt up here." Dr. Post picked up the phone on the wall and summoned his assistant in a deafening tone of voice that could have been transmitted without a phone.

"Keep cool, Al. The kid did the right thing."

"Peter McClain might have done the right thing for you," he thundered. "He's violated protocol and might have personally compromised the whole post-mortem exercise that we're undertaking shortly."

"Seems a bit extreme, Al. He hasn't altered any evidence."

I had seen Post angry before, but never quite like this. "You're a cop, for Christ's sake," he warned, "you guys live off the chain of evidence. Maybe this maneuver calls for review by Internal Affairs?"

"Not necessary, Al, let's move forward…"

"Let me remind you how sensitively we treat evidence in our autopsies, just in case you forgot how we get cases thrown out of court." There was no stopping him now, and the young man had suddenly appeared carrying an X-ray, which made things worse.

"Hello Peter," Dr. Post said acidly. I was just about to tell your detective friend here how you screwed up. First, you moved the deceased body out onto a table and then you took X-rays without a specific order to do so. How about breathing on the victim? We have just received a court order allowing us forty-eight hours to cut this young man up despite the family's protest. Everyone's watching; we've got to be extra cautious here."

"I… I… was going to tell you first thing," he stuttered, "except we started on another autopsy already."

"All right, Peter, put your bloody X-ray up on the screen."

Dr. Post prepared for more warfare; his ego had been stung. Then he slowly looked at the x-ray and did a double take. He recognized immediately where Peter was going.

"If you look at this x-ray," he said, suddenly taking over, "you can see black spots outlining part of the lower lobes of the pulmonary artery in both lungs. This is an air embolism. Where blood should be flowing, a CT angiogram will show these blockages.

“You can tell all this just from the X-rays?” I queried, with a benign smile at Peter. The young man was still sweating from the initial reaction by his boss. The mercurial doctor seemed to have calmed down and reversed his strategy to take credit for what his young associate had demonstrated, in case it turned out to have significance.

Dr. Post was warming to the subject. “We are in the post-mortem world of virtopsy, the physical autopsy combined with various scans that give us virtual proof as well. I was an early pioneer in this technique,” he said without any attempt at false modesty.

“How so?” I played dumb because I knew Dr. Post loved to offer history lessons where he was central to a procession of great scientists.

“One of the first great cardiologists was Leonardo DaVinci,” the doctor explained, “who more than 500 years ago studied the anatomy of the heart through animals and then human cadavers. He revealed that the swelling of heart vessels like the pulmonary artery indicated an interrupted blood flow, or clot, proving fatal. He didn’t have X-rays, so he used insects to eat away the flesh that might obscure his direct view.

“Skip to the present, and we can now use the CT scan as I’ve told you. Most air embolisms result from surgeries on live patients, which go amiss and allow clots to pour through arterial walls. The technology developed to spot embolisms on live patients has now been adapted to the dead ones. Sometimes the presence of an air embolism may be missed at autopsy and bubble into thin air, which is what the perpetrator of the death was counting on.”

"What are the next steps?" I asked. Peter's face looked ashen as if he had survived the gallows.

"We have an enormous CT apparatus set up in the basement that operates 24/7, so we can send Sandy down for a scan. Those results will be back late today. At least thus far, no parts of the body appear to have been disturbed. We can have a clean physical autopsy and a clean virtual one. Thus, Barney, do we introduce you to the new world of the digital verifying the physical or vice versa."

Dr. Post continued to glare at Peter, but with an undertone of pride.

The latter was blotting the sweat off his face. There were sighs of relief all around.

"Let me ask one final question," I ventured. "You said a doctor would understand the mechanics here. What about other medical personnel at the hospital?"

"You're learning Kazinski. A shame you were too dumb for med school. Any trained technician who has injected fluids with a syringe knows that a massive air bubble can create dire complications. Only a criminal mind would pull the plunger back on the syringes to allow a massive amount of air to catapult into a vein. That ability with a syringe might apply to just about the entire medical staff at the hospital except for the nightly maintenance crew and the lady who runs the gift shop."

I ignored the sarcasm. Dr. Post's mood had noticeably improved. Peter's status had gone from exile to survivor.

"Peter will alert the scan crew downstairs and have transport take it there."

Tomorrow's autopsy would be the M.E.'s first dance with the corpse. Shame on me for thinking this, but perhaps Dr. Post's delicate ego would help orchestrate a grand show to emphasize that he and not Peter McClain was still running the show.

I was out the door like a reporter with a hot scoop. The Medical Examiner had officially confirmed Peter's suspicions. A likely homicide meant we had some essential recalculating to do. I rang La-Tanya at home, and she immediately promised to call a staff briefing for the following day, after the autopsy, which I would attend.

"How can one simple death be so damn complicated?" she asked.

I could not rattle off a credible response, so we clicked off for now. I decided that I would send Gundy to the autopsy as the results sounded already pre-determined.

17. Barney Kazinski

Sunday, late morning

There was no time to rest. I figured Sandy's roommates might be recuperating from their usual Saturday night revelries while hanging out at home.

The Hillside med school dorm was an eerie, aging high-rise nestled on the street across from the hospital. The building was known for its unruly appearance, with cotton-candy pink insulation poking down from the ceilings. City health officials frequently cited the space as a retirement home for bed bugs and rodents, no doubt availing themselves of the building's poor disposal of garbage.

At the cost of over a hundred grand a year, the students shouldn't expect a vermin-free environment. I entered the lobby and passed by a security desk, with no guard or any indication of one. Lax security would have made it easy for an outsider to reach Sandy on his fateful night.

"Hey there, young man," I accosted a med student walking by in a short white coat.

"Me? Hey, what's up?"

"Yeah, you. Is there a security guard here?"

"He's probably on lunch hour. He needs a break from his nap."

I flashed my shield.

The kid put his hands up in an "I surrender" gesture, an odd response. "Okay, gotta go. Sad story, huh? Sherman/Sandy was a gregarious guy. Almost a cult figure. Got laid more than the rest of us put together."

"Oh yeah, a real lover-boy?" The kid seemed both awed and bitterly envious.

"Putting it mildly. We were all jealous until what happened. I used to date one of Sandy's conquests before he did. Her name is Rosemarie Li. Be sure to talk to her. She lives in 2E, the 2nd-floor apartment next door to mine. The walls are thin in this place. I heard enough of them to throw up.

He tried to dart away quickly.

"Wait a sec. What's your name?"

"Ralph Gruber. Third year. Apt. 2F. I have an air-tight alibi as I said, and I'll be happy to talk further after class."

"Who said anything about an alibi?"

"I dunno. Too many detective shows, I guess. There have been more cops than students swarming all over the dorm this weekend. See you."

I took the elevator up to the fifth floor, where the cleanup crew had relocated Sandy's roomies. Apartment 5G was a short jog down the hall with some wise-ass poster plastered next to the door. I knocked, and when no one answered, I turned the knob. It was open, and I was confronted by an angry young med student standing in his boxers.

"What the fuck?"

"Don't panic. I'm a detective." I flipped my identification open quickly.

"We had the entire NYPD here yesterday morning," he complained. "We don't need any more house calls. I hoped you'd be from maintenance. This place is a pigsty, and we haven't had any help in cleaning it."

"I'm sure you'll make it spotless quickly. What's your name, buddy?"

He was playing Mr. Tough Guy in his underwear.

"Where's your warrant, copper? Have you heard of search and seizure laws?"

"Ah, a physician who's a jailhouse lawyer as well."

I wanted to throttle this kid, but I knew that downtown wouldn't support me if one of the parents complained about Clint Eastwood picking on their children. I yearned to direct my borrowed taser at his wilted sword, which was peeking through his shorts.

"Look Hector, we can play this better down at the Command Center if you prefer. Might screw up your ability to get a medical degree."

"All right. My name is Hector Lopez and I'm one of Sandy's roommates or ex-roomies. You're a little old for this, aren't you pops?"

"I'll be checking into the rest home tomorrow," I retorted. "I need a couple more collars to get my pension."

We matched scowls for the moment and then Hector spoke up in a more congenial voice.

"All right, what's up? I've got an air-tight alibi…"

"Oh great, another crime show expert," I responded. "Give me a little help here. Tell me how you and Sandy were playing nicely in the sandbox a few days back."

I could hear a video game bleating like a sick animal in the background. I snuck a glimpse of someone on a couch, fingers pounding the keys of a laptop like a mad scientist.

"Detective I can't believe anyone would want to kill Sandy. No question that med school is very cut-throat, and our roomie was relentlessly out for himself. But he was under a lot of pressure from his family. They expected him to excel, but he could still be a lot of fun, especially under the influence..."

"Alcohol or drugs?"

"Mostly the booze, at least with us. Sandy had incredible powers of endurance, working the wards all day and partying all night. The guy never slept, so he probably required some chemical assistance, especially for his more intimate activities."

Hector gave me a leering shrug for emphasis.

"How many chemical stimulants would you guess he consumed?"

"I dunno. Not many. I stick to cigarettes. I'd rather die of cancer."

"How did he die, in your medical opinion?"

"Dunno, but it wasn't pretty. There was plenty of blood, plus the stench of fouling his pants."

"You seem to know a lot about it."

"I've got a nose."

"Do you have any idea where he scored his drugs?"

"Detective, I don't use. The rumor mill identified a guy called 'Pil' with one 'L,' who deals with the students, but we avoid him. Not our scene."

Oh, Pil, I thought, that son-of-a-bitch would be right in the midst, wherever the shit was flying. "If he's not your scene, Hector, what is? Maybe some peep clubs with your roommates."

"We usually all did our own thing, Pops, a little more sedentary like you." Hector was starting to get cute with me, and I don't dig cute. He got the message and reverted to playing it straight.

"We needed our relaxation when we could get it because working overnight at the hospital is very tense and disruptive to the system. I'll confess I did go to the clubs a couple of times with Sandy. At first, it seemed tame enough, just your typical urban hook-up scene, everyone on their cell rather than the dance floor."

I nodded to acknowledge that I was very aware of the club scene. Score one for Pops.

Hector continued. "Most of these joints, everyone knew Sandy by name. I'll never forget it. At one spot, called Dom XX, he'd pal around with a tall redhead, almost an older girlfriend. Great body. Nips like mommy's milk."

"Women? Men? What was the ratio there?"

"Can't exactly recall. There were all types, straight, gay, bi, trans, all ethnic groups, you name it. The boy loved the dark side, that's for sure."

Hector looked reflective for a moment. "Of course, with mixed genders, the bathrooms got a bit complicated. Some of the best partying took place there, all sexes involved. I was afraid to unzip my pants to take a leak."

"Maybe you ought to put some pants on now, Hector. But thanks. I may need you later. Can we rouse Ross Parker who first discovered the body?"

"Ross is studying in his room upstairs." Hector howled through cupped hands towards the staircase.

"Yo, Ross! Get your hairy ass down here!"

"Watch the language. Though I'm not your mother, please try to have some respect."

"Yes, sir. Um, sorry, sir."

From the stereo upstairs, I could hear a screeching performance with a rapper chanting about torturing and getting even with the cops. Such lovely guys, our hope for the future. Just then, a young man waltzed down the steps like a cross between Fred Astaire and Gene Kelly minus the umbrella. This must be Ross, the first responder. He was short, wiry, and wore tinted glasses, the Ivy aviator look. He didn't seem like the kind of guy who would be an athletic teammate of Sandy's.

Nor a candidate for murder.

I acknowledged him and asked who was playing the video games on the other side of the room.

"That's Prince Geoffrey He's one of our unofficial roomies, a scrub tech at the hospital. He's a Brit, very cool. Best hand-eye coordination in our group. He holds all the records on war games."

That was certainly something to be proud of. A quick thought tugged at me. "Somehow, you boys don't seem all that broken up about your roommate dying recently." With Ross's arrival, I suggested we grab a chair and sit bunched around a tiny coffee table.

"Sorry, detective. I was up in my room feeling down. We all grieve in our own way," Ross said.

Hector spoke up. "You can drop your big grief act, Ross. Detective's gonna find out one way or another about how we felt..."

As the outspoken leader, Hector seemed to be the man driving this dog sled. Very smart: they always said the lead dog in the sled had the most scenic view, though the dogs might look at it differently.

"Detective," Ross noted. "Hector has a flair for the dramatic. I know where he's going. Sandy was competitive, and even though we were his bros, he had an ego, an all-about-me attitude that could be very annoying."

"Can you expand?"

"The world revolved around him, especially when he was indulging in his athletic glory. Too bad he's been sidelined by an irregular heartbeat."

"Has he been getting treatment such as blood thinner or even an ablation? I'm sure this fellow Pil who is the main supplier of drugs without a license can be very helpful."

"Detective, I told you, Ross and I, we're boozers not users." Hector was again protesting his innocence, perhaps a bit too much. "We have no use for 'Pil' or pills of any kind except for aspirin or Tylenol."

Give these guys credit. They had a unified story, and no doubt pre-arranged alibis. I knew it would be difficult to pry some uncontaminated truth out of them. I should have followed protocol and talked to them individually.

Ross spoke up. "One thing you should know, the deceased had a girlfriend, Rosemarie Li. She lives in 2E. I heard she's been kind of messed up about all of this. She's very naïve, what you'd call a country girl. Sandy was her first serious boyfriend." Ross paused as if being careful about what followed. "She trusted him even though she witnessed his instant chemistry with the female crowd."

"Girl didn't know her luck," Hector said. "That boy was playing in a lot of dorm rooms. When any female supervisor was on his rotation, he found a way to charm her. You know, flirt his way into honors or at least a good night's release of tension."

"Any particular doctors or nurses you could name?"

"Dr. Dillon, or Dr. Ashley as we call her, she seemed to be his unofficial personal advisor. She's our first-year resident in surgery. They were always having coffee, or she came over here a few times. She made it look like it was very professional, with lots of scientific jargon and memory quizzes of body parts. I know he was dying to put the blocks to her. Who could blame him? Might have been the one woman who resisted him."

"You boys have a lot of respect for your roommate," I said. "Unfortunately, it's mostly booty envy. Let's hear where you were both last Thursday night."

"What do you mean?" Ross's tone had turned serious. He was quiet, clearly the most studious and analytical. A Princeton grad, apparent from his sweatshirt.

I mused privately, sometimes silent can mean deadly but we continued without comment or further suspicion.

"First of all, Mr. Parker. I understand you found Sandy dead and called it in ten minutes after midnight. The TV in his room was set to a late game on ESPN, according to our clean-up crew. Unless Ms. Li, the girlfriend, favored soccer and Scotch, I would rule her out. Sounds more like a male buddy date."

"We went through this with your crew yesterday, detective. We were bowling at Hudson Piers that night,"

Hector said. "I have no idea who might have been babysitting him."

"Ross, you found Sandy in his room downstairs," I said. "The apartment was unlocked. If he planned to do a lot of drugs without getting caught, it would have been strange to leave the door open, don't you think? Anybody could have walked in on him."

"Dude, I hope you're not accusing us." Hector was back on the offensive. "We always respect a closed-door as if it's locked. We left to bowl around five, came back around eleven after grabbing a few wings and beers. No one saw the body until Ross happened to stumble over it when he took a study break. So, maybe Sandy was spending one evening with a male friend for a change?"

"I'm just covering all bases, guys."

"Jesus, detective. We're not murderers." Hector again. He managed to look incredulous and irate at the same time. A born defense attorney.

"Hey, go check our alibis," Hector suggested. "Call the Pier. We're homebodies. Sandy was the playboy out on the town. Nothing unusual about that."

"Okay. I think I've got the alibis straight. 2E is where you say Ms. Li resides?"

"Yes detective," Ross responded. "Go easy on her. She knows very little about the clubs, the nurses, the older playmates. She was from Iowa, very rural and trusting."

I knew I was being played, but I had to let some of it go. I turned to a ruddy-faced chap who had just emerged from a bathroom dressed in scrubs, apparently preparing to go to work. He was the electronic gamer.

"And what about you? It's Mr. Geoffrey Laird, correct?"

"Oh hello. Nice to meet you. Everyone around here calls me Prince Jeff. Bit of a joke."

"Okay, Your Royal Highness," I said, "Were you 'buds' with the deceased?"

"Good pals, sir, I'm very worked up about it all."

"You don't seem worked up."

"Yo. He's British," Hector chimed in. "Stiff upper lip, this is about as worked up as he gets."

"Well then, Prince Jeff. I'll cut right to the chase. Where were you the night of Sandy's death?"

"Where was I? Where I usually am, pulling the night shift at the hospital for overtime. This city is hard on my bank account."

"Can anyone confirm your whereabouts?"

"Well, I was aiding Dr. Maura Davis on a circulatory case until very late into the night. I went home after midnight, closer to one a.m., where my girlfriend was waiting."

"And who might she be?"

"I'd rather not say, why drag her into it? Dr. Davis will support my alibi."

"I presume that means Dr. Davis will confirm your presence 'well into the night?'"

"Of course, sir. Feel free to ask her yourself. She's a big bag of fun."

"One more question. Did you know Dr. Ashley Dillon?"

"Only in my dreams, detective. She's quite a tasty bird, isn't she?"

"Do you think Sandy might have had a taste of her now and then? Maybe some leftovers?" Oh man, I was being as adolescent as they were.

"Very good on the metaphors for a cop." Prince Jeff looked bemused. "Gotta go, Detective, can I offer some advice? You might spruce up the wardrobe, get a deerstalker hat and pipe like Sherlock Holmes. It could help the image. Which seems a bit nerdy right now. Bye guys."

"One more wisecrack and we're all taking a ride." I deployed my Cagney sneer. "Okay, Mr. Parker. Your turn in the barrel. Do you want to describe the scene as you saw it on the night in question? You found Sandy and called 911 shortly after midnight. What happened?"

Ross paused a moment, almost choking up. "Detective, I came home, shut myself in my room to study. Must have dozed off. I woke up and went downstairs to raid the fridge."

Ross stopped as the color drained from his face. "I know Sandy dabbled in drugs and booze, but I never thought he would lose control like that. Lying nude in a white coat. No vital signs. He was dead and might have been for a while. The M.E. transport guys came, tried to revive him, and whisked him away. Oh yeah, an investigator, a gawky but tough broad named Jennette asked a few questions. She was from the Medical Examiner's office. That was it."

"Sorry, kid, we're almost done. The security log downstairs showed an outside delivery around 1:00 a.m. Ross, do you know anything about that?"

"When Sandy drank, he loved Chinese, and our whole place stunk of it. That was courtesy of the Mandarin place up the street, they came and went at some point, you could smell it," Ross said.

"The future doctors of America up all night. God help your patients," I muttered.

"Don't worry detective," Hector assured me. "We're just letting off some steam. This has been a terrible trauma for us all. Do have a pleasant day."

18. Ross Parker

Mid-day Sunday

"Thanks, Hector for hanging me out to dry."

The detective was gone. We were still sitting and sorting out what had just transpired.

"What are you whimpering about, Ross," Hector said, "this cop doesn't have a clue."

"Yeah, well, he's not done yet; he was just getting acquainted."

Hector was chugging his beer and not interested in any further discussion.

I went up to my room and shut the door. I felt drained, like I was a balloon filled up with helium, and someone popped the skin. Not that I cared about Sandy. Or Hector for that matter. He had sought to prevent me from further scrutiny as if my intelligence and lack of social graces would make him look guilty by association.

"Look him in the eye, damn it, look him in the eye," Hector coached me on our meetings with the NYPD. It was just what my parents used to say. As a kid, they ran me around to all the shrinks in town, and there were plenty in Chicago, the neuro-epicenter of the world.

The docs all came back with the same prognosis: I was somewhere on 'the spectrum.'

No surprise to me, I'd read all about it, more like freak-out time for my family. I will keep up my research. The latest in the DSM-5 is now called "pragmatic communications disorder," which is political correctness for what was formerly known as Asperger's. Your mind is going a zillion miles an hour, but you can't grasp or sort what's in it.

Big frigging deal. I was still categorized as "high functioning." Didn't they say that Asperger kids were born for the Internet? I was good at math and loved YouTube. My scientific gifts didn't seem to impress the Princeton girls, where I proved to be obsessive about the small stuff, such as good grades, and not very sociable.

I could tell you the lifetime batting average for every baseball player going back almost a century. No big deal, occasionally, I'd have a little emotional outburst. Every kid does some kicking and screaming now and then.

For me, it meant my parents dragging me back to the doctors for endless brain scans.

My roomie Hector had lied about my whereabouts on the night of Sandy's death, probably a stupid tactic since the detective was looking for holes in our alibis. Better get my story straight when he comes calling again. Here's how I'd game-plan it.

"Let's face it, officer, Sandy could be a first-rate prick and he probably deserved whatever happened. I'd been out with a friend that night, got back around ten p.m., and dozed off. A little later, probably around eleven or so, I could hear him downstairs watching the tv or on his Kindle in our living room, some Thursday night football game. He had the volume very high, and above the noise, I could still hear a shrill voice that sounded like a female downstairs under the influence, whining a bit."

"She sounded excited or agitated, or maybe she was a female reporter on the sidelines of the football game. Then the voices softened and turned into murmurs that I couldn't clarify. Next thing, they were most likely in his room, with the door closed so I couldn't hear anything further. Things got quiet. I never heard Hector or his bowling friends coming back. Unusual for them to be considerate. After midnight I went down for a dose of caffeine. The door to Sandy's room was partially open. That seemed strange, like maybe someone had left in a hurry. I had an intuition that I should check him out."

At least that's the story I'll tell the detective when he comes asking again. Screw Hector, he's the one telling the big lies. Where was he after bowling? And when exactly did he actually come home?

19. Barney Kazinski

Sunday, Mid-afternoon

My weekend was ruined. The boys' quarters had reeked of filth and bullshit. Once outside the door of the dorm, I was feeling dirtier than when I was inside. I needed another shower, followed by a stiff bourbon, hold the chaser.

To make matters worse, my ex-wife Jill was intruding in my thoughts again. She always shared my morbid fascination for the deviant species along the human food chain. I thought Mr. Darwin said humans were getting better, more adaptive, like the beak on a finch. Darwin must not have anticipated these med students, all their survival impulses filtered by their egos.

It was obvious these dudes enjoyed toying with authority—especially law enforcement—as if we were villains in their video games. They liked to play at murder with twitch fingers, but I still doubted they had the balls to do the job "in real-time," as they would say.

I needed a way to cool down. Here was a refreshing idea: a quick pit stop at the ice queen's office. I figured Dr. Davis would be working alone on a weekend unless she was at home yanking cat hairs out of her pet. I had a few more questions for her now that I'd met the roommates. I went over to the admin offices and, big surprise, she was there, with her door open, plucking away at her keyboard.

"Dr. Davis."

"You again? What do you want? Can't you see I'm busy here?"

"Yeah, it's me again, doctor. Shall we dispense with the pleasantries?"

"What do you want, Detective Kazinski? Make it quick."

"I just came from a meeting with Sandy Wainwright's roommates. I hope they're a little more serious about their studies."

"No one's asking your opinion, detective. Our med students are among the country's brightest. What they do with their Sundays is their business."

"Okay, let me ask if you were familiar with his roommates, Hector Lopez, or Ross Parker?"

"Not personally, detective, he stood out, but I can't micromanage everyone. My guess is his buddies were as rambunctious as he usually is. Thank God, these days we have a higher percentage of female applicants."

"Let me try you on a couple of other students."

"Please spare me."

"Just a couple more. First, Ralph Gruber strikes me as a bit of a wise guy based on my recent encounter with him."

"Mr. Gruber? Sure. He's a hanger-on, latching himself to Sandy's coattails. Very annoying to the staff."

"Dr. Davis, can you recall if Ralph was with you in surgery on the night of the murder?"

"Oh God, detective. I concentrate on the patient and not on who's observing the surgical theater. I don't recall Ralph Gruber's schedule that night."

"This is important, Doctor, because we need to know who was where."

"I've told you before, Sandy was a very bright fellow and self-impressed to the core. Ralph was a slower sort, the weak one in the herd. He was trying hard to keep up."

"Alright, doctor. We can leave it at that. Just one last question. On the night of Mr. Wainwright's death, are you aware if a scrub technician by the name of Prince Geoffrey Laird was assisting you on a case? It was after normal hours and easy to get confused."

Maura Davis rolled her frosty eyes at me. Her voice ratcheted up into anger very quickly.

"Detective. Of course, Mr. Laird scrubbed in with me! He always does. He's very reliable. Thank God for that British sense of duty. Now, if you'll excuse me..."

She offered a wicked smile. I returned serve with my most sinister look.

"Is it typical for you to pursue surgeries into the bewitching hours?"

Lucifer could take pointers from this lady. She responded, "When I am on-call, and a serious circulatory case comes in, yes, detective, I need to perform that surgery immediately before a patient succumbs to serious complications such as gangrene or death."

"Was that the case on Thursday night?"

"There are always critical cases, which you know are confidential. All that is relevant is I was there long after dark, and Mr. Laird was assisting."

"All right. Thank you for your time, doctor. I'm sorry to have interrupted your busy schedule."

"Fine. Just try not to let it happen again, or there will be ramifications."

Once outside, daylight had turned into early dusk. A pre-winter chill had set in. My mother's voice from childhood popped up: "Barney, where are your mittens? It's icy cold out."

20. Barney Kazinski

Early Sunday evening

There was time for one last call at the sports pier.

Let me confess, I've always hated sports -- whether playing them or watching them.

I was a very awkward boy, always the last guy chosen in our pick-up baseball games and exiled to Siberia in right field where I could only daydream and pluck dandelions. Individual sports like golf or tennis weren't much better. It didn't matter whether the ball was stationary or moving swiftly over a net. I could never seem to swat it properly.

Unfortunately, my job required frequent contact with the "jocks," male and female, who were in the headlines for perpetuating poor behavior before or after their match (or sometimes during it).

The sports pier on the Hudson River in lower Manhattan epitomized all that I distrusted, the uninhibited den of sports nuts. When I entered the building, I could hear the cacophony of pounded balls or slammed pucks, mixed with the exuberant cries of teammates scoring a point or a goal.

The hockey rink was on the main floor. I knew the locale well because even amateur hockey players liked it rough; they didn't lose their teeth in Bible class. A small office at the mezzanine level overlooked the rink. I knocked and found "Coach" Raymond Shaw on a hand microphone instructing a class of young skaters below him on the ice.

Coach Ray personified a coach who'd been a former player. A shock of white hair curled around the edges of a baseball cap. Under a tight sweatshirt, his weight congregated in a pulpy belly. However, he was still young of heart when it came to his job. I knew from past encounters how much he loved his work. I doubted he had any life outside of it. He was a one-man band who handled scheduling and refereeing games while medically treating those banged up.

He felt very protective of his athletes when they were accused of violence outside the rink. He did not offer a cheer when I walked in.

"Good evening detective," he said, placing a hand over the mike. "Just finishing up a class. Did you forget your pads?"

"No, Ray, I think the puck is coming at you tonight."

He waved his class good night and turned to me with a wearied expression of 'what-is-it-this-time?'

I knew he'd want it straight. "Ray, as you may know, there was an unusual death in the early hours Friday, a medical student at Hillside. Some of his roommates claimed that they were here during the time shortly before the death occurred. That would be Thursday, in the evening...."

"Are we talking murder suspects here? I hadn't heard." His face turned more hostile.

"No, Ray, this is preliminary. I'm trying to put some basic facts together."

"Look, Barney, I don't want to get caught up in a murder case. I ought to call our legal department, considering they love emergencies on Sunday night. Can we let them have peace? As a favor, we'll keep this completely off the record, okay?"

"It's off the record for now and I'm assuming it will stay that way. If this turns into an official murder investigation, then you can bring in a whole squad of lawyers for all I care."

"All right, let me check. You said Thursday evening, three nights ago."

Ray rustled through some papers and found his scheduling clipboard. "What are the names please?"

I identified Sandy, Hector, and Ross.

"Okay, let's see. Only Hector Lopez checked in at 5:57 p.m. and bowled for three hours. Out at around 10. We usually give them a little leeway on the hourly charges. Sandy was not here. When he's around, you can't miss the crowd that would gather to see him. Funny, he hasn't been seen much lately. Normally he'd come over on a Sunday afternoon.

"He has apparently had some physical issues, have you heard?"

"No, he's always putting up a brave front with me. I just heard some gossip from one of the players. He hasn't been his usual self, but is still banging the crap out of his opponents. I knew his dad whose athletic career was cut short by injuries."

"What about Ross Parker on Thursday night? He claimed to be here bowling with Hector.

"Not here on the list. Might not have signed in. We know how many games are bowled but we don't keep track of all the names unless they're in our league games."

"Ray, how well do you know these Hillside guys?"

"Oh yeah, very well. They're rarely a complete team, two or three tops, so we match them in a game that is short a couple of guys. Everyone wants Sandy on their team. He's legendary: big and fast, not an ounce of fat on him for all the burgers and fries he stuffs into his mouth. He was a big star in college. He should go pro instead of messing around in medicine. When he gets rolling, let's just say I've had to use quite a bit of tape patching up the opposition."

"Sounds like he has a reputation for more violent behavior."

"Oh, that's not the half of it. You want to know what is unusual about Sandy?" Ray said. "He can be a monster in the games, yet he's a pussycat before and after. He's mentored a ton of young players who all look up to him. The man has more patience than I do. Even with the little ones, boys, and girls, some of them can barely skate. He'll lace them up and give them short sticks so that they can get a feel for whacking it into the goal. You should see how hard they work to please him. A natural coach."

"That's nice to hear, a real sportsman. You said he didn't show up on Thursday with his group?"

"Nope, it must be exams or his health. They say he likes the nightlife so maybe he's just worn out."

"And you're sure about the other guy, Ross Parker?"

"No, I don't recall him. Here, take a look at my clipboard and see if you recognize any other names."

I ran down the coach's log. Bingo. There was Ralph Gruber, popping up as usual. He'd checked in at 6 p.m. and left a checkmark for when he left, no time notation.

"Hey Ray, do you know this fellow, Ralph Gruber? I met him in the dorm at Hillside. Was he part of the gang?"

"To be honest, I don't recall. He isn't one of the regulars. We have a few Hillside kids who come down here to play or show off for their girlfriends. The gals are plenty damn tough on the ice too. And they don't steal equipment." He shrugged and waved his hands in mock despair.

"Ray, what about a lanky guy with a British accent? The first name is Geoffrey or Jeff. I don't see him listed here."

"We got a few Canadian accents but no Brits that I remember. No matter how I split the teams, everyone wants Sandy because his presence determines the winning side."

"Hey Ray, I see a woman's name here, Rosemarie Li? She signed in a week or so ago. Is she a regular?"

"I recall she sometimes comes with Sandy. Pretty Asian gal. Didn't seem the type who would like to watch big oafs smashing their brains out."

Ray paused for a moment. "So, who is dead? A medical student?"

I stopped to compose myself. "Sandy is the deceased, Ray. We're not sure if it might have been an overdose."

"An overdose, you shittin' me?" The color had drained from Ray's face. He sat down, almost falling back into his chair. "Sandy, dead? The kid was the real deal. Cocky, but he could back it up. A nice kid deep down, a natural leader. No way he overdosed. Maybe hit the sauce a bit, but all the med students indulge. So much pressure."

Ray couldn't stop shaking his head. "He's dead? It can't be. And certainly not by himself."

"Sorry, I've got to ask you a few more questions, Ray. Did you ever see any sign of Sandy or his pals drugged up?"

Ray nodded. "You know it's funny now that you mention it. The kid, he would come in here occasionally, and he'd seem a little glassy and slurring his words, from liquor not drugs. I can tell the difference."

"He could still go out and play normally?"

"Oh yeah, he always works with the kids, and then he plays. I'd worry that he might injure himself. I make sure we keep our liability waiver up to date. In case the rumors were true about his medical issues. Or possibly, have you thought if someone wanted to pay back an injury?"

Ray looked sadly at me. I could see a glint of moisture in his eyes. "God, he was a special kid. Everyone treated him like the king. Their idol. Hey, is there a wake or something? I'd like to pay my respects."

"Not sure Ray, the family wants to rush the body back to California. Probably not receiving visitors. Thanks, I gotta go."

I left and closed the office door behind me. Reentering the tumult and loud voices of weekend athletes in action, I swear I could hear Coach Ray pounding on his desk and sobbing.

21. Barney Kazinski

Sunday later evening

I drove back and wandered around the apartment, too depressed to read or stream something. Finally, I hopped in my car again and drove over to Hillside for some quick takeout. I could see the shadowy light cast by the food truck. A woman's voice carried through the darkness. She was ordering a Jamaican meat pie.

For a moment, I got closer and stood transfixed. In the silhouetted light, she displayed a calm manner and a slim, dusky frame with ample cargo up top. Her scrubs made it clear that she was most likely a doctor, probably one who preached nutrition to her patients while playing the coronary lottery game by stuffing down meat pies on the fly.

This young woman was a looker. The light from the truck amplified her natural beauty, like a model or a movie star. No amount of fatigue could bury the charisma. The ghost of Jill came back to haunt me.

"See something you like down there, old boy? I'm up here." The mellow voice was aimed in my direction. Oh damn, I must have been squinting a bit too long at her nameplate and its environs.

I cleared my throat, trying to recover, and glanced sheepishly at her face.

I didn't need her nameplate. I knew who it was.

"I'm sorry, Dr. Ashley is it? I'm Barney Kazinski, NYPD."

"Well, nice to meet you, Officer." She stuck out a graceful hand, giving mine a hard squeeze. Our eyes met for a brief second.

"One meat pie!" Alessandro, the overnight cook manning the food truck, called out loudly. Business is business. He didn't care about my Romeo and Juliet moment.

"Right here!" She responded; our instant connection was broken.

"Hey, let me get that," I offered.

"Oh, you don't…" she started to protest, but I was too quick. I swiftly produced the necessary bills and forgot to order for myself. She grabbed her pie and started dashing back to the hospital.

She was about thirty feet away and almost back to the building when she half-turned and yelled into the night air: "Hey thanks, Barney Kazinski, NYPD."

"No problem…" I shouted back. Too late. She was gone.

I ordered a pie and contemplated what to do next. Most normal single guys would grab the take-out and chug a brew, preparing for Sunday night football. I checked my email for messages and was pleased that the boss lady, La-T, had texted and wanted to see me on the double. Work must also be her antidote for loneliness in a late evening.

I decided to walk the mile or so to our Command Center. In the prevailing darkness, I arrived at the shadows of slumbering brick. On a bulletin board inside, a handwritten note posted a warning that the "basement plumbing is out" and the holding cells "down there" were not to be occupied.

I wondered if that meant we should invite our perps home for the week.

The place was deserted, but through the glass of her office, La-T waved me in with a friendly look that could stop a charging rhino in its tracks.

I gave her a thumbs up and scurried towards the men's room. The pit stop offered a simple moment of reflection. La-T and I had jointly experienced plenty of history in our relationship, dating back to our days as partners and road warriors in a pothole-punished Ford Taurus.

My mentorship had helped her leap over numerous veterans on the force to become one of the first black women to attain a commanding officer position.

Heading back to her office, I knew something was bothering her, as she never tolerated fools. Despite her success inside the system, she always tried to maintain the stubborn streak of a rebel and an outsider. Thus, we had a lot in common. Yet she was very private, and I knew almost nothing about her personal life.

"Where the hell have you been?" she asked, employing her usual tactic of putting me on the defensive.

"Everywhere I should have been, except resting at home on the weekend. I was hanging out with the roomies. Eating meat pie and a load of errands. What's your beef?"

"Oh, we're in wise-guy mode tonight. I can see that."

"As it happens my dear T, I gave up my court-side tickets to the Knicks tonight, so I could be out there hustling for you.

"Good try, Detective Barney; the Knicks are playing in Toronto. And the only decent seat you've ever had at the Garden is in the men's room."

For emphasis, she raised a querulous eyebrow, but only one, an encouraging sign.

"Just so we're clear," she said. "We must pivot quickly now that murder seems to be on the docket. Meanwhile, it's been hard to get a handle on the deceased," she continued. "Not a lot of close male friends. We've interviewed a few blushing nurse practitioners, not much intel there. It comes down to this: Sandy Wainwright was a self-centered young devil with a soft side that made women forget everything their mothers warned them about."

"He wasn't alone in having a strong faith in his competence," I chided her. "Gotta have that ballsy psyche to be a good surgeon."

"I'll say this," she concurred. "Sandy's report card suggests he was a good listener and very intuitive in diagnosis, given all the static surrounding a new clinical student. Our colleague Becky says a few members of our street force cited his empathy and special connection with seriously ill younger patients. He apparently liked to hang over at pediatrics, possibly a girlfriend there. What do you think?"

I gave her my most affable shrug. I could use a breather from today's quest that had turned up very little. What I needed was some relaxed companionship. "Hey there La-T, how about a quick nightcap down the street? Our friend Mick has a generous spirit when he pours for the troops in blue."

"You are kidding me?" She made a disdainful face. "You know socializing rules." Then she turned more pensive, like a stone softening back into clay. "On the other hand, it's a Sunday night, and we're the only two dummies that are working. Give me a minute while I get my coat."

Flashback: 60 Days Ago

22. Dr. Ashley Dillon

Surgical Blues

Accuse, Blame, Criticize, and Deny, all surgeons learned to recite these ABCDs as if they were a pillar of religious faith. It might provide an inside moment of humor, but, like any good joke, profound truth lay behind it.

Surgeons rejected blame for an unexpected patient disaster to deflect guilt and insulate us from the frightening truth that tragedy is often random and inexplicable. Sometimes we couldn't retrieve answers within the realm of medical logic, so doctors reverted to the simple dichotomy of the operating theater: We save lives, we can lose lives.

Yet, for a young resident, the pain of causing an actual, live patient's death was unbearable (made worse by the hovering presence of malpractice lawyers).

I should have kept my ABCDs in mind, but the growing feelings for Sandy clouded my judgment.

After our initial drink date in August, Sandy and I had both chilled into a disciplined reserve over the next month.

We were frequently doing rounds together as part of a team and trying to quash any rumors of greater intimacy. From his occasional ripening glances, I sensed Sandy was waiting for me to make the next move.

One late afternoon, we were doing our final rounds for the day. I scanned the surgery chart for the following day, posted on a whiteboard by Dr. Davis. My quest focused on finding the best case of the day and hoping that we'd scrub in as a pair.

Maybe I was looking for trouble. In retrospect, I was foolishly setting myself up for failure. Sandy was preparing soon to move to another resident's surgical rotation. This case might be my last chance to show off my medical acumen and nail down our relationship.

The patient was a middle-aged woman in generally good shape. An avid jogger and yoga devotee, she had whipsawed her body through over-zealous exercise. Her symptoms included constant pain in her neck and shoulders as well as numbness in her fingers. An MRI indicated a major pinched nerve beneath her breastbone caused by pressure from her uppermost rib.

Bed rest and physical therapy did not improve the condition, known as Thoracic Outlet Syndrome. Her pain persisted, and she couldn't find a comfortable position to sleep so that she was begging for increasing dosages of opioids. The surgery aimed to re-set and remove a portion of the offending rib.

I had studied and practiced this procedure on cadavers until I had it down cold. I jumped at the chance to impress Dr. Davis, whose open animosity toward Sandy had generated a dark tide washing over my reputation as well. As it happened, he would not be involved in this procedure after all, so I felt alone and disoriented.

The surgery did not start well. Dr. Davis stood opposite me in her usual starched and arctic manner and didn't say a word. I could feel her glacial eyes burning into my body, which disrupted my normal surgeon's composure and rhythm.

Her manner made it clear: 'This is your show, kid, don't blow it.'

The primary threat in any vascular surgery is the welter of major arteries and other vessels surrounding the point of attack. In this case, that's where things went wrong. I nicked a vital artery, and it erupted like a geyser. The blood was spurting everywhere. No one could stop it. Dr. Davis made a half-hearted attempt at intervention; and then, a backup emergency team rushed in to help while I tried to clamp the bleeding arena.

We were too late. The patient bled out. It was well into the night when we finished trying to save her.

The whole OR was stunned. Even Maura Davis looked overwhelmed by the outpouring of so much blood. Dazed and disoriented, I helped with the cleanup and then said dejectedly to her: "I've got to get out of here." She looked at me with annoyance, but she didn't try to stop me.

There was nothing more to be done.

I dashed out of the OR and raced back to my apartment as fast as my clogs could carry me, with my long white coat doused in scarlet. I could feel tiny droplets of blood still simmering on my forehead. Following surgery, the protocol was to wash off any exposed plasma particles quickly, the universal precaution from exposure to an infection.

This time, I didn't care.

After what happened, I needed to get the hell out of Hillside and call Sandy.

He would hold me, wash my bloody face, console me.

I dialed his cell with trembling fingers. "Can you come over?" My voice was quaking.

"Oh my God. What's wrong, Ashley? You sound horrible."

"Just come. I need to see you now."

There was an awkward moment of hesitation before he responded. "I'm studying right now, be there as soon as I can."

I could hear partying sounds in the background and ignored them. I sat on the couch, my mind regurgitating the surgery mistakes for what seemed like hours. Finally, he showed up on my doorstep shortly before dawn. He was a burst of fresh air tainted by alcoholic fumes on his breath. I greeted him at my front door, almost comatose, still wearing my bloody scrubs.

"Ash, you are shaking! You are covered in blood. Come on, let's get you out of those clothes."

He disrobed me gently in the entrance hall, then scooped and carried me into the bathroom, where he drew a warm bath. He delicately placed me in the bathtub as if I were an infant and began scrubbing the caked residues off my face and neck.

"It was a nightmare, Sandy." I paused as his hands threaded through my bloody patches of flesh. He was like an avenging angel turning the bathwater crimson. I was still shivering as tears started to gush down my face.

"We, I—lost control. There was blood everywhere. We couldn't clamp the rupture. And that bitch Dr. Davis watched me as I crashed. She knew perfectly well that I'm an intern, and she had final responsibility."

I stopped talking for a few seconds, put my head down, then lifted it, stiff with rage and remorse. Sandy was quietly trying to 'interpret the data' as he would say.

"Where was my pal, Prince Jeff?" he asked. "He's a pro at exposing and protecting the field. That's why Maura Davis always wants him by her side."

"I don't know," I said still tearfully. "He wasn't there. Maybe they both wanted me to fail. What difference does it make? I killed her, I killed a nice woman who took too many yoga lessons and sprained her neck."

My guy remained silent, thoughtful, always the ever-professional diagnostician.

For the moment, I wanted to take out all my frustration on him. Where were his emotions in my crisis? After a failed operation, it didn't seem cool or noble to be a doctor. I felt myself coming apart, more logically preparing to occupy a mortuary slab next to my dead patient.

Sandy wanted to say the exact right thing to alleviate my pain, yet he could find no words. He seemed almost detached as he idly soaped my back. Was he in a drunken stupor?

He helped lift me out of the tub, wrapped me in a towel, and led me back to the sofa. He cradled my head in his lap. I listened to his breathing, steady and soothing. I could feel his hands inside the towel, stroking my body in a gentle massage and then inevitably ranging with greater urgency over my breasts and down into the pelvic core. His heartbeat was starting an up-tempo riff.

Suddenly, he felt like a barking dog straining on a leash. He wanted my flesh. His natural tendency was to crave sex in any intimate situation. Yet, my tears weren't stopping, and he finally got the message that I only wanted to be held.

As if in sympathy, it started pouring outside. We reclined tightly, our arms and bodies overlapping, while we listened to the raindrops drumming on the roof. Sandy was snoring lightly; I ignored his sour breath spraying out in tiny staccato bursts. I couldn't sleep, yet at that moment, a resigned calm blanketed my senses.

This meant real love, or at least I thought it did, the intimacy when you're not having sex, simply lying quietly entwined on a cramped couch. I was enveloped in a blissful cocoon, watching daylight burst into the room. At some point, I must have dozed off, and he left.

Having expected a massive witch-hunt that would culminate in my being relieved of duties, I was surprised when I reported to Dr. Davis's office later that morning. She maintained her usual icy manner, yet she kept our conversation on a factual level without emotional recriminations. She could see my authentic bereavement. No doubt she felt validated by my comedown.

She also knew this was a cover-your-ass moment for her as the attending physician.

"We try to learn from our mistakes," she said, with a faint scent of sarcasm. "We'll have to prepare the patient's case for the Morbidity and Mortality conference next week. We want our peers to understand that this was a one-in-a-thousand instance of bad luck and a camouflaged blood vessel."

I was heavy-hearted and relieved. Yet, I also knew that the unexpected loss of a patient would leave a permanent stain on my record if she had anything to do with it.

I walked over to the residents' team room and sat alone, processing what had occurred, and writing up notes of the previous night. Sandy was nowhere to be seen as I stumbled through my rounds.

The day moved slowly—the gigantic wall clock at the nurses' station seemed paralyzed. As I returned to the team's staging room and peeked through the tiny window, I realized it was dark again outside and, per usual, I had missed most of the daylight.

Sandy reappeared with a group of students. He ignored me; he probably felt a botched operation was not the moment for an outpouring of affection. I slowly put on my backpack, waiting for everyone but Sandy to leave.

"Coming Ashley?" One of the senior residents called out. "In a minute," I sighed. It looked suspicious as class was over. Sandy turned to leave. "Wait." I grabbed him by the arm. "Come with me." I took his hand and whisked him down the empty hallway, through a thick door, and into a series of twisting corridors.

The two of us arrived at the anatomy lab. The cold antiseptic smell brought back memories of the practice lab during my first year in med school. God, that seemed like a lifetime ago. Yet the overriding smell of death filled my nostrils, reminding me of the time with my then pal Wendy Jamison in our med school lab.

For the first time, I appreciated the sanctity of death in our work. Many of these patients had donated their bodies to science; the cadaver drawers were their burial grounds. The opportunity to learn through bodily dissection was a rite of passage.

My time for reflection was over. I had come to this lab for a reason. I gloved up and pulled the plastic off one of the cadavers dedicated to the residents' education. I was obsessively determined to re-explore the torso and redo the operation correctly.

"Sandy," I pleaded. "Please come help me."

I assembled a 10-blade knife and—in one fluid motion—slit the body precisely as if performing the surgery again.

"We were right here, damn it—*right here*!" I pointed to the anatomical spot. An hour elapsed while I reviewed my mistake, teeth chattering in the cold air. Finally, Sandy responded.

"Ash, it's late. I'm exhausted and starving. And freezing. We must get out of here."

He pulled me back into the present moment. I approached him like prey, slowly, deliberately, as if stalking him on all fours. I could almost feel my tail twitch.

"Wait!" he exclaimed. "Wash your hands first. I don't need my cock preserved in formaldehyde, thank you very much."

I erupted in laughter: "You are a sick fuck, you know that?"

"At least right now, I'm *your* sick fuck…"

I walked over to the scrub tank, grabbed a betadine brush, and, with theatrical aplomb, scrubbed my hands and forearms for several minutes, exactly as if I were completing surgery.

"That's better." He rolled his eyes and performed a quick rinse of his hands and arms. The mood tensed, desire beckoned, and his muscles bulged.

In a flash, we loosened our scrub pants, followed by savage kissing, panting, rubbing: two animals in primordial concert.

The intoxicating aura of my man overtook all other sensations. In the logistics of sex, he radiated self-assurance. Exorcising his frustrations from the previous night, he stood roaring, ready.

For a freeze-frame moment, we came up for air. "We're about to consummate anatomy lab sex. Are you sure about this?" he asked, clawing off more clothing.

"I guarantee you that this is the most action these stiffs in here have enjoyed in quite a while. They will be cheering us on from the afterlife," I noted wryly.

Sandy let out a small laugh and drew my body against his. He was totally enjoying this fantasy exercise where the anatomy lab had been converted into a bordello. Blindly responding, I could hear the metal anatomy tables shaking as he reached for a blue Operating Room towel and forced it against my mouth, muffling my ecstasy.

Just then, we heard a voice and a banging door.

"Oh God, we're not alone!" We hastily pulled up our pants and discarded torn clothing just moments before two surgery students walked into our section for their practice session. We calmly replaced the plastic cover over our silent witness as if we were making up a bed together.

"Hey Joe, Steve…" I greeted them like classmates waiting for a lecture to commence.

They didn't seem to notice my very red face. Or Sandy's devilish grin. We bolted out of the fume-filled room and reversed field down the dark corridors, checking nervously behind us.

We split up quickly. I went home and fell asleep immediately, squirming under a succession of cadaverous nightmares.

23. Dr. Ashley Dillon

Flashback: The next day, two months earlier

When I woke up in the early afternoon, I needed to clear my head via some diversionary impiety from my friend Wendy Jamison. I immediately called her, and fortunately, she was still available, with enough time to squeeze in lunch before reporting for her late afternoon into evening shifts.

We met in a small café a couple of blocks away from the hospital, where we could avoid the prying eyes and ears of medical gossip. As we sat down, I could feel her shoulders slumped, a shining beauty in dull gray repose as if her mundane academic life was diminishing her radiance.

Wendy had always sparkled in medical school, where she had cultivated a unique life. She was a tall, rangy brunette, slim through the middle and tightly knit from many hours in a gym. She liked to call her upstairs charms "the peeping Toms" because they would pop stealthily out of her profile when she threw her soldiers back. Way up top, her cobalt blue eyes could melt any male's defenses and offer the promise of an evening to remember.

She had worked her way through med school as a part-time hostess on a cruise line and managed to sail the seas while pursuing her studies. We all covered for her absences. ("She's got fibroid problems, you understand." No male wanted to delve into details.) Remarkably, she was a quick study who maintained decent marks back on land at home.

Unfortunately, her academic record had been only good enough to qualify for a pediatric internship. She wanted

Hillside, but she also craved an adult specialty. Nonetheless, she had been a great tutor for me in the social realm. I was still locked down about sex. She had produced my first magic wand and its clandestine delights. Yet, when we would double-date, I never seemed to click, while Wendy always managed to have that post-coital glow the next morning.

Her pallor told a different story today. She had reluctantly tried adapting to a new city: new faces, new colleagues, and the rigors of holding a steady job where she couldn't dash off to the high seas at a moment's notice.

I always thought that nothing could change her implacable free spirit. But Wendy wasn't the same in captivity as when she'd been a free-range sailor. I was too caught up in my own fantasies to worry seriously about her migrating off track. After all, she had watched me fail in social circumstances throughout medical school. Didn't I deserve a small taste of male adoration?

"What's up, babe?" she asked, trying to overcome her depressed mood.

"How's pediatrics treating you, Wendy? I know this specialty wasn't the pick of the litter for you, but you can move later into other fields."

"You know, Ash, I'd rather be cruising the Mediterranean and hooking up with an exotic Catalonian type. I guess I must grow up," she admitted. "I'm scheduled for a research fellowship that might lead to the loftier realm of *adult* surgery."

"Don't grow up anytime soon, Wendy. You're my bestie for a reason, and I need you for *my* sanity!" I burst into a smile worthy of a theatrical spotlight. She didn't respond for a long moment.

"Geez, girl," she finally said. "Back atcha. You're my lifeboat to sanity also." My heart registered a twinge of guilt. For her, the strict hospital regimen was like a prison sentence. For me, a sense of being trapped was the natural course of life that I had accepted, starting from my mother's womb.

"So, Wendy… not to change the subject, but I HAVE to tell you something."

"Do tell, what is it? Please channel some sunshine into my dark mood."

"I'm working with a guy, Wendy. He's independent, smart as hell, and freewheeling. He grew up in a California lifestyle. Rich family, maybe a bit spoiled. If he weren't such a schmuck sometimes, he could be everything I've been looking for…"

"Quite an endorsement. An alluring jerk. That's today's number one most popular attribute on the female bucket list. Okay. So, let me guess. He's a tall, smart hunk, a brilliant doctor, comes from the right family stable, and best of all, he brings a potential parental stamp of approval from your mom. Have I left anything out?"

Wendy knew me too well.

"Well, yes. Unfortunately, there's a slight catch. He's all the above and also *my* med student."

"What? No way. Not possible." She had turned pale, genuinely shocked, hardly the reaction I was expecting. She wasn't typically so judgmental.

"Your student? Now you know me, the last person on earth to follow the rule book, but you worked so hard for this position. Are you going to risk throwing it away over a younger guy who's probably using you for bragging rights?"

Bubble burst. I couldn't believe this was my same friend, Wendy, the burning rebel who had been blowing up societal conventions at every moment.

"Oh God, I know you're probably right. Tell me there's hope," I said.

"I'd normally agree, 'follow your bliss,' except this is treacherous territory. You're a brand-new Resident swimming in shark-infested waters, and you may not have as many friends as you think. You're beautiful, smart, romantic, and naïve. If you're below deck with some stud med student, people are bound to take notice. Never underestimate the power of jealousy…"

Wendy paused to consider more practical concerns. I wondered: *was this attitude a lesson for herself?* "What's the guy's name anyhow?" she asked. "Does he have a twin who might be unattached? How did he come on to you?"

"Well, I think he was flirting with me during some recent surgeries. Hard to tell. We were in a tight space."

"My dear, was he putting the woody to your hindquarters? That's always fun. Of course, dealing with the patient and giggling in front of Doc Davis becomes a bit more complicated."

We both laughed, diverted by memories of earlier sexual escapades.

"What's his name?" she asked.

"Sandy Wainwright."

"Wainwright, eh?" Wendy ratcheted briefly into exaggerated concern, then chilled a bit. "At least you hooked a nice wealthy guy. Any relation to the donors of our surgical wing?"

I nodded.

She paused and gave me a contrived look as if to say, "Are you sure about this?"

Then she spoke up more gently. "I know this dude, kind of a Pied Piper, with plenty of young patients in tow. Plus, the older staff is lining up for a fling. No wonder he's so self-impressed, unlike the other five hundred males in this zoo."

"My dear, don't get any ideas. This is my golden fantasy. But I've got a good possibility for you. A hot British scrub nurse, we call him Prince Jeff. From what I've seen, a muscular build, seductive accent, bedroom eyes, and succulent lips. Very smart and competent in the OR, sought after for assisting major surgeries. The whole package. Could be your type. We can double date."

"Are you performing surgeries or soliciting for Porn Hub?" Wendy frowned. "On the other hand, maybe I could give the prince a try? What the hell, I wish it didn't seem so condescending: doctors for you, scrub nurses for me, eh? Not that I've minded trading down now and then for immediate needs. A bit randy these days."

"He's a perfect match. Prince Jeff is right up there in the romantic five-star category. Even the robotic Dr. Davis seems to 'fancy the lad' beyond his medical competence."

Wendy had turned ponderous again. Was she annoyed that while she sulked alone, I might be coming out of my shell? "Think of it this way," she noted sadly. "Now that I'm here and land-logged, things have been a bit slow. The babies bore me. The doctors bore me. Pediatrics in general bores me. I'm sorry if I'm not myself. This city, this place, it's not me. I'm doing my best to embrace it. Maybe we need a short break from this dungeon and taking a romp into greener pastures."

"Well, I'm down for that, girl. Don't leave without me. Our friendship has always survived the most trying circumstances."

Wendy and I split the tab and walked out together, each lost in our troubled thoughts. Despite my brave words, I couldn't help feeling a bit uneasy about Wendy's loyalty if Sandy was signaling her some interest on his part.

24. Dr. Wendy Jamison

Wendy's flashback

Give me the Oscar for best actress. I had to sit there and listen to Ashley showing off her gleaming new boy toy, whom I wanted as my boy toy as well, only I wasn't going to tell her. At least we both agreed on the dangers of consorting with the students.

How ironic that after months of doing the pre-mating ritual, Sandy and I had edged closer to fulfilling our mission a few days ago. It wasn't quite a Cinderella romance. The slipper didn't fit yet. I'd started scouting convenient locations: a single bed in the hospital with electrical problems and a current vacancy for my reckless objectives.

Sandy came down on a mid-week visit to my department, and he was thinking about "it" as well. He had shucked the scrubs and was wearing a t-shirt and tight-fitting shorts that screamed out for attention. Perhaps my kids with serious illnesses had taught us both that life can pass by swiftly, grab it when you can.

This opportunity turned out to be a big tease. The kids loved the fact that his shirt had some animal characters on it. They lined up like he was handing out popsicles. What magnetism! I stood next to him and watched as he talked patiently to each child. It was very disarming: the gentle, empathetic side of Sandy that made his bedside manner so appealing. I was quite prepared for a bit of bedside manner myself, but alas, it was not to be. Off he scooted upstairs for a valve surgery conducted by none other than Maura Davis.

Rats. I was feeling defeated by the karma of Ashley Dillon. So much for friendship, and let's forget the hospital regs while we're at it.

Sometimes the hormones take over, and you gotta do what you gotta do.

There was one laugh. Dr. Ashley was trying to pawn me off with Prince Jeff so we could double-date. The Prince might find it enjoyable that I was warmed up for some action after spending an evening double-dating with Ashley.

I wanted to warn Ash that Sandy is not the type to settle down with one person. You can't pin him down or pen him up. She wouldn't listen. Thus, my Plan B would mark my own subversive turn to the scrub nurse. Since he and Sandy clearly enjoyed making trouble together, I wouldn't mind joining up for the bad-boy behavior team, singular or plural.

Unfortunately, Jeff was probably not the kind of guy who would want to play second fiddle on the junior varsity if he figured things out.

I had to tread carefully. Jealousy will make you do dumb things.

25. Ralph Gruber

Flashback 60 days

I made a terrible mistake today. It all started when Rosemarie Li, my next-door neighbor, knocked on my door late last night. She told me that Sandy was acting strange, and she was worried. "He's been erratic lately," she revealed in confidence because she didn't want to get him in trouble. He'd been getting a hefty stockpile of drugs from Pil and hitting the bottle hard as we were facing a heavy load of clinical work and exams coming shortly.

Of course, I was sympathetic. Rosemarie was "my girl" before Sandy stepped in. Frankly, I wanted her back. She was a sweetheart, very gentle and buttoned up. Her parents owned a farm and had brought her up with the proper values. She could see the good side in everyone. Otherwise, she'd never have gotten involved with Sandy.

I knew his real problem was too much cruising the nightlife with his pal, known as Prince. (This guy was no prince, believe me.) Sandy flaunted his amazing stamina. He liked to say pridefully, "Life rushes by too fast for those slowing down for sleep. Only the sleep-deprived shall rule the world."

After I calmed Rosemarie down last night, I decided I had to take some action. I went into the hospital early this morning and managed to find Sandy while he was having a cup of coffee in the cafeteria. I told him that Rosemarie was worried and he needed to be careful.

That was the mistake, right there. Sandy did not appreciate my intervention. He blew up as I should have anticipated. He didn't relish the fact that I live right next door where walls were thin. He resented my presence, invading their privacy.

Rosemarie was angered because she didn't need *that kind* of help, just a chance to talk things out with a discreet confidante. So now I had made two enemies, and that creepy cop Kazinski was on my case too. *Maybe I should apply for a room transfer. I didn't need all this drama.*

Monday, Day Four

26. Barney Kazinski

Back to the present, Monday morning

The one absolute rule taught to rookie detectives was to treat every encounter in criminal investigation with a certain skepticism. My rule of thumb as a cynical older hand was to consider the witnesses as "guilty until proven innocent." First impressions, especially good ones, could mislead you and throw an investigation off track.

The biggest mistake in the book for males was falling for the charms of a seductive female.

After 27 years, this wariness became automatic. Sure, we were supposed to make a careful appraisal of each witness as individuals: Their body language, their state of mind, their lifestyle, background, and so on. Those details and impressions were part of our reports, now set up online. We also had to maintain a strong pretense of objectivity for cross-examination of testimony in a possible trial later.

I had met Dr. Ashley momentarily at the food truck, so I'd received a brief impression as she was dashing back to work. Even in those few seconds, she radiated an attitude that life with her would be more intense, more passionate, and more exciting. Hers was a subtle come-on for susceptible, weary detectives like me. I decided that this time I would catch her unprepared amidst her rounds and try to un-ring the warning bell sounding in my head.

I flashed my shield and raced through the security on the main floor of the Wainwright wing. I rode the elevator up to the daily surgery wards on the 6th floor. A receptionist directed me to a small conference room where Dr. Ashley was finishing up morning rounds with her students. She spotted me through the open door and signaled that she would be available shortly.

After the students filed out, she waved me into the room. The grungy conference table was littered with donut wrappers and empty water bottles. She looked uneasy and unkempt, her bristly hair shooting up and out like parts of her brain were firing scatter shots everywhere.

Even without makeup, there was no hiding her sensual appeal. The bumps in her lab coat intimated a body to die for.

Perhaps Sandy-boy had learned that lesson the hard way.

Dr. Ashley was subdued, as if she had her guard up. Her body language seemed precarious, like a house of cards anticipating a strong breeze. Her eyes bore an inscrutable, inky darkness.

As she no doubt intended, I found myself immediately off-balance, sweating, and a bit breathless. I would learn that she could turn her charms on and off like a light switch. Yet today felt different. I could detect a slight tremble in the coffee cup she was holding as if she was still recovering from the trauma of Sandy's death. My interior shit detector caused me to question if this was an unusual moment of self-doubt?

Or perhaps a subconscious inkling of guilt?

Despite my suspicions, I wanted to play it straight as I didn't trust my instincts right now. I repressed a desire to throw my arms around her and offer parental comfort. The bell in my brain chimed again, warning that she might be "playing" me.

Now I needed to stop thinking and start talking.

"I'm Detective Kazinski. We met briefly at the meat wagon. Hope the pie was good."

"Yes," she said, "I'm not into food right now, but I appreciated your kindness."

"Well, today it's all business, I'm afraid. I have a few questions for you regarding Mr. Wainwright."

"Sandy? Oh yes, he was our student. We're all pretty freaked out."

Her mood shifted faintly, eyes flickering into caution.

"Dr. Ashley, you seem a bit downcast today."

"This is not a pleasant subject, Detective. Our medical student died. We lose older patients now and then, but a young student is a different story."

"Doctor, I would think a surgeon such as yourself would be very accustomed to death. You are a Resident physician, are you not?"

"No amount of experience can prepare you for this kind of tragedy." Her eyes now appeared wary like an animal, sizing me up as a predator. "When our patients die, we've rarely gotten to know them before death. I had worked with

Sandy for a couple of months, often in long, hard surgeries. That's a bonding experience. I became very fond of him. We're not robots, you know."

I paused for effect, preparing to ask the most challenging question.

"Doctor, can you please describe your whereabouts on the night that Sandy died?"

She was anticipating the question and responded instantly, as if from a script.

"I was here, detective, in the hospital where I spend 90 percent of my life. I heard and saw police cars outside. There were shouts of concern from a crowd forming near our building. The death rattle usually takes place inside the Emergency Ward, not in the street."

"So, what was your response? Running outside? Is that standard protocol for a resident on duty?"

"Everyone seemed to be racing outside to see what was going on, even some patients. I have emergency training to revive a potential victim. It was almost reflexive to rush to the scene. The first hour of resuscitation is critical, the so-called golden hour. Maybe I could have helped."

"One thing perplexes me, though, doctor. I understand that you were delaying the medical investigator when the M.E.'s assistant was trying to get the body moved downtown."

"Am I in some kind of trouble here, detective? You seem very suspicious. I thought there might be a bit more casual conversation between us."

There she went again, playing the vulnerability card. The dark eyes were now pools of moisture. Big trouble loomed for a stupidly smitten male. I stalled for a moment, hoping to re-assert my professional composure.

“Doctor, I’m here trying to collect some preliminary information. That’s all. Trying to do a job. I need your help in answering some questions.”

“Detective, I didn’t know who was in that body bag until the transport team unzipped it. The word coming from the clean-up crew was only that a male med student had died. I have worked with most of the clinical students at one point or another. I was devastated to hear that one of those students had died tragically, and I still hoped that he might have been salvageable. When I learned it was Sandy, this vibrant, handsome young man, I went into total shock. My memory before and afterward is foggy.” She paused and looked at her watch. “I really need to see some patients now. Can we wrap this up?”

“Then let’s cut to the chase. You said you were here most of the evening, correct? Did you leave the building at any point?”

“I took a dinner break somewhere around 10 p.m. I don’t recall the exact time.”

“This was at the meat wagon?”

“No, I walked over to a small café and sat for a while to clear my head. I must have returned about an hour or so later.”

“Were you with anybody?”

“Well, my friend Wendy Jamison joined me for a cup of coffee. She’s a resident in pediatrics. We were both on call for the duration of the night. We had to get back to our patients; you can check her out.”

"To clarify, what time did you leave the hospital for the night?"

"Very late, or early, depending on how you look at it. It was before the sun came up. I was wrung out by Sandy's death and yearned for my own bed."

"All right let's turn to your relationship with the deceased. You seem to have been fond of him. Maybe a bit more so than the customary professional relationship?"

"I resent that… shall I call a lawyer?" Her face was flushed, eyes sharpened like animal teeth. Who was the prey here?

"Let's be specific. What exactly was the nature of your relationship with Sandy?"

"What do you mean? Like, how did I know him? I already told you. He was my student."

"So, then, your relationship was strictly professional. You would swear to that?"

"How many times are you going to ask? Yes, we were strictly colleagues, or rather, I was his superior, but I also considered him a friend. He was very bright and had a promising future. Great sense of humor. A bit cynical at times. He didn't buy into all the crazy politics that we run into here. It was refreshing to hang out with him."

"Excuse my naivety, doctor, I thought that residents and students were instructed *not* to fraternize—aren't there clear rules about keeping them separated off-campus?"

"Of course, that's true, exactly the way we played it. He participated in my rounds, assisted in the OR, and did some workups for our Morbidity conferences. He was a diligent student and remarkable in diagnosing medical issues. I take exception to your prying into my life as if you are a gossip reporter."

"Okay, fair enough, but some members of the hospital staff seem to feel there was a special closeness between you. I heard he was quite the ladies' man."

"Let me stop you right there." Her eyes were blazing now, as if her head might explode. I was not surprised to see that this lady could be a potent adversary when things weren't going her way.

"He was my student, Detective. Get it? Nothing more. Do I miss him? Sure. He was a student who comes along once in a lifetime. End of story."

"Okay, 'once in a lifetime,' let's leave it at that."

I'd pushed hard enough. I wondered whether I was jealous of this young man or merely following my quest for facts in a contentious interview.

Her mood softened. "Detective, I have a question for you." I noticed a sheen of tears was diluting her anger. "I've heard that Sandy might have committed suicide. He was a former athlete being forced to chill by a heart irregularity. That might have driven him foolishly to living on the edge."

"Can you clarify what it means to be living on the edge? Are we talking booze or drugs or simply too much carousing? Do we know how serious the heart issue was?

"You'd have to ask cardiology or the M.E. about his ticker. But the booze was a given. That's S.O.P. for med students. Maybe some drugs were in play that night. The investigator tending the dead body couldn't tell me for sure what a puncture wound in the thigh represented. Sandy's friend Pil is a walking pharmacy and might have been over-prescribing dangerous stimulants."

She paused as if to gauge my reaction while she subtly offered a veil of tears.

"The crazy thing about all this is Sandy didn't need chemical assistance. He felt everything about life had possibilities. His natural enthusiasm was infectious."

"An interesting word, 'infectious' as in poisonous?"

She ignored that comment. "A deeply passionate man, he never wanted to let go of the moment, even after mopping up a head wound at five a.m. He would say, 'Sleep is the enemy.' I'll have plenty of time to lie down when I'm dead."

"Well, he got his wish on that one."

A low blow, yet she didn't respond. For the moment she seemed distracted as if her mind was elsewhere, reeling backward in time to make Sandy come alive again.

I decided to make a quick exit. I worried she might suddenly lash out as reality set in. I grabbed my coat and departed after a quick "thank you doctor" and a half-wave goodbye.

27. Dr. Ashley Dillon

Monday, early afternoon

"Hey Wendy, I'm glad I caught you."

"I'm late for rounds. What's up? Can I call you back later?"

"This will only take a sec."

"Go ahead, shoot."

"I just met with the cop, Kazinski, who's investigating. He's been talking to all the doctors, friends of Sandy, the usual routine. I might have made a mistake."

"I don't like the tone of your voice."

"Nothing to worry about. He asked where I was between 10 and 11 p.m. on the Thursday Sandy died. I told him you and I were grabbing a bite."

"You did what? Are you crazy? I can't recall where I was off hand, but why drag me into this thing? Thanks, a helluva lot."

"Wendy, you hardly know Sandy. No one will be suspicious. If the detective calls, his name is Kazinski. Tell him we were together; I need you as a witness."

"Wait a sec, where were you, Ashley?"

"I couldn't remember. I froze up. I had done a take-out from the meat wagon and wandered around and then gone back to the hospital. I wasn't anywhere near the guy."

"Then why didn't you use Alessandro's name? He's the nightly boss at the meat wagon. He would do anything for you. "

“I don’t know. I froze like I told you.”

“Oh Ashley, I know you were over there with Sandy having Chinese on that night, weren’t you? Maybe the last one to see him. Perhaps you had slipped him a special goodbye cocktail?”

“Don’t be ridiculous. We broke up a while back. You know that. Never mind. Forget it.”

I angrily broke the connection.

28. Barney Kazinski

Monday late afternoon

I checked in with La-T and the crew at our headquarters. We all agreed that, given the likelihood of Sandy's becoming a murder case, the resourceful Becky Muller, following up on field reports would double check her final chronology of his last day, emphasizing who might have been the most likely final person to see him alive.

I wanted to go back to the student dorm to interview Sandy's "official" girlfriend, Rosemarie Li. Becky had said her reputation at the hospital was 'misguided innocence.' She would logically have been a possible contender for assisted suicide or, if innocence soured and she sought revenge, she might try to take him down altogether. We agreed that my partner Gundy would accompany me, as it was better to have a witness for these critical interviews. I regretted having done Ashley solo.

I knew enough about Sandy already that being his "girlfriend" was like riding in very hilly terrain. No woman could last long in his saddle. Our colleague Becky's instincts pegged Sandy as the type of guy who might leave behind a few ex-partners thirsting for revenge.

The question remained: how much did Rosemarie know about his wavering loyalty and when did she find out? This afternoon we might confront a woman who had nursed a grudge and deployed a syringe, another typical case of a bad boy attracting a good girl. In a wistful moment, I wondered if I had favored the dark side instead of trying to stamp it out, I'd be attracting more potential mates.

Becky's research subjects had characterized Rosemarie Li as a farm girl with limited knowledge of Sandy's wide-ranging quests. How would she have become a potential suspect in a murder? Gundy and I hightailed over to the dorm, hoping that we might catch Rosemarie while she was still hanging around her room. She'd been avoiding my calls, due to her state of mourning, although a devilish side of me felt she should be celebrating. Her voice mailbox was full.

In the dorm lobby, no security existed once again, only some loose garbage left by the night guard. An eager rodent picked away at it. We headed up to the second floor. When the elevator opened, we encountered the startled face of Rosemarie's neighbor, Ralph Gruber, who seemed to have found a ubiquitous place in my life.

He wore a crumpled Yankees hat, turned backward. I wondered if this was a clue as to his general state of mind. Nothing had changed his cocky, wise-ass routine. "Hello Sherlock, still sniffing out those clues?" he asked.

I would have liked to put my fist through his gaping front uppers, but my anger management training suggested a restrained approach would be more appropriate.

"What room are you living in?" I asked him.

"I told you, I'm in 2F. Right next door to Rosemarie in 2E, which may be where you're heading. I haven't heard a peep in several days. In the good old days, I lost a lot of sleep playing along with those two lovebirds. It's gone deathly quiet now, so to speak."

He flashed a goofy grin.

"Hey, buster," I said, "get all your alibis lined up and straighten your cap. You look like a complete jerk."

"A very good day to you also, Detective." He started to saunter off. From the rear, I could see he was wearing jogging pants with the front zipper showing. Everything was backward with this kid. He'd be fixing the wrong knee someday.

"I'll try to catch you tomorrow," I called out. He shrugged and continued to walk away.

We headed down the hall. I knocked at 2E and heard nothing. Gundy tried his linebacker routine, a forearm stinger bashing into the doorframe. "Open up. Police."

A faint sound: "Go away, I'm not here."

Next step, my more official police voice: "Rosemarie, we need to talk to you. There's some new information about Sandy."

The faint response once more: "Oh hell, I knew it. Go away and find his killer."

My tongue felt like it was caught in a lawnmower.

"We need help, Ms. Li, your help."

We waited, and a few moments later, a latch turned, and the door opened.

This is what personal hygiene looked and smelled like after a few days without bathing, sleeping, eating, or brushing one's hair and teeth.

Yet, I could see this unkempt woman would still be appealing after spending 40 days with wolves in the wilderness. She managed to project an image both sultry and reserved, with saddened eyes projecting from a wrinkle-free face. It seemed she wore a bland mask where the imperfections – and passions – dwelled under the surface. No doubt Sandy had been cultivating her steamy inner heat.

At this moment, her body was buried in an oversized terry-cloth robe, most likely belonging to her deceased ex-boyfriend. We'd want the robe for evidence to see if there had been any other companions besides Sandy inside the folds, including Ralph next door.

I glanced at Gundy and watched his face, trying to anticipate our next move. His poker face gave nothing away.

We shared a tacit glance as if to say, 'Sandy, you'd have to be crazy to go looking for playmates outside this lady's sandbox.' Even the sensuous Dr. Ashley might run a close second in this derby.

Rosemarie went to freshen up. Gundy grabbed the opportunity to pull out his cell phone and film a 360 video panorama of the apartment. Like a dancer, he whirled through the room, aiming at the framed wall photos, and her bookcases, moving in a few close-ups of notebooks and textbooks in disarray on a circular table where she must have been studying. Even her coffee cup was targeted by the eye of Gundy's camera.

She reappeared. Her flawless cheeks were moist, the tears still trickling.

She motioned us to chairs around her table while she sat stiffly on a stool overlooking her schoolwork. She'd clearly been trying to study while in mourning, as the floor was littered with tissues.

We introduced ourselves and then allowed an awkward silence. Small talk seemed insulting when her world had been torn apart in one crazy night. Yet, we needed to know where she was that night.

I read her name into my digital recorder and dove in without preliminaries.

"Ms. Li, how long were you and Sandy 'together?'

"Practically right from the beginning when I started med school," she said. "Our anniversary was a few weeks ago. We met at my very first party. You might say it was love *before* first sight. I saw him initially from the back. He had a taut, muscular body with a vulnerable face turned in profile. He was leaning into a conversation, joking with a couple of guys. I felt an urge to climb like a monkey on his back, and I knew this was it."

"That's pretty fast."

"A farm girl quickly learns to diagnose the natural order of things. When he fully squared around, I gasped for breath. I had never come close to falling in love, so maybe my antenna was picking up a false reading."

She started to cry profusely. Gundy produced a handkerchief. She wiped her face and handed it back. He gave me a private wink. He was wearing gloves and quickly folded the cloth into a small evidence pouch for DNA purposes.

"We'll make this fast, Ms. Li. I know it's painful," I said. "After that first night, can you tell us what happened?"

"My initial instincts were right. He was sweet and gentle. He bought me flowers and candy almost every week, and he sang to me on his guitar. He was in a band you know."

"A band? What was it called?"

"It was a nerdy Hillside band, The Four Syringes, something stupid like that. He could be so wacky. We laughed a lot. We spent most of our free hours outside the hospital together. Within the hospital, he liked dragging me into a vacant room. I was raised to be cautious with men, though he broke that barrier down quickly. I'd never felt the intensity of being loved by a male in that way before."

She gave me a soft, wistful look. "Detective, have you considered the possibility that he was murdered? He would never take his own life. Sandy had a joy for life that was rare. He hated the idea of sleep. No wonder I was exhausted most of the time. Who would want to kill him? Everyone loved Sandy, maybe too much affection being offered sometimes by the wrong female friends."

"Let's talk about those women, Ms. Li."

"All my girlfriends were jealous. He was so hot and so fun. They wanted to include him in our study dates and have an excuse to start flirting. It made me angry. They'd make jokes about his going home with us. I suspected he wouldn't be opposed to entertaining a small crowd."

"That might be a logistical nightmare," Gundy remarked, as his mind whirred with numerical calculations.

Rosemarie ignored him and continued.

"Even the older doctors, Dr. Ashley, or Dr. Davis, would act like adolescents when they were on rounds together. I thought about carrying a baseball bat to protect our relationship."

Gundy threw me a "woman-scorned" shrug, happy to let me take the lead while he observed.

"What about male friends such as the roommates, partners in lab work, that sort of thing?" I asked.

"There's no question the roommates or 'the delinquents' as I called them were a bad influence. Most of them were drugged up half the time and living on stimulants. Naturally, they got tired after all their nights boozing and trying to nail everything in sight."

She launched into a talking jag after so much seclusion. "Pity their patients. I always thought boys don't know any better, but this was an animal farm, which I understood quite well. I knew Sandy wasn't like this pack of beasts, although in retrospect, he wasn't the type to stay isolated either. If we were watching television or spending a quiet night, he'd want to go out and light up the town. I needed sleep, so I'd let him go. God knows what he was doing."

"You had some indications he might not be totally faithful? Can you give us some names of his closest companions?"

"Sure, there were the roommates. They played sports together, accompanied by a couple of deranged buddies, like this fellow Pil; he was the pharmacist, a real lecher, controlling everyone with his mobile medicine cabinet. And don't ignore the scrub nurse Prince Jeff who tried to flutter around Sandy's discards. That should have been a warning. Last and least, poor old Ralph, my neighbor, made a chronic pain of himself. I dumped him practically 30 seconds after I met Sandy. He might have his ear to the wall right now."

"Was Jeff a roommate?" Gundy asked.

"Practically the fourth roommate. He would stay on a couch after a long night. I always said he was a Brit that rhymed with twit. It made Sandy laugh. The two of them incited each other into boorish behavior. I tried to ignore them when they were together. I grew up in a small town, and I will never get used to these nerdy doctors acting like they are rock stars. Dr. Davis attached herself to Jeff like a postage stamp. She made Sandy's life miserable."

"Ms. Li," I jumped in, "you're not suggesting that jealousy might turn Maura Davis into an accomplice if this were a murder case?"

She thought for a moment, a long moment. "Dr. Davis was always a bit of an ass. She took special pleasure in criticizing Sandy; he would rail against what a bitch she was. I think she was intimidated by his brilliance at such a young age."

"Ms. Li, is it possible that Sandy and Dr. Davis were, shall we say, intimate at any point?"

"Good God, no. He had some degree of taste if you don't mind. He wanted to apply his charm to win her over. His ego craved getting everyone to like him, not to mention she could be important in his career."

"Any other friends who might have an axe to grind?"

"Since you asked, come to think about it, Prince Jeff might have gotten jealous that he was getting the leftovers. But I keep coming back to Ralph Gruber, the weirdo listening through the walls. He would constantly be inviting himself over and borrowing stuff from me like he owned the place. After we broke up, I know he could hear us getting loud, he must have felt that I owed him."

Rosemary had broken out in a mottled blush. The tears had dried up. Blemishes on her skin were surfacing. "Ralph was trying to break us up. He would tag along and report back all the news of Sandy's antics. You can imagine how I loved hearing that news. I wanted Sandy at home tucked in safely between my sheets."

I felt compelled to offer a little zinger.

"It follows from your attitude that there was a lot of nasty stuff and jealousy coming down. Why would you put up with it? Doctors in training are supposed to follow their oath to do no harm, including to themselves."

She shrugged. "When you're in love, all your old-fashioned values fly out the window. I know my parents are appalled when I tell them some of these stories."

"Did they meet him?"

"They didn't like him. We went home to their farm over one Christmas. This was not their idea of a perfect match. Sandy was restless at night, and they forced us to stay in separate bedrooms. Not a good scene, although they could tell how much I loved him. No way you could miss it. My parents tried hard to make allowances for the behavior of city folks. But he was not their choice of a suitable mate."

The tears came again, and she dabbed her face to recover.

"I'd say you might have had some doubts also," Gundy chimed in.

"That's right detective, then again, isn't the girlfriend always the last one to know?"

"What do you mean?"

"Well, for a long time, I thought that he was faithful. I knew he was flirting. The hospital staff isn't above playing touchy-feely. Medical treatments require some intimacy. A hug can do wonders for psychological treatment."

"So Sandy was a big hugger?"

"Well, Detective, I'm embarrassed to tell you. I'm not usually a stalker, one of these psychos you read about. One night I was walking home. I saw Sandy stop outside an apartment near the hospital. A woman came out dressed in scrubs. She jumped up and wrapped her legs around him. They began kissing passionately."

She unleashed a brief fusillade of tears, replaced by a stern, angry look, the first indication of rage that she'd shown.

"Ms. Li, I am sorry to make you re-live this. Do you have any idea who the woman was?"

"Do I know who she was? Of course, I do, that stuck-up whore, the one who I heard was acting so lovey-dovey with him on rounds. I'll never forget that sight, my boyfriend locking lips with his resident, Dr. Ashley Dillon. Do you know the four-letter word that rhymes with hunt? Sandy taught me that term. We only used Christian words in my day. I felt like a complete fool hiding behind a tree. There they were, carrying on about fifteen feet away and I was embarrassed and furious.

Now her face had turned fierce, wrinkles suddenly popping up and careening across her cheeks. The mask of innocence was ripping apart.

"Oh my God," she said, "that nasty, self-righteous worm. I thought if I only had a scalpel right now…"

"I've heard Dr. Ashley's name mentioned by others. You're certain it was her."

"You could put me at a hundred line-ups, and I'd point to her."

"What happened after that terrible night? Did Sandy break up with you? Did you confront him?"

"Nope. Sandy continued to pursue me like crazy. He sent chocolates, we ate together in the cafeteria when our schedules coincided. He seemed almost desperate to spend some time together. There was the usual physical energy, plus he was considerate and almost tender. I wanted to believe that deep down, he loved me so I could forgive…"

"Do you know how long the other relationship with Dr. Ashley was going on?"

"That I don't know. My girlfriends all warned me. They said he was more than a big tease. I felt some of my friends wanted to take my place in his bed, so I ignored their concerns. Flesh begets flesh in a hospital; it's the natural order. I trusted him even after I saw what I saw."

"Ms. Li. When was the last time you saw him?"

"I don't know, a few days before his death was the last chance we had for real intimacy. The time for med school boards is approaching. We were both busy with our studies."

"So, you didn't see him the night of his death?"

"No, only during the day. I went to his apartment around noon, hoping that we might go out for a quick bite. I worried we were moving apart. He had plans of some sort, very vague, so I left. I was certainly not in the mood to throw myself into his arms."

"It sounds like you were fed up, maybe planning on breaking it off with him?" Gundy said.

"I was confused, detective. I'd been so naive when I arrived here. Despite it all, Sandy had a good heart. As a teenager, he'd assisted 'Doctors without Borders' over the summers, sponsored by his parents, going to countries where there was famine or malaria. That's why he loved dropping down to the pediatric wards and hanging out with the kids in trouble. He believed in being a doctor who could cure all their ills, from their diseases to their poverty."

Gundy had a touch of moisture in his eyes, and he was not the sentimental type. I tried to swing the conversation back to her anger.

"You mentioned one disturbing scene, any other specific cases of infidelity?"

"No, just that one. I hoped it was a brief fling that would pass. I'll confess there were moments when I'd get upset, angry, betrayed, whatever you call it. Then Sandy would show up with a bundle of roses. He knew how to play my emotions. You know, love sucks sometimes."

"Perhaps, ignorance is bliss," I paused and then popped the key question. "Ms. Li, were you ever angry enough to have wanted him dead?"

"I can't believe this," she flared. "First, my boyfriend cheats on me, then he is murdered, and now you're asking me if I killed him! You're a little too advanced for me. I think you'd better go now."

"Sorry to upset you. One last question. I see you're managing to keep up with your studies. That must be difficult amidst your grief."

I pointed to the pile of medical books on the table.

"Are you going to arrest me for studying, Detective? As messed up as I am right now, I must keep up with my workload. I still have a career ahead of me. It provides some diversion in any case."

"I wasn't insinuating anything. I'm appreciative to see you're finding the strength to move on. Just to confirm: You're sure you only saw Sandy once in the middle of the day?"

She didn't respond, but her face had transformed into a sneer. Gundy tugged on my sleeve. "Leave it for now and let's go."

We walked to the door, and I looked back. Her initial pristine beauty was clotted by red marks of ventilating anger. Her facial muscles were twitching like maggots on dead flesh.

29. Rosemarie Li

Monday evening, a few minutes before midnight

A restless evening; those frigging detectives; time to break out of the Kleenex factory. I picked up on the first ring. "It's about time you called."

"Busy day, darling, a couple of surgeries mopping up for my dear Doctor Davis."

"I had a lovely afternoon with the two detective goons. They're so annoying, grasping for culprits."

"This is normal procedure. Nosy buggers in training."

"You'd think they'd realize it's so obvious: the lovely Ashley stalking my boyfriend, maybe with assistance from the older porn dancers. Or Ralph, he's an obvious candidate, the horny little creep."

I was getting worked up by all the imposters surrounding Sandy, including his former British trouble-making companion on the other end of the line.

"Okay, bollocks to them all. The main thing is, *we're better off* with your ex-boyfriend gone. Now we start anew."

"Well, my Prince, you were always panting for me long before Sandy was around. I'm getting bored, studying mixed with an occasional Netflix. I'm starting to go stir-crazy. Sandy always said a girl needs to sow some oats too. Why should the boys have all the fun?"

"Maybe we can have a spot of supper, very soon, so I can start looking after you."

"Good idea Jeff my love, how about tomorrow tonight?"

"Very possible. Let me check my diary and see how the day goes."

"That doesn't sound like a firm invitation. Shall I sit and wait like a dog for its master?"

"Don't whine, darling. Take a shower, clean up the place, pamper yourself, maybe a manicure and pedicure; you'll feel better. I'll try to scrape some time away from Doctor Davis."

"Here's a novel idea, my friend. Click on FaceTime, have a look."

"Give me a sec. Oh yes, now there's a sight."

I could hear his slight intake of breath and a long pause. "Good camera angle, darling, I like that, down there, a bit of a jungle, wild and curly, isn't it? I guess it's unexplored territory lately; since the boy is gone, no time for a razor."

A moment of silence for effect.

He exhaled loudly and responded. "Got the itch, have we? Tomorrow night then."

I clicked off the cell and slammed it down on my table.

Flashback: 12 Days Before Death

30. Dr. Ashley Dillon

A weekend interlude.

My weekends with Sandy were an intense mixture of pleasure and pain. We usually carved out a day when we were both off-duty, a rare opportunity for relaxed, spontaneous affection. Or, as it often turned out, spontaneous affliction given the bumpy status of our relationship.

We'd been avoiding contact outside of the hospital when Sandy showed up on my doorstep one mid-Saturday afternoon. He must have checked my schedule. To my further surprise, he held twelve long-stemmed red roses in one hand, a basket in the other.

"Is that a picnic basket?" I asked. "I've got a lot of work to do right now."

"Maybe you need a break. We both do."

"Are we starring in The Sound of Music? Should I put on a dress made from recycled curtains?"

"Is chivalry dead?" Sandy asked with a touch of dismay. "What's wrong with a romantic afternoon? You are a spoiled brat; do you know that?"

He seemed hurt. My spontaneous man with a chink in the armor? Per usual, he recovered quickly.

"Come on, get dressed. We're going to the park."

"Yes sir. We haven't spoken in weeks, yet you're still in command of our relationship."

It suddenly dawned on me that I was standing at the open door in nothing but a loose T-shirt and panties. I tried pulling the shirt down before one of the neighbors walked by. Sandy seemed to appreciate my outfit as he put down the basket and handed me the roses. I stood holding them proudly like the prom queen that I had dreamed of being in high school (with a dress on).

Total panic: I doubted I could find a vase that was large enough. There had been few if any flowers coming my way in med school.

We went inside. Sandy sat on the sofa, thumbing through a magazine while I rummaged in the kitchen. A pot? Would that work? I found one that was deep enough. It was too wide but would have to work for now.

"I need a beaker for these," I said. "Maybe I can pilfer one from the pathology lab."

"I have a vase. I'll bring it over later."

My 'hero,' this boy had a solution for everything.

I excused myself and hurried to get ready. Sandy knew I wouldn't refuse his invitation, the bastard. The element of surprise worked in his favor. I put on a dab of make-up, a pair of very snug, cutoff jeans, and a ratty college sweatshirt. I brushed my teeth and ran a brush through my hair.

I had missed him terribly, although I wasn't quite in the proper mood for a picnic right now. Mechanically, I filled a water bottle and exited the bathroom.

"You look…"

"Very earthy?" I cut him off. "We're going to be rolling around in goose droppings, right?"

"I was going to say you look beautiful. Luscious. Natural, not all done up."

I blushed. Was I usually done up? I felt naked. Sandy always made me feel self-conscious.

He stood and motioned to the door. "Come on, let's go. I don't want to miss the sunset."

I locked the door, and we walked toward Central Park. Suddenly, Sandy stopped in front of a vintage-looking car, bright red with a white top and ascending alligator taillights.

"What is this?" It reminded me of the model cars that younger boys liked to push around on the living room floor while making revved-up engine sounds.

"It's a 1958 Plymouth Fury. Fully restored. You like it?"

"You want to drive to Central Park, less than a mile away? Are you sure we don't have to push this thing?"

"I wanted to impress you. It's a classic, Christine's twin from the Stephen King movie."

"I've never seen it."

"You have clearly been missing out on Classic American cars and Classic American horror films," he said with a touch of amusement.

"Life has enough daily drama without watching more of it," I replied. Why were we both being so nasty? I preferred a warmer duet of foreplay.

He held the car door open as I slid into the passenger seat. The motor growled into ignition, producing a vibrational response through my cut-offs. I was living dangerously, but I couldn't stop. I propped my legs up above the glove compartment for Sandy's viewing pleasure.

Maybe we could skip the bugs and grass stains.

Sandy was enthralled with his toy and accelerated dangerously down Central Park West, lurching into a parking spot. Only he would manage to find parking instantly. His timing for seduction was impeccable. The sky was a silvery blue, the grass a sparkling green turf. The heat of the day was ebbing as if he had manipulated some weather knobs. Central Park was still shimmering in the fading sunlight.

We walked to a patch of shade. Ever the magician, he pulled a neatly pressed blanket from inside the picnic basket and spread it out on the ground. Out came a parade of gourmet vittles: Kumamata oysters, Cornichons, a moist Brie. He lifted an oyster and slid it into my mouth, where it melted like the puffy clouds passing by.

I grabbed his arm and wrestled him to the ground, throwing my pelvis against his.

He flinched. "Wait, Ashley. These are contemplative, not tantric oysters."

"When did you become a monk?" I had to laugh. Yet, I was flattered. Sandy wooing me with clothes on? Could this be real love, grandly rekindled?

"It's okay to lie around quietly sometimes," he said. Who was this stranger? He ran a finger down my spine and gestured at the scenery. A triangle of birds rose in a swirl, then swooped, calling to each other. The sky was shading into a darker blue, lined with traces of crimson.

I leaned back onto his chest as we watched the receding sunset. Sandy planted a simple kiss on my forehead, a kiss that could mean, 'I've missed you; I love you,' more clearly than any words did.

I realized sadly that since puberty, few men had offered the intimacy of wanting to hold me without the implicit precondition of sex to follow.

Would he tell me we were renewed as a couple? It seemed like the perfect setting to do so.

We reclined on the blanket, sipping wine, as the time slipped by, watching the sky shut down for the night. The temperature started falling abruptly; time to leave. We packed up our leftovers as the wind prodded us swiftly back to the car.

"You're it!" I tagged him and ran.

He chased after me and caught up. He was breathing heavily. His left arm held the basket, while the right one circled my waist. I pretended to wriggle free. He spun us around so that our faces pressed together. I had never felt so vulnerable and yet so in sync with our romantic potential.

Then suddenly, a husky voice bellowed out of the darkness.

"Well, hello. A Saturday study date?" I felt Sandy jerk backward, his posture stiffening.

The burly woman with the short pixie cut was an eerie nightmare, cast from the park's deep shadows. What were the odds? The magical words, 'I love you,' were stuffed back into my throat.

"Dr. Davis. Um, hello! We were just…" I tried to recover, straightening my clothes.

"Yes, Dr. Dillon, I see what you were just…" Her tone was mocking in her patented gotcha manner.

The glow beating in my chest contracted into a fierce spasm of fear. We were exposed, wrinkled, and stained; our emotions crushed into an awkward silence.

"See you Monday, Dr. Davis." I pretended we'd just completed rounds as we walked away without another word.

"What does this mean, Ashley?" Sandy's arms were trembling, his usual bravado repressed.

"Nothing. It means nothing. We've done nothing wrong," I said bravely. "Just a picnic in the park."

"There must be some rule we've broken. There's always some bloody rule."

"Of course, it's frowned upon," I conceded, "the faculty manual has warned us. Let's hope the interpretation will not be driven by revenge."

"Does that mean a reprimand rather than a burning at the stake?"

"Maybe she won't do anything," I muttered glumly.

"Ha. And maybe those creatures won't unload all over the park." He pointed to a flock of resident geese, dimly outlined a few yards away, stepping gingerly over their own carpet of excrement.

An ominous feeling suddenly lurked between us, poisoning our tryst. Maura Davis could turn from being your best friend into your worst enemy, and despite my reassurances, I feared that we had aroused the latter.

When we drove home, Sandy seemed eager to drop me off. I started to panic. What if we did get in trouble? What if my job was compromised or even led to expulsion? What exactly did Dr. Davis see us doing in the dim light?

I didn't know.

Despite the unsettling situation, I needed my old confidante, Wendy. She would know how to manage this situation. I picked up my cell. She answered right away.

"Wendy? Hey girl! I miss you. Need a little help from my bestie..."

"What is it, you're in trouble again? You only seem to call when you need something. I thought you'd broken up with the golden boy. Maybe try the married senior docs again."

"Oh Wendy, please don't be so nasty. No, we haven't broken up totally, and yes, I'm in trouble. Sandy and I were having a picnic in the park. Our tormentor, Maura Davis, walked by and saw us canoodling, as the tabloids put it."

"Jesus, Ashley. Why do you keep getting yourself into this craziness? Can't you learn not to foul your nest? I used to find men in every port, but you never saw me bringing them home."

"I guess you're right, Wendy, I'm in kind of deep, let's face it, I've fallen hard for this guy."

"Love? Ha. That's a good excuse," she sneered. "You're falling in love with an adolescent brainchild? A bit over the top, isn't it? Ashley, this sounds like a bad trip, maybe a bit too selfish. Hopping in the fountain of youth after robbing the cradle."

"What? Why would you say that, Wendy? He's a mature guy, the type whom I've been wanting for a long time."

"Better to wait for your trip to Mars. I've lived in this God-forsaken place for a few months when it feels like years. It's usually the men who think with their groins. They like the Oedipal fantasy of the older woman with her young buck and daddy gone."

"What is this, Psych 101?" Now I was both hurt and furious. How had this happened to my carefree best friend? "What about your guy, the British chap? Not my type, that's for sure."

"Jeff is a good guy, and we have a lot of fun. He's my emoji man, always offering a different mood with a different adventure in store. He satisfies my needs right now and breaks the monotony of dealing with kids all day. We're still day-to-day, a rental not a purchase."

I remained silent, seething without words. Wendy paused and seemed to return the anger. "Wait a sec," she declared. "Let's not get stupid about our boyfriends. I don't have to defend Prince Jeff. He is a bit loony all right, as you know because you introduced us. His major fault is that he looks up to your boyfriend, who's even crazier. Now I've got a ton of studying to do, so good luck."

And with that, she abruptly clicked off.

What had just happened? I had lost my lover, my best friend, and possibly my career in one day. Was Wendy right?

Maybe she had fallen in deeper with Jeff and repressed the same insecurity that I felt for my guy.

I poured myself a stiff bourbon; Vodka appeared too tame for the moment. The bliss of drunkenness started to float from top-down. Dark thoughts made total sense. Pink Floyd crowded into my skull, “the lunatic is in my head.”

To hell with them all, I gobbled down some melatonin, knowing full well that combined with alcohol, it could only lead to greater anxiety.

I closed my eyes and prayed for sleep.

Tuesday, Day Five

31. Barney Kazinski

Back to the present, early morning

I decided to walk uptown and clear my head, watching New York City awakening to all its workday glamour.

The poop-laden pavements.

The open wire trash cans overflowing with garbage.

The patrol enforcers playing "gotcha" to make their quotas exactly one millisecond after the parking space timed out.

The double-parked trucks and sprawling construction sites tying traffic into knots.

The ear-piercing jackhammers and sirens.

It was another tense morning in the Big Apple as November meant preparation for the holidays.

Like millions of New 'Yawkers,' I mentally absorbed every hint of chaos. *Let all our neuroses rise and shine, indulging our anxieties until lunch.*

And then a query to self: why did I stay here? I could have taken early retirement, transferred to Hilton Head or the Florida Keys. Rested my weary bones while sucking frozen margaritas with tiny flags.

New York presented an irresistible gravitational pull, and so did my declining checkbook. Perhaps I was clinging to the fantasy that, at any given moment, the quality of life might get better. New York was the angel on your left shoulder, devil on the right shoulder luring us with promises, and warning us of dashed dreams.

So, buy a ticket and sell your soul. How had Sandy gotten caught up in this web? Or a better question, how had I gotten caught in *his* web?

Now our case pivoted to finding the one silver bullet. I was a block away, and I could see our former firehouse up ahead, its squat frame wearily lording over the neighborhood as if it was tired from the commotion.

Inside, there was already a hint of hysteria in our chambers.

I had hoped to do my morning Case Management catch-up and prepare for our staff briefing. Too late. Speaking of the devil, the boss lady, La-Tanya, was already here; through the glass, I could see her with the door closed, frowning, and cursing to herself over several spreadsheets.

She shouted my name, rattling the glass, and waved me into her office.

"Good morning to you there, detective. Aren't you an early bird today? I hope you're catching some worms. May I ask, any progress?"

Her manner made clear that the frustration of this vexing case rested on my shoulders. She had blamed me right from the get-go for the unusual circumstances of death that started our misadventure. I nodded and looked at her blankly. Best to let her get it out of her system.

"The troops downtown at One P.P. are not too thrilled with our humble group's performance to date."

"Oh, really?" I said. "We've got 1000 suspects on a medical campus. Maybe the chiefs would like to give us more resources to find the culprit."

"And perhaps you'd like to go back to traffic control. Detective, the ducks are quacking downtown. We need some progress."

Screw the poultry. My morning coffee was already rumbling in my guts and churning with gastric intentions.

"Let me study what intel the team has brought in from the field," I grumbled. "We'll try to narrow the odds in our favor."

"Brilliant plan, detective. I like you better when you're wise rather than a wise ass," she observed with a look that seemed to carry a warning signal.

"Got it. I'll see you in a few." I stood up and made a swift retreat down the hall for some stomach relief.

We assembled in the conference room shortly thereafter. I was expecting to lead the discussion until Becky jumped in. She could be one tough broad, and yet today, her high-strung energy provided a welcome counterpoint for the distressing lack of progress in our case.

"We have to ratchet up the murder protocol," she said with growing fervor. "We know that most murderers are close to or familiar with the victim. Let's do the full-court press on the possible perpetrators who were involved in Sandy's daily life. That means friends, girlfriends, doctors, supervisors, maybe a deranged patient, or the Mandarin deliveryman. In short: anyone who might have a grudge to bear and a discreet way into the apartment shortly before midnight last Thursday."

"Grudges to bear," Gundy piped up, looking frustrated and perplexed. "We need more resources."

"We get it," Becky cut in with a patronizing scowl. "Sandy was a magnet for trouble, our very own Mr. Lothario. All this in a few months of his first clinical year."

"Thanks Becky." La-Tanya was trying to keep things on track. "We know he had a reputation, and it could have made a lot of males jealous too." She turned to me. "Barney, what have you found so far?"

I ran through my meetings with Sandy's immediate circle: his two roommates and the women he had attracted, including Dr. Ashley Dillon, Rosemarie Li, and Dr. Maura Davis, the surgery supervisor. I added the suspicious hangers-on outside the inner circle, including Prince Jeff, who was almost a fourth roommate, along with Ralph Gruber, next door to Ms. Li, known for an open history of resenting Sandy's conquests.

"Not much to go on," I concluded lamely. "More alibis than clues. Of course, we were once thinking suicide, but now with the likelihood of murder, some tougher questions need answering."

"Well, I got a couple of leads." Becky again. She was all pumped up, her ruddy cheeks were bursting with the excitement of a schoolgirl on holiday.

"A couple of clues from the clean-up squad," she said. "First, let us address the late food delivery. I noted the roomies said there was a faint scent of a Chinese meal, perhaps consumed in Sandy's room. The take-out carton was found in the kitchen garbage, the remains of pasta in chili sauce. Spicy and a bit moldy."

"We followed up with the restaurant," Gundy jumped in. "They confirmed the delivery, and the deliveryman checked out. That meant enough take-out for two. But where are the chopsticks or the extra carton with rice that Sandy usually ordered? Somebody must have had dinner with Sandy and tidied up the evidence of it, possibly wearing gloves and taking all the DNA with them. We need to find that 'other' person, male or female."

"Good point," Becky conceded. "Here's an even better one. In Sandy's white coat, crumpled under the corpse on his gurney, Forensics found a pack of matches with the name DomXX and an address. That's a possible game-changer. I have spent some time in the past tracking down witnesses at this fine establishment. It's known as a place where young men can bring their 'mothers.'

The insiders called it Cougar-Ville.

First the ducks, and now the cougars. The day was shaping up as an Animal Kingdom episode. I said that I would hightail it down to DomXX at noon when the joint would be open for the popular, triple-martini business lunch. Gundy broke into a wicked smile and quickly volunteered as a chauffeur for a visit.

Horny goat, another charter member of our bestiary.

"Thanks gang. You're a bundle of laughs. Can we move this investigation above the waist?" Becky shook her head and slipped me a conspiratorial wink. Maybe there was hope for her after all.

The boss lady, La-T glanced over her flock (now we're sheep?) with an anguished look as she closed out the meeting.

32. Barney Kazinski

Tuesday lunch hour

The "nooner" has long been a tradition relished by men and women who find the middle of the day best suited for catching a little action outside the bounds of monogamy. To cover tracks, this establishment was known on its credit card receipts as The Art Domain. Small wonder the patrons had diverse backgrounds that ranged from the young hot-shot Wall Streeters to the bejeweled older ladies who drank their lunch and escorted their younger companions downstairs for a post-meal flirtation.

A big part of the appeal of DomXX was its unremarkable and fusty appearance that provided perfect camouflage amidst this blossoming Chelsea neighborhood of posh galleries and gentrified lofts. Inside, the only hint of bad behavior was an artistic strand of neon body parts, arrayed like Christmas lights, flashing above the long bar near the entrance.

Due to the respectable clientele, the police had given up busting the place, which claimed to be a legit artistic and spa emporium. The management strictly observed safety and fire laws while the bathrooms were mopped up hourly. The private rooms were renovated in a sleek, modern Danish style. Security officers patrolled the hallways discreetly and curtailed any rowdy misbehavior immediately.

In other words, leave the customers alone to enjoy their harmless playground.

We walked inside the front door, passing through a security sentry and body scanner. I noted many of the faces seated at the bar showed traces of having been renovated along with the whitewashed interiors.

Cougar-Ville was in full swing.

I wondered how Sandy the golden boy had found this place. He seemed to have an instinctive nose for the sordid.

As we approached the lobby bar, Gundy and I immediately confronted the elusive whiff of the magic fragrance: alcohol and pampered bodies perspiring in the thrall of naughtiness. We passed through a second security station (we had called ahead) and were directed straight down a marble staircase that opened into the underground warren of rooms.

A young male dressed in torn jeans and a dingy wife beater stood lethargically mopping up the floor.

"Hello," I interrupted his exertions. We flashed our shields.

"Yeah, boss. You're expected. Let me get Miss Shannon."

He moved away, leaving a whiff of nuclear B.O. behind him. He could use scrubbing with the cleanser diluted in his bucket.

A few seconds later, a tall, striking red-head, her hair crinkled from too many blow-dries, appeared in a pencil skirt, more-midi-than-mini, with dark stockings, and a shamrock-trimmed sweater. She looked the part of a corporate executive managing a financial portfolio.

On closer examination, her obviously enhanced boobs, along with her nipped and tucked face and neck, were losing the age-old battle with gravity. She directed us to be seated in a small nook that had an obstructed view of other visitors. We all sat down, and she crossed a thin pair of legs, modestly covered by the stockings.

"What can I help you with, guys?" she asked.

I'd known her vaguely over the years as a source of street intelligence. Her Irish brogue had once been as thick as the foamy head on a British stout. Now the voice was gentler with an inflection of bridge-and-tunnel twang. This merger of tongues was effective.

I'll say this for the aging hoofer: she still had senior cred as an object of pleasure. Sandy could well have thought so.

She ignored my pudgy-faced partner and homed in on me, knowing that I was running the show. She reached over and tapped a painted scarlet fingernail on my thigh. I could sense why her come-hither manner translated into generous tips from the patrons.

"Not that kind of rodeo today, Madame," I said. "We have some questions for you."

"Okay, okay. No need to get testy. How can I help?"

"First off, do you still go by Miss Shannon?"

"Yes. For you both, that will do."

"That's your given name?

"I've got a lot of given names and a few nicknames. What's it to you?"

"Maybe you're in trouble, or you're hiding something?"

"I cause trouble every day, detective. It's all legal and very much appreciated by our clients."

"Let's not play games, Miss Shannon. I'm not here on a prostitution bust; this is murder we're talking about, so you can chill and take a load off."

She turned wary now. Murder was a very dangerous word in her world. "Let me cut to the chase," I said. "Did you know this young man?" I flashed her a headshot of Sandy Wainwright.

"Aw, Sandy, he was my cutie. Loved the boy. We had so much fun together. I heard he fell into some bad stuff."

"Yes, he's gotten into some real bad stuff about six feet in the ground."

"So, I heard. Made me very sad." A tear, a real one, broke out and tried to ski down one cheek through the pancaked furrows.

"Fair to say," I asked, "that Sandy was more than just a typical Joe to you?"

"He was special, you know. Not like the usual young guys hanging with their lady meal tickets. Or the old cockers looking for one last pop. Sandy was a genuine fave for the girls. They begged to be his companion. And yet, believe it or not, he could be timid and vulnerable. He was a definite candidate for a little mothering."

"Your girls aren't exactly like the mothers I've known. In your case, did you ever see him outside of this club?"

"He usually came here with his friends, but we went out a few times. He would ask me to get dolled up for a special night on the town."

Gundy had a dreamy look, which meant he was not paying attention.

"Miss Shannon. Were you aware of any other women in Mr. Wainwright's life?"

"Ha! LOL. There was no such thing as 'the *only woman* in his life.' My God, the boy lured in groupies as easily as rock stars. He always spoke of wanting more freedom, maybe to get back at *his* mommy, which is why he liked me. I'm an old broad with no rules, no obligations, no guilt. Just plain, innocent fun."

"Did you ever meet or have a conversation with any of his other women?"

"Not really. He complained that his latest girl, the Asian one, wanted him to give up the good life and come home for dinner and the local six o'clock news."

"Did you ever meet her?"

"Nah. Don't even know her name. Sandy told me our joint wasn't her scene. She's more the monogamous type. I always figured he'd break up with her out of boredom. He liked the spicier stuff, being tied down with a rope and not a ring."

"Did you ever get jealous or want Sandy for yourself, Miss Shannon?" She sighed, and for a second her eyes turned moist.

"Look, detective. I cannot believe he's gone. I liked the boy, sure, I looked forward to his visits. I've been a professional manager in the adult pleasure business for a long time. One thing you learn here—human nature can go way out of bounds, so you should ride along only as far as you feel comfortable and then hop off."

Her tears were sliding freely down the slopes. She continued. "He was a young lion. You can't cage a young cat like him. What energy! The med students, all genders, and sometimes their teachers, would tag along. We have a Champagne theater designed for spectators."

Speaking of spectators, I noticed Gundy had totally stopped listening to our conversation. I reached into my pocket and produced two photos.

"Have you ever seen this woman?" It was Rosemarie Li.

"Nope, she must be the Asian girl."

"How about this one?" I could see in her eyes that the full-length picture might be hitting pay dirt. It was Dr. Ashley Dillon.

"I don't know, Detective. He was always surrounded by a crowd.

"So, you don't recognize her?

"If I'd seen her in the flesh, I might remember her. She's hot—good shape, tight body, velvet legs. Probably more my type than his."

"This is a specific question, Miss Shannon. You're sure you don't remember?"

"There's a lot to choose from in this joint. I make it a point not to remember."

Miss Shannon took a breath and glanced at Gundy. She shook her head. "Who is this guy anyhow? Not very talkative, are you? Hope you're not going to play bad cop."

"I need a burger," Gundy said.

She laughed and punctuated it with an Irish growl. "You men: kill it, eat it, or shag it. Three settings in the gearbox, Detective Gunderson, go order at the bar upstairs. Tell them I said it's on the house. Get the burger lunch special, French fries included with a brew to wash it down. Any further trimmings or companions are on your nickel."

He wandered off, and I resumed. "So, Miss Shannon, when did you last see Sandy?"

"Some night a couple of weeks ago. We were hanging out in the Champagne theater, everyone getting acquainted, warm, and friendly. One of his buddies, the British one, a real putz, had a complimentary liquor card and was buying for the crowd."

She gave me an unguarded shrug. "I hadn't thought about it until now. That was our last hurrah."

The tears were digging deeper and trundling down her cheeks, carrying bits of her make-up like ants with popcorn. She was having a tougher time speaking, the way a witness tries to recall a painful memory at trial and loses it on the stand.

"Did you know if any of the others from the last time were Sandy's roommates or workmates from the hospital?"

"I might have seen some of them around a few times. I can't remember all the faces that I see in a night. Sandy was the guy I noticed, always the center of attention. Few men had that kind of star power and were so modest about it. He always made me feel special, even when the younger girls were practically tugging at his belt.

"So, you've missed him?"

"Well, yeah, though our business booms in the fall. I've been busy here, with school starting and stuff."

"School? You go to school?"

“Third-year law student. Detective. I can’t be Miss Shannon forever. Look at me; the body is hanging on. If my professors only knew…”

“Last question. Let me ask you this: can you think of anyone who might have wanted to kill him?”

“Holy shit.” Her face stiffened. It was drier now. The make-up had crusted into small hives. “I can’t imagine anyone with that kind of hostility. Guess I’d be a poor material witness.”

“You sound like a lawyer already. Won’t speculate. Okay, Miss Shannon, your turn in the barrel. Did you personally have any reason for wanting this man dead? Were you jealous of the other women in his life?”

“Detective, I should slap your face. I’ll give you a pass for naivety. I’ve been down in this joint for fifteen years now. There’s no crying in baseball and no being jealous in our world. We’re a business, like any other, take good care of the clients, they’ll love you. A girl with a delicate heart wouldn’t last here two minutes.”

She stood up. “If you’ll excuse me, I need to go get ready for the mid-afternoon shift.”

I walked upstairs to retrieve my partner at the bar. Gundy sat finishing off some apple pie while flirting with an attractive older woman on the next stool. A great help he’d been. I was tempted to hit the road and leave him there.

Then I had a shock. And I don’t shock easily. Speaking of the devil, sitting further down the bar, in an animated discussion, was none other than Prince Jeff. He didn’t see me, and I don’t think his senior companion looked up either.

It was Dr. Maura Davis. I gave Gundy a quick nod. He couldn't get his phone out fast enough and started snapping photos of the two of them in tight conversation..

I gave Gundy the high sign and we were out the door shortly.

33. Barney Kazinski

Tuesday, mid-afternoon

After our visit, Gundy drove us back to the office and I entered my notes into our case file. I decided to see if I could pin down some alibis (or lies therein) about the victim's final hours.

I was especially eager to see Dr. Davis, the Mother Superior of Hillside, if she was back on her sacrosanct admin perch. Perhaps she and Prince Jeff had decided to take the whole afternoon off and grabbed a "quickie." I doubted they would be so brazen. Prying into her inner glory would be like ratcheting the cork off a tightly sealed bottle of champagne -- with your teeth.

I was in an energized and yet cranky mood. Seeing Prince Jeff and Dr. Davis looking cozy had provided a special note of pleasure for my possessing an outrageous piece of evidence that could come in handy later. Right now, I'd keep my cards face down. I imagined the look on Dr. Davis's face when I accosted her about occupying the most embarrassing locale in New York.

Not to mention her companion, that equally pompous British chap.

Talk about fraternizing below pay grades.

A devilish fantasy took hold: Post a Facebook snapshot of the chummy twosome on line, and see who responded with "thumbs up" or "hearts." Probably the entire surgery wing, maybe the whole hospital community would participate in noting this happy coupling.

OK, stop it, I cautioned myself. Don't be an adolescent jerk. I knocked on Dr. Davis's door, which was already half ajar. Her coat lay thrown over a chair. Most likely, she'd just arrived back at the office.

"Come in!" She hollered. Did I detect a bit of a loud alcoholic warble? She quickly sat opening her computer screen as she swung around to face me. A sense of silent rage darkened her demeanor. I could smell stale cigarette smoke snaking through the freshly minted aroma of mouthwash.

"Detective Kazinski! I thought I told you not to come back here," she glared, her eyes a fiery red. "I have a busy program to run and enough paperwork, so I must resist your absurd curiosity. You need a warrant this time."

"No, Dr. Davis. I'm following up now that we know Sandy was murdered."

"I heard that several days ago. Good news travels fast, Mr. Kazinski. A bad boy from day one, though I'm never sure we can totally trust Dr. Post, who has a flair for the front page."

She flashed a lubricated grin. Maybe the Brit had popped her cork after all. Nah, not enough time. Might take a couple of gallons more of alcoholic primer.

"I'm not at liberty to say much more at this time, doctor," I said softly, "I'll be needing more details from you. The manner of death is consistent with an inside job given the medical expertise required. Surgeons or their assistants might be especially qualified for the task."

"We have a lot of competent doctors here. Our mission is to save lives, not destroy them," Dr. Davis snapped back. "My office is dedicated to making sure we maintain high standards of ethics. The med school devotes a huge chunk of the curriculum to the subject. "

She buried her head in the computer. "Now, are we through here?"

"No, I have a few more questions…"

"I'm afraid not. Your insinuations are uncalled for and distressing." Her mood had leaped into the dark side. "Let me write a prescription for you, detective. It's the name of our lawyer. Any further discussion will be arranged through her."

She wrote something quickly on a pad and looked up at me with a chilling stare. "I suggest you might take some medication for anxiety, Detective Kazinski. I'm a member of our local precinct's community board, and your reputation precedes you, not too favorably. Perhaps a transfer might be in order, or early retirement."

She tore off the piece of paper and handed it to me. Underneath the lawyer's name was a neatly doodled skull and crossbones.

She waved me out.

I intended to pay a visit to Ross Parker, Sandy's roommate who had falsely claimed to be at the hockey rink before the murder occurred .I needed a breather from the case. La-Tanya had left a message to call it quits and go have a stiff one. "It's been five straight days non-stop, and you need some relaxation," her text said.

How unusual was her concern, coming from our round-the-clock boss? I headed home and decided to follow La-T's advice. My neighborhood pub beckoned even though it was not yet five o'clock.

I walked inside the establishment; where Mickey, the central casting bartender, indicated someone was waiting for me. I put my hand inside my coat and unlatched the safety on my gun.

Then I saw her.

It was my ex-wife, Jill, sitting with slender legs crossed and sipping a martini while she scrolled through her cell phone. God, she was beautiful, just as I remembered her.

Suddenly it hit me. I must be losing it. How could my ex-wife be here, sitting in a bar and turning back the clock over 25 years?

"Hello, Dad," she said softly, putting the phone down. It was my daughter, Sarah, who had grown into a mesmerizing adulthood.

"Oh my God," I cried out as I stumbled into a seat at the table. There was another drink, a dirty martini, sitting across the table with just a hint of lipstick on the rim.

"Hello Barney, are you surprised?" I heard the voice behind me. Now I got it. Mother and daughter had been waiting. What were they doing here, and how did they know where I'd be?"

As if reading my mind, Jill said, "We called and spoke to La-Tanya. She said she'd try and get you here as a surprise."

Mickey appeared with perfect timing and handed me a double bourbon with a touch of soda. The three of us were seated facing each other. I was confronting a pair of reddish blondes, their ponytails swaying in sync as they sipped.

I couldn't stop shaking. It felt as if my skin had melted away while my nervous system plunged onto the table. Only later would I be able to process what had transpired.

The three of us talked for a few minutes before Jill excused herself so that I could speak to Sarah one-on-one. I hadn't seen her in a long time. Where the hell had I been? Too many cases, too many personal issues keeping me wrapped up in myself. I knew these were lame excuses, so I didn't bother offering them.

"I've thought of you often, Dad," Sarah said, her emotions measured and under control. She was always the calm one amidst the emotional jabs flying back and forth between her parents.

"Mom and I decided on the spur of the moment, to take a quick trip to New York, and do some shopping, theater, that sort of thing. So here we are." Sarah looked at me plaintively as if unsure whether I still wanted to be a father.

I took a large swig of bourbon, trying to plow through the shock of this moment. Words failed me as the liquor kicked in.

"Mom's happy," Sarah brightened. "She's put her life together. My dad, I mean my second dad, has been great to us both."

I shrugged as guilt mixed with the disappointment of being replaced.

She picked up the cue, her earnest Jill eyes imploring me to hear her out.

"Dad, you are part of me, and I'm part of you. We never change. I'm finding my way through an important time in my life."

She held up her left hand with a twinkly blue sapphire glowing on the fourth finger.

I tried to react happily, rising beyond autopilot, thrashing through more than twenty-five years of memories.

Sarah did not want to let go of the moment. “I’d like you to come to the wedding, dad, give the bride away. It will be in the spring. His name is Tim, he’s with the LAPD. Funny coincidence, huh? I figured what better than to marry a cop, right? We met online.”

“Oh yeah,” I suddenly retrieved my parental voice. “I love cops. We have a ball. Maybe today isn’t the best time.”

Then my mind blew out. I put my head down on the table, tears assembling quickly, and my shoulder knocked the bourbon all over the surface as Sarah yelled and scrambled to salvage her cell phone. I felt her behind me, patting me on the shoulder, like a parent would comfort a child. Her voice was soft but clear. “It’s all right, Dad, I’ve missed you. We’re gonna be a family again.”

34. Rosemarie Li

Tuesday, dinnertime

"Good God, Jeff, this has been torture. Confined to the barracks, taking virtual classes, while the world swirls around me."

We had cleared out the tissues on the floor of my pad and wiped down the kitchen table. The so-called Prince was sitting in white linen, shoveling my hastily prepared Rao's Marinara pasta into his mouth. I loved the way his lips attacked the pasta, No slurping, just one predatory bite per wad of noodles. I envisioned feeding him a nipple. Maybe a little painful fun now that his buddy was gone?

I could feel tiny tremors emanating from my underbelly. Ambivalence fought against my hormones, my needs punching through sadness. I needed sympathy, a bit of foreplay, and then an assault by his gluttonous lips. Shame on me.

I had showered, put on clean underwear, and coiled my hair into a controlled mass. A yellow sundress barely covered an open expanse of oiled legs. My mother would be proud. Not that it mattered. Jeff seemed distracted; damn him, food and wine were his preoccupations right now.

"The detectives were brutal, Jeff," I told him. "Have you met the one named Kazinski.? And Gundy, what a creep, collecting DNA. They could have asked consent for these intrusions."

"Wankers all, ignore them." Jeff loved his new role as the Prince of Darkness in the Hillside royal court. He 'fancied' being the center of attraction, a British novelty now that his romantic field was clear. We had been friends before Sandy arrived. It was his turn to fit the glass slipper.

The hell with a dead ghost, I needed some flesh and blood.

I dredged up my best coquettish smile. "I've been saving myself for you, haven't I? Where have you been?" God, it felt good to flirt again.

He said, "I'm in the mood to give Ralph next door a bit of a flutter." His lips parted into a pasta-crusted smile.

I started unbuttoning my blouse. "My mother always told me, 'Don't give away the milk because then they'll never want to buy the cow.' Coming from the farm, she ought to know."

"I want the cow *and* the milk *and* the farm, darling. It's been a while for me too."

Wednesday, Day Six

35. Barney Kazinski

Early morning at the Command Center

I have always maintained a protective coating of pristine skepticism, while polishing it over with each day's accumulation of grime. My mother, bless her soul, liked to remind me, "Jesus re-creates the world anew every morning," I would like to have shared her faith.

I was sitting at my desk, indulging in self-pity, and fighting a hangover from the bourbon, along with a chaser of remorse after our cocktails. My two angels were occupied this morning with tailoring their wedding dresses and catching an afternoon plane back to LA. I guess they had figured that one night of family togetherness would be sufficient for now.

Today required a special effort to put all the frustrations aside and bring an unvarnished perspective to our case. The pressure was increasing even as our mission mushroomed into a complex investigation of murder, while the bosses at

One P.P. insisted on a desperate strategy for wrapping the case up.

We were sitting in our squad conference room, pretty much walking the evidence around the block, and getting nowhere. Following Becky's mandate, the neighboring precinct detectives and beat patrollers were out interviewing and re-interviewing just about everyone with even a slight connection to the deceased.

Becky was carefully culling the DD5 reports flooding into our Case Management System. As usual, many were clotted with irrelevant details. Becky meticulously weeded them out for valuable clues, starting with the roommates and dormmates. The surgeons and their staff might have harbored repressed anger. Ditto for the DomXX ladies. Every local merchant was covered, anyone who might have seen Sandy or served him on the fateful last day or night.

We scoured the security staff in the dorm and surgical wards. They were typically as clueless as the spotty video cameras. (Most conveniently, the dorm's video security system had been out of order for the past month.)

Credible alibies flourished. Big surprise: no one wanted to admit they were the last to see Sandy alive. Finally, Becky dropped a small bombshell. "Our Forensics team has come up with additional evidence concerning the lady of Dom XX."

She explained, "One of our investigators found a hidden copy of a small broadsheet in the roommates' living room, which announced that DomXX was having a special 'Champagne Evening' on the Saturday, it turned out, before the murder. On the backside of the flyer, a small note urged in a feminine hand, 'Don't be a stranger.' That sounded like a specific invitation."

It also sounded like a potential game-changer. For one thing, we now had reason to believe that Sandy might have been at DomXX five or six days before his death and not "several weeks ago" as Miss Shannon had tearfully described his last visit. She was also the most likely candidate to have written and delivered the note. In any case, another suspect with a memory lapse had joined our parade of witnesses who lied. Furthermore, we needed to know who attended that party (including Sandy). My gut told me there might have been some tense rivalries uncorked, a prelude for violence almost a week later.

Meanwhile, our distinguished first liar, Ross Parker, deserved attention. Like the victim, he was a highly pedigreed student with a rich father and the audacity or mendacity to offer a false claim that he was bowling or playing hockey on the fatal night.

It sounded more like he'd been playing hookey, but with whom?.

I drove back to the Hillside dorm, Room 5G, the new quarters of the roomies. The downstairs security guard was absent, probably out on an extended coffee break at 10 a.m. The new lobby garbage can was shiny, with a top that could be sealed. No rodents in evidence. Progress!

I took the elevator to the fifth floor and knocked at the door to 5G. No one answered.

I knocked harder, turned the handle, and the door opened, unlocked. I walked into the apartment, which was not a good idea without a warrant. To cover my tracks, I crept up the stairs halfway to the living quarters for the other roommates since the arrangement was the same as their old configuration where only Sandy lived on the ground floor.

I could hear music bleating with sounds like a chainsaw crossed with the wailing of a primate in heat.

"Someone up there?" I yelled.

The music hissed off. "Yeah, c'mon up."

I took that as consent to talk to a witness, whoever he was. I rushed up the remaining stairs and peeked into the room belonging to one of the guys, messy and vacant right now. When I got to the second bedroom, Ross was reading at his desk, with a single speaker nearby.

He had turned the music back up.

"Ross! Please shut off that damn music!"

"What?" He finally looked up. "Oh, hi, Detective. Sorry." He yelled at the speaker, "Alexa, down girl."

Alexa lit up and responded: "I'm sorry, sir, I can't find a song called 'down girl.'"

"Alexa, turn it off, please." She obeyed, and we sat in blessed silence for a few moments, my eardrums still palpitating.

"Mr. Parker. I'll get right to it. I want to know why you weren't at Hudson Piers the night of the murder."

"Detective, let me try and recall…"

"You're a smart Ivy League kid. Please try hard. Let me emphasize, *very* hard, so you don't wind up in handcuffs."

"This was which night?"

"Last Thursday, easy to forget, just another night on campus. Nothing memorable, other than you said you discovered your roommate's dead body around midnight. Happens all the time."

Parker looked stunned. His brain was like a roulette wheel whirring in a casino. He was trying to gauge where on the truth spectrum his mind would stop.

"Maybe your memory will improve if we take you down and throw your butt in jail."

"No detective, wait!" Ross started sorting through excuses like a Las Vegas dealer shuffling cards. He lowered his head, knowing he was cooked. "You are correct. I wasn't at Hudson Piers with the guys."

"Well, would you mind telling me where you were until the wee hours?

"It wasn't exactly wee hours. I was with our friend Pil from around eight or eight-thirty or so. I then came back to the apartment at about eleven, and no one was around, so I went upstairs and grabbed a quick nap. I woke before midnight and went downstairs to raid the fridge. Sandy's door was partly open, which meant any visitors had gone home. I walked in and saw him sprawled face up on the bed in his half-open white coat. I screamed and tried CPR. The body was still warm, but he was a goner. Then I called 911."

"So, you were hanging with Pil Potter, the illicit drug dealer of choice for med students. Were you loading up on sedatives by any chance? I gather you didn't see any of the roommates when they got back?"

"That's correct. I might have heard a couple of voices before midnight, but I was half asleep at that point."

"So, you couldn't tell if they were male or female voices? Any angry words exchanged?"

"No, sir, more like background noise. Maybe a video was playing, hard to tell."

"Let me ask you this, Ross. You're a bright boy, Ivy grad and all, wearing expensive duds with your parents giving you a free ride to a doctor's shingle. What is it about you young punks that you cannot wait to screw up your lifetime opportunity with a loser like Pil who can't even spell his name right? I'll bet he wears his cap on backward too."

"It isn't what you think. Pil is a very convenient full-service guy who makes deliveries. We cannot go through med school without a bit of off-license help. I needed some Adderall to help me study and some Cannabis to calm me down to sleep. Pil's the only guy around here we trust to maintain quality and keep his trap shut. Using pot is grounds for serious detentions here."

"You said the body was still warm?"

"Yes. His white coat was sprawled half on top of him, it was a tepid warmth. No rigor that I could spot, but some blood lividity creating discoloration of the skin. Possibly from blood thinner. We'd heard he was being treated for an irregular heartbeat. I cannot predict exactly what the time of death was. It had to be recent."

"Presuming he died between ten and midnight, that means you were alone for a period of time between 11 p.m. and midnight when you discovered the body. Is that correct?"

"Not totally correct, Detective. There was another faint voice downstairs in the interim, as I just told you when I was half in a fog of dreamland upstairs."

"Listen, Mr. Parker. I understand your need for secrecy, but you weren't bowling, and lying about your whereabouts to an officer is a serious offense."

"I know, I was wrong. It was an awful experience. Sandy always drew a crowd around him. Here he was alone and crumpled up."

"Just to be clear, when was the last time you saw him alive?"

"Hard to recall exactly. It was sometime earlier that morning, Thursday. I was up at dawn studying downstairs, and Sandy was prowling around the kitchen looking for something edible. We said hello, and he said he was heading down to see his girlfriend on the second floor. She always maintained a full-service kitchen for him."

"Very convenient. So, you never saw him alive after the morning."

"That's correct."

"How about this? He was a very flashy guy who seemed to have attracted a lot of friends and possibly girlfriends. Did you feel any jealousy about his prowess in class or with the women? Competition in med school is prevalent for a lot of reasons."

"No, detective! I want to be a primary care physician. Sandy was surgery-bound. We were not in competition."

"Just to be clear: You felt no animosity toward Mr. Wainwright?"

"Detective, he was an operator, always had everything figured out. What a mind. He could diagnose illnesses faster than many of the senior staff. We all loved and hated him for making everything seem so easy and under his control."

"You are certain those moments of jealousy never erupted into a plan for taking his life?"

"No, sir. I am not the killing type. I admired the guy. I only hated his attitude towards others, especially women. It wasn't just about sex. He had to assume power and control. He wanted to win; thus, someone else had to lose, just like knocking guys down on the hockey boards for the hell of it. The women always fell for his audacity. He could sense their vulnerable spots because he was oddly vulnerable himself. Then he'd torture them and dump them and look for some fresh conquest."

Ross paused and looked at me for the first time straight on, without any noticeable filter of expression. "I'd look there if I were you. Women scorned. Hell, hath no fury, right? That's all I'll say. Just my gut."

"Any particular names?"

"I suppose you'd have to consider Rosemarie Li since she was the current girlfriend and had been for a while. She was up in our pad quite a lot lately. Towards the end, I mean before the death, she seemed a bit desperate. I think she had figured out he wasn't going to settle down."

"Any others?"

"I'd start with Dr. Ashley. It always seemed they were cozy at the hospital or at our place. They tried to pretend it was professional, but I dunno. His door would often be closed. She has an apartment nearby, so who knows what was going on."

"How about any of your other roommates or close friends like Prince Jeff? There may have been reasons for jealousy from several quarters?"

Ross flashed a genuine look of disbelief.

"We may wise-ass a bit, but we're a serious crowd. Moments of jealousy, absolutely, but murder? No way."

"OK, Ross. Go back to your books and your heavy metal. We're done for now."

I hustled back down to the lobby, only to bump into, you guessed it, Ralph Gruber, full of his usual "earnest" concern for my well-being.

"How's the case going, Columbo?"

I vacillated between a right uppercut and a left hook. Which side of his jaw might relinquish the most teeth?

I smiled and walked down the steps and out the door.

36. Barney Kazinski

Wednesday mid-morning

After the Ross interview, my mind was throbbing, and my stomach was growling. I was preparing to go for another meat pie when my cell rang. Becky told me to get back to home base immediately. Indigestion diverted for the moment.

I raced back to find our team reassembled in the conference room. Becky started dialing a speaker phone centered on the table. The medical examiner, Dr. Post, answered. He sounded psyched up as if he had just won the Nobel Prize for his discoveries of the genetic composition of bullshit.

Evidently, he was still following this case and the technical data closely.

"Hey there Kazinski, how are you feeling today?"

"Just great, Dr. Post. Even better if I could get one witness to tell the truth."

"I always say, only the dead give it to you straight from their guts."

"Very reassuring, doctor, now what good news prompts this call?"

"As you might expect," Post said bluntly, "in Mr. Wainwright's case, it's his restless sword and the cutaneous contacts with women that have provided us the truth serum."

"What is this, Game of Thrones? I have never heard of a restless sword. Out with it then, doctor. You're on speaker." My comrades had gone silent and were looking at me expectantly while indicating disbelief.

Post charged ahead in his usual bombastic manner. "Our super sleuth Peter McClain has given me the news. We've got some interesting results involving vaginal fluids on the victim's genitals, along with lower abdominal trace smears collected by Jen Park in the hours after the murder. The boy had plenty of intimate contacts, and it appears there was no cleansing shower during his final day along with some sloppy condom protections."

"Vaginal fluid present," I replied. "Big surprise. That narrows it down to Sunday's attendance at Giants Stadium. Most staff members at the hospital don't have to provide DNA swatches."

"Really? You don't think this might lead to *your* murderer?"

"No, Dr. Post, not unless each of the strands of DNA comes with its own social security number. But it's a start. Hold on to that evidence. We have a few likely prospects..."

"Not so fast, Kazinski. You haven't heard the best part."

"Go ahead, make my day. Very promising; you and McClain have discovered female DNA on the most prolific lover-boy in New York. What took you so long?"

The ebullient doctor ignored the question.

"This might be a little help. Our analysis took some time. We've sorted things down to two distinct types of female DNA present, meaning two different women were recently involved in intimate relations. The strands were lifted off his genital region and the white coat he was lying on. The lack of a shower helped."

Dr. Post. paused, letting this information sink in before expressing a dramatic, and logical deduction. "My dear friends, you have two women, and thus the possibility of a little jealousy taking place. There's also some evidence of male DNA and unrelated prints around the murder scene that are not Sandy's. Those might lead us to his dinner partner."

"You're halfway there, doctor," I said with a calmness that I certainly didn't feel. Were you able to run any of these DNA samples against the entire surgical group?"

"Didn't help. As you said, there's no requirement that all staff provide DNA samples. That's the hitch as you suggest. Meanwhile, identifying the other male who was present will be more of a problem because we know that the roommates had a vast circle of friends."

"One last question Dr. Post," I said. "My associate detective Gundy attended your autopsy and said that it confirmed Peter McLain's theory of a murder taking place."

"He's a very well trained diagnostician," Post said proudly, "so of course he was right. We were surprised to find several deep vein clots in his lower body so we aren't sure which clot was ultimately responsible for turning out all his lights. I suspect the killer was caught by surprise as to how fast the injected air bubble worked because the victim had such a propensity for clots."

After we hung up, Becky looked as if she continued to be sickened by the speculation of Sandy's errant sexual behavior.

She was not alone. Give credit to that old medical codger, Dr. Post. He might have opened the possibility of finding the so-called “smoking gun” in the case, or perhaps we might call it the “smoking sword.”

I wisely didn’t pursue that line of speech out loud.

While the others grumbled among themselves, I tried to assess the various female suspects who might have participated in Sandy’s final spasms of life.

First came the femme fatale, the seductive Dr. Ashley Dillon, whose provocative manner had drawn me deeper into confusion about my own feelings of value as I aged.

Then there was the “good girl” next door to Ralph, Ms. Rosemarie Li, an innocent transfer from a farm in Iowa to the harder reality of life in the big city. Her soulmate, the first real love of her life, had led a double or triple life with other women.

Innocence, like cow milk can curdle quickly when monogamy proves duplicitous.

I presumed Dr. Maura Davis should be on the persons-of-interest list, although I doubted the Vegas bookies would accept bets on her possible participation. If she had been Cougar-ing, Prince Jeff was more likely her prey.

Among other medical residents, Dr. Wendy Jamison’s name had been introduced by some pediatric nurses. Coming from a lower floor, Wendy was not well known to the surgical group. Still, Sandy enjoyed her young patients and was trying very hard to win them over and perhaps secure her romantic interest as well.

Finally, we could not rule out the older Irish lass, Miss Shannon. Despite her law school aspirations, she had managed to find time for more personal engagements. How many subway stops would it take to go from downtown

Dominatrix to uptown Murderess? She presumably had lied about when she last saw Sandy. We knew she had been present at the Champagne blast on the Saturday night before he died. What raw feelings were carried over from that affair?

Meanwhile, there was a host of males who might have been dinner-mates, ranging from The Prince, Pil, or the roomies, including Hector and Ross Parker. Finally, Rosemarie's neighbor Ralph Gruber, ears pinned to the wall, was a long shot, but we couldn't take him off the list yet as a "pain in the ass of interest."

Unfortunately, we needed to get some missing DNA samples. We could start back at DomXX.

I gave the group a sanitized summary of my hit list and grabbed my trusty steed, Gundy, as we made our way back to the enchanting confines of DomXX. Miss Shannon was on a small downstairs couch, with a law casebook in her lap.

She sat sipping an early bull shot. Her eyes had an icy, frozen quality, suggesting this was not her first cocktail of the day.

The unpowdered face gave her away. It had more wrinkles than a discarded shopping bag. She looked like a tired drunk. I doubted Sandy would be turned on right now. Then again, maybe it was his absence that had stimulated notions of revenge and tweaked her body into looking its age.

"Ah, you two boys are back," she greeted us with minimal civility. "My friendly neighborhood coppers. What can I do for you this time?"

"Well, Miss Shannon," I volunteered, taking out the crinkled flyer discovered in the roomies' apartment. "Seems to me that you have omitted some details regarding when you last saw your deceased boyfriend. This flyer advertised a 'Champagne and Cougars Evening.' On the back, there is a generous invitation to the party less than a week before his murder.

She studied the page, turned it over casually, and made a half-hearted attempt to pretend this wasn't her handwriting.

Meanwhile, her lubricated stare was defaulting into belligerence. I pushed ahead. "Are you sure you don't have anything else to say about that last Saturday night?"

"Well, detective. I admit I may have omitted a detail or two. We try to preserve confidentiality for our customers. We have parties almost every night. They run together in my mind, so my memory might have been faulty."

Her face revealed the glazed expression of a witness trying to salvage an alibi. She continued in a slurred voice. "As I recall, we were in the Champagne Theater, everyone getting acquainted, a lot of friendly conversation on the couches. Our boy had his posse there, and I supplied a few sweet companions to brighten the atmosphere. All I distinctly remember is that the chick Dr. Ashley, had brought a flask, showed up and started screaming when she saw Sandy dancing with me. Things got a bit physical, and she had to be sent home."

"Any other jealous lovers show up?" Gundy asked. He liked love triangles that almost always trapped at least one bad actor and maybe the whole trio. His wily mind was trying to sort out who was the leading culprit in this situation. For once, he was paying attention.

"There might have been a couple of others. With Sandy, it was always a crowd," she said, offering a mixed look of regret and reproach.

"Did the Brit play peacemaker?" Gundy asked innocently.

"Don't know him well," Miss Shannon said. "The girls aren't amused by his Princely pretensions. I will say he liked to throw his inheritance around and they didn't mind enjoying his booze and his tips."

"Did you see Prince Jeff leave with anyone?" I asked.

"Yes and no. It seemed like a magic trick, one female would disappear, and a new one would take her place. In Vegas, they used to do that routine with elephants. Fortunately, Prince Jeff's charge card had no ceiling. For all I know, Buckingham Palace was backing up his credit."

Time to bring this freak show to a conclusion. Here came my favorite question that always seemed to produce sobering reactions. "Miss Shannon, do you think Dr. Ashley Dillon could have been a murderer?"

"Hard to tell. He always said she was trouble." Her face clenched into a mode of exasperation. "I mean, he made her sound unstable enough, but hell if I know."

I flashed my eyes at Gundy, who has the quick hands of a purse-snatcher. As soon as Miss Shannon placed her drink down and turned her attention toward me, Gundy grabbed the lipstick-stained napkin crumpled next to her glass, a perfect specimen of DNA.

"I hope today has been the whole truth," I warned her. "I want your absolute assurance that you didn't see Sandy on the day or night of his death."

She turned very solemn and pensive, suddenly clearheaded for the moment.

"If I'd seen him, I would have saved him."

Thursday, Day Seven

37. Barney Kazinski

Early morning

Our increasingly frustrated boss, the hard-wired Captain La-Tanya, called at 6 a.m. to announce an "emergency" briefing in two hours. I had been thrashing through one of my ever-more-frequent nightmares about unsolved cases. La-T's phone call produced a wakeful relief from the nightmare.

Our unruly group managed to make it in, bitching and growling, shortly before 8 a.m., which is precisely what La-T anticipated. There were a couple of NYPD investigators present from the neighboring provinces. They did not look happy at being called to appear at such an early hour.

In our conference room, La-T had set out a cardboard canister of dark black coffee without any donuts. This meant there was more serious business to discuss, or else she had started one of her periodic low-sugar diets.

In either case, her mood was as dark as the coffee. She didn't bother to pull up a chair as she addressed us in a speech without a podium. "Ladies and gentlemen," she declared. "One week is too frigging long for this thing. One P.P. downtown is having their usual shitfit, only it's your butts that are going to be back walking the streets."

"Excuse me, La-T," I interrupted her. "As you all know, we've got a very delicate situation here. Our best piece of evidence is that our victim may have had relations with two women in his final hours. I'm going to need some help in speaking to his potential partners and possible perpetrators. I don't want any complaints that I was harassing his lovely lady friends."

The group exhaled a kind of collective groan. "Two in one day," Gundy surmised, "maybe he did kill himself after all to get a rest."

"All right, that's enough," La-Tanya realized we were diluting her briefing's purpose to move the case toward closure. "Tell you what," she said. "Becky, you divide up the most likely witnesses that we need to finalize the chronology of the deceased's final day. Let's meet here again tomorrow at 8 a.m. That's a Friday, so be prepared to cancel your weekend plans."

There was a collective groan, but La-Tanya wasn't finished. "In 30 minutes, I want Barney and Gundy to escort me over to the suite of Ms. Rosemarie Li, Sandy's latest and possibly last girlfriend. Class dismissed."

In the car, La-T was unusually quiet and reflective. "How does one simple case get so complicated?" she muttered loudly enough for us to hear.

"They're all complicated," I replied. "It only seems simple when you solve them. The secret here is to reject as many solutions as possible and hope that the last option is the missing piece, which has been obvious all along. That's Gundy's specialty."

"You'd better be right," La-T shrugged. "I don't especially enjoy peering into female va-vas for the silver bullet."

For once, Gundy kept control of the speed as we moved patiently to the hospital. We found a suitable fire hydrant as a temporary parking spot for a police vehicle. I had called ahead, and Rosemarie was waiting for us when we arrived at the door of her pad.

She had made a definite attempt to clean up her apartment since our earlier meeting. The floor was free of tissues, and her clothing looked freshly laundered. The textbooks were still strewn on her desk—an indication she wasn't neglecting her studies. Sandy's picture remained prominently displayed on her table with a ribbon across one corner.

She was still in mourning or at least pretending to be.

Gundy started darting around the apartment, snapping photos on his cell as I introduced La-Tanya. "Hope you don't mind a few photographs," she said. We waited awkwardly while Gundy went into the kitchen nook and disappeared into her bedroom.

"Get out of *there*," she rasped as Gundy quickly re-emerged, and we sat around the table in the living room. She was sipping a cup of coffee but did not offer us anything. Up close, her eyes looked puffy. Her freshly applied makeup accentuated the lumpy effect caused by swelling from her continuing tears.

I decided to go for the jugular right away.

"Ms. Li, we have a bit of sensitive business this morning. That's why Captain Lawson has joined us. Feel free to meet privately with her at any time."

"No need for privacy here," she said. "I want the same answers you do as to how he died." A tiny band of tears had settled below her eyes. La-Tanya produced a handkerchief and offered it to her.

She declined as if sporting a war wound with pride.

"OK, then, let's get right to it," I said, trying to appear sympathetic.

"It seems that there was a prominent amount of female DNA on Mr. Wainwright's body when he died. We were able to take some DNA samples off the white coat he was lying in as well. You have told me that you saw the deceased early that morning, but since you were his girlfriend, we'd like to confirm that you had sexual relations with him and at what time."

"My God, detective, is this standard procedure? Haven't I suffered enough without reviewing the details of our sex life?"

"Afraid so, Ms. Li," La-T jumped in. "This is a relevant part of our investigation. If it makes things easier, the male detectives will step out of the room."

"No, let's get this resolved, so I don't have to deal with the police department again."

"Okay," La-Tanya nodded. "Then let us have the answer."

"Sandy and I had relations a little later than I had previously indicated. It was midday. He arrived here at lunchtime. That is all you need to know. As it happened, my annoying neighbor Ralph Gruber had stopped by a few minutes before Sandy arrived and I had barely pushed him out of my apartment when my man showed up. I was preparing a salad for his lunch."

"Exactly what time was this?" I asked.

"About 12:15, or thereabouts. I'm sure Ralph will recall, Mr. Peeping Tom."

"This is a different story than you previously told us, Ms. Li," I said.

"I know, detective, I was confused when we first met. Frankly, that last day was a very mixed-up one. Sandy could typically materialize out of nowhere at any time."

She gave us a look of such sadness that I would have stopped right there, except that La-T had flipped on her patented cynical glare.

"Here comes the hard part. Ms. Li," La-Tanya said using her usual method of plowing ahead with a lack of tact. "There is evidence from the Medical Examiner's report that two strands of DNA were present in many of the erogenous regions, meaning at least a second woman was involved."

"And no shower in between," Gundy added with surprising gusto.

Rosemarie's face wrenched from sadness into anger in one nanosecond. "What? That little shit," she sniped. "It's lucky he's dead. I can imagine who it might have been. No doubt, our resident with the big boobs, Dr. Ashley Dillon. Or maybe the woman who runs his favorite bordello, the Irish redhead. He loved going to those porn bars, and I had to draw the line. I knew how those girls liked to drink and party."

She paused and practically spat it out, “My advice is to get them all prepared for a firing squad, don’t bother with a trial.”

She suddenly rose and dismissed us. “All right, we’re done now. I am not discussing this further. Any additional conversations, talk to my lawyer. Now please get out of my apartment before,” she hesitated, “before I call the police.”

We all rose almost as if in sync. “Ms. Li, we’ll be in touch,” I said. “Please plan to make yourself available, with or without a lawyer.”

Back in the car, Tanya looked over her shoulder at Gundy a bit skeptically. “I notice you walked out holding a Styrofoam cup. I don’t recall you bringing it from the office.”

“Oh, good detection there,” Gundy spoke up from the back seat. “I must have grabbed it from her kitchen table by mistake. So sorry. We’ll have it swabbed for DNA just to verify it matches Dr. Post’s sample. Then I can return it if you wish.”

Gundy offered one last tidbit. “She must have gotten her coffee outside the apartment. There was practically nothing in the fridge and nothing on the stove, which seemed a little early for Thanksgiving or Christmas break. Where might she be going and with whom?”

38. Barney Kazinski

Thursday mid-day

In our conference room, we had a luncheon deli spread laid out like a banquet. La-Tanya was showing her appreciation for our round-the-clock work. Detective Becky Muller could barely wait to tell us about her meticulous job organizing the troops from three precincts. "We've managed to interview over 50 personnel in surgery, pediatrics, pathology, and various outside retail establishments that might have had some involvement with the deceased in his final hours."

"And the winner is…" Gundy loved to pop the balloon at the first inkling of self-congratulation.

"There is no winner," Becky retorted. "A couple of staff, male and female, were blushing in their descriptions of our golden boy, but that's as far as it went. The consensus is that there was a bitter contest taking place between Rosemarie Li and Dr. Ashley Dillon. The rivalry might have been sharpened due to a third party, the pediatric resident Dr. Wendy Jamison stepping into the fray. She's a latecomer to the Sandy Wainwright fan club. At least, that's the nurses' station view, and they have a pretty good intuition about these things."

"Cavorting with Sandy in pediatrics, Dr. Jamison was certainly in the right department to rob the cradle," La-T interjected. The laughter exploded around the table. Becky smiled and joined in our outburst.

"While I appreciate what I overheard, does anybody at Hillside take death seriously?" La-T asked. "We're like dogs sniffing for clues. You all know just where canines like to sniff other dogs."

Even in a crisis, hand it to our leader. The woman was flashing her dimples and breaking the tension.

We all bubbled up in chatter and overcame our fatigue for a moment before quickly turning serious again. "Not sure about Dr. Davis," I noted, "we haven't confronted her about her recent mid-day visit to DomXX. She and her haughty scrub nurse seem to have glommed onto each other. Feels a bit odd, an unlikely pair. There's been a rumor that she caught Sandy and Ashley playing kissy-face in the park, after a picnic together."

"Oh yes, almost forgot," Becky continued, "Rosemarie's next-door neighbor, Ralph Gruber, keeps showing up when he's not wanted. He's trying to move in like a mafia don now that the deceased is out of the picture. Rosemarie is not encouraging him, but he's very pushy and he plays on her vulnerability."

Becky stared sternly at me: "Someone needs to go ask a few more questions in the dorm. A little more legwork, and maybe we can put this case file in completed status."

I nodded, realizing her intent. Becky was looking at me as if to say, "Our reputation is on the line. You and Gundy have always been the miracle men pulling perps out of a hat. Can you do it one more time?"

And then it hit me. Becky had been in the office for over twelve hours almost every day. She was still charging ahead, although her clothes barely looked ruffled. What discipline! Maybe each day, she'd taken twenty minutes for a tuna fish sandwich from the fridge. Hers was dedication beyond all endurance.

Yet here she was putting out an SOS to all nearby sources. All her investigative work had not done the trick thus far, so the job was back firmly on Gundy and my shoulders.

I realized we had to deliver. My banged-up shield reminded me of the responsibility for taking on the greatest responsibility of all: closure of this case.

Flashback: Weekend before Death

39. Dr. Ashley Dillon

Emotional Roller Coaster

The ups and downs with Sandy had been playing havoc with my emotions. I vowed to clean up my life, purify my romantic intentions, and find a way back to sanity. That lasted about ten minutes.

Before Sandy, I had never been in a sex club. I had only heard about the depravity of the participants.

We didn't want to "get it on" directly with strangers, or at least I thought *we* didn't. He mainly liked to go watch the conjugal dances as a prelude to our own private nights. We had to be especially careful after our incident with Dr. Davis.

By day, I was a perfect boss, calling the shots for the medical students, which was a blessing and a curse. My white coat had a bright and a dark side. Along with the recognition of power came the fear of exposure. I knew further moral laxity could only lead to career disaster. Dr. Davis would certainly not have forgotten.

In Sandy's arms, I kept ignoring the consequences and let him take me down.

At times, I was falling hard: deeper, lower, into the depths of hell, and yet, I rationalized, this was the sunny patch of earth I had been craving. His brilliance as a student was unquestionable; his peers and teachers all confirmed that this was a special man, a rare clinician who keenly felt his duty to solve and heal his patients' woes. He seemed especially sensitive in his work with children and was winning plaudits from many quarters, a chorus led by Dr. Wendy Jamison.

My fantasy of the future was still taking shape. Sandy would be the man who unshackled my inhibitions going back to adolescence. I was tired of pretending to be my mother's perfect little girl, the dutiful child repressing all joy. Every minute with Sandy was an adventure, a journey, a rite of passage to an intensity of feeling that I'd never previously experienced.

Did I love him? Always. Did I hate him? Outside of bed, my exuberant fantasy could vanish into his callous behavior where I barely knew this man.

Despite the encounter with Dr. Davis, we continued to push the envelope at every opportunity. In the end, I knew that I had to submit; there were plenty of volunteers to take my place in his crazy life.

Occasionally, reality intruded; our futures were hovering in the balance. Only his parents' largesse might save us. Rumors abounded that the med school dean, Dr. Michael Grant, had a folder in his top center drawer with architectural renderings for a new Wainwright building.

Sometimes when we had a snatch of time off duty, Sandy would bring his guitar over to my apartment and present subtle melodies of seduction and sadness that he had composed. This was the vulnerable side of Sandy, who, despite his outward bravado, would take any slight personally.

How could I not be overwhelmed, with my devotion overriding common sense as my own self-identity struggled for reinforcement?

A harrowing question loomed in my more rational moments. Was he prepared for a permanent, monogamous relationship? At one level, I didn't want to seek the answer and risk bursting the euphoric bubble that engulfed us. Nevertheless, I spent many days mustering the courage to seek an answer. I was waiting for the right moment.

A post-coital afterglow would be the best time to ask.

It was already mid-November. I dreaded the Thanksgiving and Christmas holidays coming up with their bogus gaiety. One night, while lying in bed, limbs intertwined, I was lolling into the conviction that Sandy was "The One." My hands and arms were languidly folded around him as if I wanted us to be a statue preserved in this pose forever.

Just then, I heard two beeps, the all-too-familiar ping of his incoming phone texts. Normally, in these moments, he would ignore them. In this case, he brushed me away and jumped up, grabbing his phone at warp speed. With his back to me, he read the message, inducing a tiny chuckle.

Suddenly, the mood had shattered, and a painful shift occurred.

"What's so funny?" I asked.

"Oh, it's nothing," he said.

"Doesn't sound like nothing." I sat up and rested my chin on his shoulder. "Can I see?"

"It's nothing, I told you." He pulled his phone away. "Just one of our boys' nights getting organized by my friend Prince Jeff."

My antenna was alerted. I was curious and frightened. I knew that although Prince Jeff was now involved with Wendy, he was a poor influence on Sandy when it came to behavior involving other women. It was also highly possible Wendy might be pursuing her own unresolved fantasies about my boyfriend.

"Yeah," back in our moment, Sandy said brusquely, "Jeff's got our buddies a gig at Dom XX in the main Champagne party room. It's a premium experience."

He beamed, like a mad scientist or someone high on an incendiary substance.

"You mean *our* sex club?" I asked, trying to maintain a neutral tone. I wanted desperately for him to show his loyalty and invite me with his friends.

"I wouldn't exactly call it *our* sex club, babe. I only took you there a couple of times. Either way, it's just guys hanging together—a harmless boys' night out. Only the big spenders get the full Champagne treatment."

"How can Prince Jeff afford premium service on a technician's salary at an upscale club?" I asked with a gnawing pang of dread.

"Connections, I guess. He's pretty cool about it. British royalty enjoying a trust fund. He doesn't need the money—

he's a scrub nurse for the hell of it. Anyway, gotta go, babe. See you on rounds."

And with that, Sandy got dressed so quickly that it felt like Maura Davis had entered the bedroom riding a witches' broom.

"Okay, see you." I was speaking to his back. So much for having 'the talk.' Deep in my soul, my spirit was squelching the wedding bells that had been chiming a few minutes earlier.

There was a definite chill in the atmosphere. I watched silently, confused, and hurt as he half-waved and slipped out into the night.

40. Dr. Wendy Jamison

Flashback several days before party night.

There is always a turning point for the significant events in our lives, good and bad. With 20-20 hindsight, we can look back and think about how things might have turned out differently. For all of us around Sandy, everything "came to a boil one Saturday night," as Prince Jeff described it.

It had been a strange week, and believe me, I was very accustomed to "strange." I had been an army brat crisscrossing the world as a child. The early years were so turbulent that I felt most comfortable living in the cracks of daily life where I could endure family storylines without expecting a happy ending.

The tension became palpable during the days before our upcoming Saturday night revelry. Sandy had been distracted when he paid one of his mid-week visits to my pediatric ward. He could barely focus on the names of the kids with whom he typically hung out. When I asked him what was wrong, he replied dismissively, "Lots on my mind."

I knew from Ashley that she and Sandy had been caught in the park by Dr. Davis, practically *in flagrante delicto*, which my wicked Brit liked to call "knickers down." I warned Ashley about keeping tight-lipped and close-legged around her boyfriend, but I was hardly one to give advice when I was looking for a little personal attention from the glam stud myself.

Any attempts at converting flirtation into seduction had met Sandy's sidetracking me to his 'best buddy' the Prince.

This was a pointless exercise because I had decided Ashley's friendship was not going to stop me from standing in line when I knew Sandy was intrigued by me.

My default option had been the not-so-royal Prince, who appeared strangely reticent in the romance department. We were dating as friends without benefits, while something was holding him back.

Imagine my frustration, hanging around with two of the biggest womanizers on the upper west side of Manhattan, and neither one was making the ultimate move. Normally, I had men crawling all over me, so I took a page from their playbook and pivoted to an intellectual strategy. Prince Jeff asked for help in preparation for the MCAT exams, following Dr. Davis's encouragement to apply for med school. Suddenly, he was getting serious about his future.

We would meet at his very swank apartment on Park Avenue, where I prepared to share the fruits of my wisdom plus some other treats for the boy rendered by my microscopic skirt.

We had experienced one unpleasant moment earlier in the week when Jeff and I were walking together out of our medical building while Ashley was headed for the meat wagon. She gave me a chilling look. I recoiled, although she had initially set us up. Jeff likewise felt insecure in that instance and wrapped a muscular arm around me as if to declare ownership of one of his possessions.

Ashley started to turn away when Jeff decided he might create a little mischief. He sensed that her relations with Sandy were fraying, and perhaps might incite some action from both of us. Out of nowhere, he called out, "Dr. Ashley,

I hope you've heard about our little party on Saturday night. You know the spot. The Champagne is on me."

"No, I hadn't heard. I've been working." Ashley looked back at me as if she would have preferred taking an axe to my neck rather than participating in our Dionysian revelry. Yet Jeff had learned from the master how the three of us could play this game. I detected a sudden twist in his laid-back British demeanor.

"What's the matter, your boy toy doesn't fancy your being there?" he yelled. "We certainly welcome you as our guest, right Wendy?" He threw me a very smug look that warranted a hardy kick in the balls.

I didn't respond, but I could see he had gotten Dr. Ashley nicely wound up.

"Maybe you boys need to find some older toys and grow up," she sniped. Then as we all continued to separate, she looked back. "On further thought, if I get a second wind, maybe I'll stop by. I can always hang with my pal Wendy, right?"

She gave me a venomous smile. At that moment, if you handed me a scalpel, I would have plunged it right into the midst of her overflowing boobs. As events played out, I would have been justified in taking her down right then and there.

41. Prince Jeff (Geoffrey) Laird

Flashback, Saturday party night.

Wendy was right to question my thinking when I invited Ashley to our 'knees-up?' Looking back later, I realized too many crossed wires and frayed connections would ignite into a royal mess. For starters, Sandy was a bit off-tempo, making the rest of us so wobbly that we began a mindless race to get sozzled. The bodily focus in medicine can easily breed intimacy, where personal familiarity overwhelms professional distance. Add a little fermented jealousy, and the evening bubbled up out of control.

We all started at DomXX in the usual fashion, close to midnight. The corks were popping, while inhibitions were like a corral of animals being let loose. My girl Wendy was quite the life, or so she thought, a bit cheeky while she tried to interest Sandy in some of her sexy bits. Miss Shannon, the head scrubber, had put her aging legs into play with Sandy in some sort of contorted dance. I was quickly too drunk to settle down and shimmied around the room in sync with the spiraling disco ball on the ceiling.

For his part, Sandy found his stride in the maze of confusion. He thrived on being the chaos-meister, joined by a sizable crowd of outside collaborators that had weaseled into the room. He guzzled a Champagne bottle as if being filled up with petrol. No doubt he'd purchased an illegal energy boost from Pil, for he was a pumped-up creature of the night bent on mayhem. Later he planned to have his pick of temporary companions to take the edge off since he was officially unattached for the evening.

Then, after midnight, Ashley showed up, and everything turned into chaos.

Yes, to be frank, here was my opportunity to multi-task in the romantic sphere. Why must I always be in the shadow of that unfaithful arse Sandy? Maybe the alcohol had liberated my tongue and my power of reasoning from a sensible mooring.

You might say I knew enough to be dangerous but not enough to know how to sort it all properly.

42. Dr. Ashley Dillon

Flashback: Saturday Party Night

Plain and simple, I should never have gone to that party. Relations with Sandy had chilled, so I was desperate to find out where we stood. I attempted to go to sleep that night, but at midnight I was still wide awake. I could almost feel the thrumming sounds of a disco beat in my bed from miles away.

Operating on autopilot, I wanted to tart it up better than the young sluts who were the customary accessories at these gatherings. For a foundation, I picked my most explicit pink thong and a satin bustier. Then I corkscrewed into a very tight red dress, with stiletto red heels topped off by hard black eyeliner and blazing red lipstick. In the mirror, I saw the reflected glory of my tightly contoured body, totally blowing its lid off. In one hand, just in case, I held a small flask of 151-proof rum that Pil had provided. It was about 75% alcohol, a useful preparation for the Uber 'carriage' taking me to the ball.

The rum was considered dangerous due to its flammability.

Hence my nerves would be on fire all night.

Prince Jeff had left my name at the door, good boy. From the upstairs lobby, I could hear the sound downstairs blasting through the whole building. It didn't take long for my eyes and ears and legs to find the Champagne Theater.

I walked in or stumbled in, making a grand entrance where the mood hit me immediately. This was no boys' night out. I'd never been to a party before where everyone seemed to be so completely wasted. I looked around: Sandy's roommates were there, with women draped over their respective laps. On the dance floor, my boyfriend was practically smothering Miss Shannon while mixing calisthenics with uncoordinated thrusts of his body.

As for BFF Wendy? She was out on the floor, engaged in a drunken caper, wrapped like a snake around Prince Jeff. She resembled a pole dancer; her skirt was climbing as if on a ladder up her thighs. Jeff was enjoying that sideshow immensely.

What the hell was I doing here?

How had I arrived at this surreal scene where my best friend and presumed lover were both betraying me? Flask still in hand, I was in a wanton mood, ready to defend my turf. I raced over and started beating my fists against Sandy's back.

Before I could say a word, he grabbed and practically choked me, then dragged me over to the side of the dance floor.

"What are you doing here?" he asked, eyes sizzling.

"You may recall that Prince Jeff invited me," I said drunkenly, groping to engage in some quick damage control.

"I thought you understood this was a boys' night."

"Yeah, I see that now. You didn't mention it was girls' night too."

"You should go home *now* Ashley," he said acidly.

"Sandy, can I talk to you for a minute? What is happening? This thing between us?"

I was tottering badly as he propped me up. Then, he delivered a deadly blow.

"Ash, what are you talking about? We were having sex. You know, like animals in heat. I already have a girlfriend, and I'm not ready to be tied down, especially by a woman of your age,"

"My age? I'm 28! I'm not exactly a spinster."

"Approaching thirty, you should date more mature men. They'd be overjoyed to find someone like you. I'm 25. It's almost embarrassing, hanging with my very own M-I-L-F."

I looked at him in astonishment as my bleary eyes filled with indignation. "Your Irish lady friend over there is not exactly the fountain of youth."

"Listen, Ashley, we had some good times. You've been a fun chick for a few hot nights. And you've served as a good mentor at the hospital; I'm grateful, but now we're both moving on."

I was appalled. I had to leave this scene before I strangled his fat neck. My God, what had happened to my sweet tender soulmate? I whipped around, unleashing my rage… at Wendy.

"You…" I gave her my best death stare as I raised my voice.

"What did I do?" Her arms were flapping in space, reeking of innocence.

"What did you do?" I responded. "You were my best friend. We would never betray each other. Isn't one guy enough?"

She was speechless. I started to run out of that God-forsaken place. I heard footsteps behind me and began to turn around.

"Sandy? You didn't mean all those cruel things, did you?" Only it wasn't him. Prince Jeff stood there, looking at me with a combination of pity and lust. This man was ghastly drunk, and his timing was off.

"That boy will never love you, Ashley. Let me take you home."

"I'm fine, you bloody fool. Is this your idea of a party? Have a good night."

"Just let me put you into a cab. You're in no condition…"

"Go back to Wendy, right behind you, and your other birds."

"Okay for now," he said with a slithering smile. "You haven't seen the last of me." Jeff's eyes alighted on a young Asian woman who had started to walk past us. Wasn't this Sandy's girlfriend? I wasn't sure, having seen her at medical school functions a couple of times. It looked like Jeff was playing Sandy's game of multiple partners.

Right now, I just wanted to get out and get home.

Later, as I practically fell into bed, I heard my cell beeping. I couldn't deal with it. I switched the phone to "Do not disturb."

The next morning, I checked my messages. Five texts? I scanned them quickly, hopeful that Sandy had sobered up and come to his senses. Instead, I received disturbing news. They were all from Jeff, with solicitous concern.

I deleted them quickly as if they might transmit a new Covid-19 variant.

Unsettling thoughts rattled through my hangover: I still loved Sandy. I still hated him. I still needed him. Maybe I was in love with the idea of love, rather than the real deal. For the first time, it occurred to me that I barely understood the full depth of his dark side. I only knew that being cruelly rejected in public was going to require retaliation.

Some options of revenge sprung swiftly to mind.

Hey, hold on, get a grip. My brooding ideas were soon slowing and sifting calmly through a list of how to even the score.

Maybe the British lad could be useful in showing his appreciation for me after all.

43. Dr. Ashley Dillon

Continuing flashback

All day Sunday I felt overloaded. Where was the off button?

By late afternoon, my brain felt like it was shredding apart. Alcohol consumption during the day had become a depressant, while breathing, sleeping, and daily functioning were highly irregular. My heart felt like it was in atrial fibrillation, creating spurts of cardiac irregularity.

The stress points were adding up. Every aspect of my life seemed to be unraveling.

I needed to take stock. The boyfriend had dumped me and was most likely carousing with my best friend. Make that *former* BFF. My self-doubts were raging, but there was no going home again. My career was in jeopardy from a bloodless, jealous superior who seemed transfixed by her scrub nurse.

What perfect synchronicity: all the ex-es in my life had coalesced at DomXX!

The danger in being a physician was that too much knowledge could be a hazard to calmly analyzing one's health. How could I limit further pain?

My condition required drastic action, effective immediately. I couldn't solve my pain by taking two aspirins and calling myself in the morning.

I also couldn't turn to doctors at the hospital. My woes would be common knowledge before sunrise. I needed a sudden fix, a chemical uplift, and no doctor would prescribe what I needed without an extensive examination.

One emergency recourse presented itself. If I was acting like the diva princess of woe, then I needed my personal prince. After midnight I dialed my savior. Scrub nurse Prince Geoffrey Laird answered his cell, sounding as if he'd been riding his own drug-propelled high.

"Um, is this my Prince? It's me, Ashley."

"Hey, good to hear from you. Have you dumped that playboy yet?'

"I thought he was your best friend."

"Just like Wendy is your best friend, right?" Touché. I could hear hysterical laughter in the background and wondered who was participating in the drunken orgy on this day, wherever they were. No doubt Sandy and Wendy were thriving in a threesome now. I was desperate and couldn't worry about anyone else.

"Jeff, I'm in bad shape. I need your help."

"Say no more, *darling;* the doctor is on his way. I know just who to call."

Within minutes, faster than a pizza delivery, Jeff arrived on my doorstep accompanied by his sidekick Pil with a small rolling suitcase bearing the usual pharmacopeia of drugs. I was in curlers and must have looked as if the Grim Reaper passed by, took one glance, and moved on in disgust.

Pil was at his best as he unveiled his traveling medicine show. He reassured me in a somber voice that his anti-psychotic cocktails were winning five-star reviews for curing mental breakdowns, depression, and convulsive madness along with such lesser symptoms as adrenal malfunction and insomnia.

Furthermore, Pil claimed to have special treatments for dozens of potential suicides and catatonic tragedies with his patented formulas for the most desperate, broken-hearted and despondent lovers.

All that he lacked was a Medical Board Certification in snake oil sales.

My God, I thought through my fogged-up brain, I must be out of my frigging mind. Was I about to take heavy doses of Pil's drugs for the first time? After almost ten years of non-stop drudgery from pre-med to post-med, I was relying on this instant salvation.

My mother would have axe-murdered both of us if she knew.

Pil was on a roll. He smiled almost sweetly while his eyes magnified his narcissism. "I always wonder why the ER doors start spinning after midnight?" he said.

"Don't know. Surgeons tend to wait until daylight," I replied, still in a daze.

"The traditional western medicine doesn't understand the pathogens that can produce such panic," Pil cautioned. He paused and looked at his friend Prince Jeff for approval, which was eagerly bestowed upon him.

I was approaching a state of hysteria, regretting my tacit cooperation in this total farce. I tried to rationalize what was happening.

Pil's merchandise was no doubt several levels below generic grade. Cue my fluency in Eastern medicine. I recalled that the original snake oil offered salutary benefits for soothing neuro-disruptions, according to Chinese holistic healers.

With exquisite timing, Jeff handed me some pills and a glass of water. The next thing I knew, I was stretched out face-down on the couch as a mellow golden haze cascaded down from the upper registers and dispersed through my body.

Pil made a hasty exit, and I could hear Jeff's soothing voice over the buzz of a hand-held, deep-tissue massager. It moved up and down through the chakras, hitting all the nerve bundles and knotted organs. Where had that powerful little machine come from?

At some point, my pajamas had been discarded and replaced by a towel while I lay on the couch. I vaguely tried to object, but Pil's cocktail and Jeff's wonder toy were turning all my tensions into a vortex of release.

"Jeff my Prince. You know what I wish?" I asked, half stoned and half asleep.

"What is it, Princess?"

"I wish Sandy would die. Either him or me or both of us together."

My last sensation was Jeff flipping me over and lightly running the massager directly over the sensual front of my body as I receded deeper and deeper into the embracing cocoon of sleep.

When I awoke, the sun was peeking through the curtains into the living room. I was covered in a blanket, apparently having been untouched overnight. Prince Jeff was sitting in a chair. He rendered a laconic smile and looked over at me through blistery eyes.

"Welcome back to earth, my love," he said softly. "I think we can agree to live without Sandy in our daily lives, don't you?"

I gasped at the underlying message that was dead-on so to speak. We were tired of being a disposable part of Sandy's libido. Life without him made sense, great sense. His absence would present an alternative for all of us.

Hey, wait a minute? Please, let's not go so fast. Jeff couldn't be serious about life without Sandy.

Friday, Eighth Day

44. Barney Kazinski

Back to the present, lunchtime

Despite my unwelcome fantasies about Dr. Ashley, it was time to ramp up her status from a person of interest to a possible suspect in a homicide. We also needed a clean slice of DNA to confirm Dr. Post's analysis of Sandy's final sexual glory.

The best place to start would be the residents' team room on the ninth surgical floor. As luck would have it, Dr. Ashley appeared to be waiting for me. Well, not really. Her half-concealed frame was perched in the doorway. She was talking to someone inside the conference room, preparing to leave.

She seemed disturbed when she saw me. But, ever so gracefully, she reversed field and, like a ballerina, pivoted back inside the room carrying her meat pie. Gundy and I followed her quickly before she could slam the door.

Gundy had his cell phone out, camera-ready, and I tapped his shoulder to acknowledge our priority was a quest for a clear DNA sample.

Thinking of La-Tanya's impatience, maybe we should have raced in and twisted Ashley's arms back into cuff position. More practically, recalling Rosemarie's possible role, I was struck by the amazing grit that our deceased victim must have shown trying to nail both these ladies in one day. What determination, what arrogance, given the fact he had succeeded. And what about Wendy, the pediatric resident? Had she made it a trifecta at some point, perhaps for the final blow?

A spark of jealousy lit up my suspicions again. Sandy seemed to have had few restraints in living the profligate life. Or at least he did until his sudden finale.

Any one of the obliging mates could have treated him like a black widow spider; lulled Sandy into a post-coital sleep with a special sedative and killed him thereafter.

Ashley's harsh voice pierced my thoughts. "Detective, are you here with some purpose? This is a big surprise, though not a pleasant one. Let's get it over with." She flashed her teeth in a razor-like smile. I thought of the spider image and cringed inwardly.

"I see you're still on your health kick, doctor?"

"Don't be a hypocrite, detective," she said, "I know you're hooked on these meat pies as much as I am."

She picked up her pie and took a savage bite. My entire body recoiled while Gundy's investigative mind popped into action. Oral tissues are a DNA haven.

"I didn't know whether they put opioids in these pies. They're so damn addictive," she said, bringing me back to our mission. "Now, what can I help you with today, detective?" A woman of many moods, she favored her Mary-Jane smile. It reminded me of my former wife Jill, in the throes of our worst marital spats, suddenly melting into marshmallow affection.

An inner voice warned: a woman scorned could be compliant or aggressively perturbed by the alpha beast. Gundy quieted me with a disarming look that said, "Let's chill into anger management default."

I regained composure, sort of, but there was something about Dr. Ashley that was pushing my anxiety button. I couldn't help myself. Was it time to charge ahead La-Tanya style?

"Dr. Ashley, I'm not going to play naïve detective here. Your ex-boyfriend, Mr. Wainwright seems to have been intimate with two women on his final day. I would certainly hope you made the finals."

She looked at me in total shock. Gundy's expression was a red stop sign. Ignoring them both, I plunged ahead in blatant violation of NYPD guidelines for a proper interrogation.

"That's right, doctor, you haven't confessed your sins. There is strong evidence of your having an illicit romance with the victim." Our eyes took on claws and warily stalked each other.

"Look, detective, my job is on the line here! Surely you can understand why I couldn't exactly go around advertising my love for Sandy…" Her voice was quaking, her features clenched as if fighting to hold back an avalanche of tears or maybe spittle.

"Did you say, your love for Sandy?"

"That's right—love. I loved him, and I had no idea he was cheating on me."

"I find that hard to believe, considering just about everyone else at Hillside knew of his escapades."

She pushed back hard. "You're a first-rate jerk for walking in here like you know anything about me, or Sandy, or our relationship."

Her features had mutated into hatred. Eyes dark. Cheeks crimson. Chin uplifted and teeth ready to rip. I regretted not having strapped on my body camera. One frame shown to a jury would erase any shadow of a doubt about her capability for vengeance. Somehow calling a timeout for a selfie of us did not seem advisable right now.

She verified my instincts by smashing the remainder of her half-eaten meat pie down on the conference table. "What happened between the two of you?" I asked. My hands were bunched into boxers' fists.

She paused. "Why would I kill the man I loved?" She was backpedaling into a more rational mode, but I was not buying it.

"Why would you kill? Because you are a proud woman and he dumped you like yesterday's trash. You're certainly not above lying, doctor. We both know that."

"It's like I told you, detective. I denied the affair to protect my job!"

"I'm going to ask you this one more time," I said, keeping up the heat. Gundy was frantically making a calming hand motion. I wanted to maintain my edge. "Where were you the night of the murder?"

"I told you before," she said very calmly now. "I was right here, the resident on call. We had broken up a few weeks prior. I had seen him with another woman. Are you happy now?"

"No, doctor. I'm sorry you were hurt, but how am I supposed to trust you? One last time: when were you with him the night of the murder?"

"I'm not suffering from early dementia, Detective Kazinski. I was here that last night doing my job. The only time I saw him was his cold, dead body lying ready for transport."

She paused, building up steam again.

"OK, got it? Now go away and stay away from me. We're done."

She jumped up and stormed out of the room, slamming the door.

"You certainly have a way with women," Gundy noted, his features scrambling from concern to amusement.

Gundy grabbed a tongue depressor from a plastic cup on the table and made his way over to the remains of Dr. Ashley's meat pie. He scraped some of the teeth-marked residues into a small evidence bag. Forensics would be appreciative of this large sample. We wanted to be sure we had a match.

I had little doubt she would qualify as the second female based on DNA. And yet, despite our encounter, I was partially hoping she had not been present that night in Sandy's room.

I opened the door and peered down the hall. There were no doctors in sight, so we snuck out like shoplifters trying to escape with a bag of sweaters.

45. Barney Kazinski

Later Friday afternoon back at Command Center

"I just heard you had a friendly conversation with Dr. Ashley." I nodded, knowing *this* conversation was certainly *not* going to be friendly at all. La-Tanya had just received a call from the Dean's office and summoned me immediately for one of her "woodshed" conversations.

I was sitting, and partly cowering, in Captain La-T's office. Her eyes had scoped themselves into a double-barreled shotgun. Some official documents sat on her desk. I knew La-T rarely kept correspondence in plain sight. She made a point of shuffling some of these papers for my benefit.

"Detective Kazinski, with one stroke of my pen, you could be tending a garden for the rest of your life."

"There's not enough space for a garden in my neighborhood, Captain. Perhaps you'd like my shield?"

She looked at me quizzically and then more gently. "Barney, we've been on the force together for over 25 years. You've taught me and mentored me and bucked up my leadership cred, all of which I found flattering. But badgering a key witness given the sensitive subject of DNA in her privacy zone, that's beyond crazy. All the nurses in the hall enjoyed hearing the show and invited our Internal Affairs group into this case."

"I know, I'm sorry, so where do we go from here?" There was no point in arguing.

"I'll tell you where you're going: over to see Dr. Maura Davis, the hospital's Director of Surgery. She called this morning and has some important information that she wants to give you personally."

"That's it? I don't have to kiss her ass in Macy's window?"

"You keep talking like that and you'll be arranging the mannequins all right. That's the end of the lecture, which you'd better take to heart. I have spent an unpleasant hour explaining to the top brass at One P.P. that Dr. Ashley baited you and, frankly, you're still the best guy to solve this case. It would take days to bring someone up to speed, even Gundy who's been trying to help you. I gather he was trying to calm you down."

"Big mistake on my part. I'm a bit stubborn when someone pushes my buttons."

"Witnesses love Gundy for one main reason, among others: honesty and integrity and trust, not to mention keeping his cool. Words like that," she said. "He's already got the car pointed in the right direction, and it's about a mile and a half to the hospital admin offices. Let's see if you guys can make it without stirring up more trouble. You'll be meeting in the dean's office, so that should be a warning. You're dealing with the Wainwright family guardians. They're considering a huge donation of another facility. Proceed with caution and humility."

"Yes ma'am. Thanks for having my back." I wondered if the meat wagon would be serving a special batch of humble pie today for me to devour. It might be tastier than the usual fare.

"I have your back for now," La-T warned. "Keep that in mind, detective. You are on a special watch, don't blow it. We're set for the staff briefing tomorrow morning, an 8 a.m. start no less on a weekend. I'll be anxious to hear about Dr. Davis's urgent message. Becky's still trying to piece together all the details of Sandy's last day. We seem to have missed a few clues the first time around. Is there a Ralph somebody in the dorm possibly involved? Everyone is sick of this case and wondering why our star detective can't crack it."

She turned back to her papers, which meant the meeting was over, no excuses allowed. Traffic was light, and Gundy liked to floor it, accompanied by his siren's highest decibel level. Pedestrians were shielding their ears and dashing into stores for shelter from the sound.

We found ourselves in the Hillside Medical Admin office within minutes. There was no security. The corridors on this floor had a distinct academic look and feel, with creaky wooden floors, high ceilings, and an occasional tinny voice sounding down the hall. It felt like a sealed-off convent, where a shocking death barely roiled the dust.

The dean's office was open and without any sentinels, so we marched on in. There were two walls filled with diplomas and honors, presenting a backdrop of a man put out to pasture. I expected to see clods of cow dung piled atop a crumpled oriental rug.

The dean officially noted Dr. Maura Davis's presence while I introduced Gundy. We grabbed some coffee from a sideboard and arranged ourselves, negotiation-style, around a small conference table. This meeting had the ripe smell of an ass-covering exercise. I held my tongue while Gundy sat quietly, prepared to take the lead on damage control.

"Your attitude has been well short of professional standards," Dr. Davis glared at me first, then Gundy. "While we're all very upset about Sherman's death, that's no excuse to barge onto our campus and harass us."

"We've finished the first week of investigation, Dr. Davis, and uncovered a lot of 'misrepresentation' by possible suspects. Perhaps you can help us clarify the situation." Gundy had tactfully turned defense into offense. I practically beamed at him while Dr. Grant maintained a fixed expression as inscrutable as the statues in Central Park.

"We have a new piece of information that we want to share," Dr. Davis said almost joyfully. "You've been inquiring as to whether Mr. Wainwright had been having intimate relations with Dr. Ashley Dillon. I believe we can offer conclusive proof without further Forensic vetting."

"What is that proof?" I asked. "We've been hearing rumors and wished to avoid rushing to judgment."

"Yes, I've heard about your great concern. Well, detective, here's what I've been trying to tell you. I happened to be walking in the park a few weeks back, and they were also walking, exposed in an intimate position. I'm referring to Sandy and Ashley, the lovebirds."

"This wasn't a friendly peck on the cheek?" Gundy asked.

"No, definitely not. Their arms were entangled, and they were surprised and embarrassed to see me." Her look of scornful pride made it clear she considered this a significant a-ha moment of scientific discovery.

"Can you be more specific about the precise nature of the physical contact you witnessed?"

"Good grief, detective, you know it when you see it. Their bodies were pressed together in a partial embrace. Our handbook warns against personal indiscretions between residents and their medical students."

"So how exactly does this relate to Sandy Wainwright's death?"

Maura Davis looked perturbed and insulted by this line of questioning. She glanced at the dean for support. But his mind was wandering. She sighed and pushed ahead.

"Detective Kazinski, you've been intent on proving that Dr. Ashley Dillon has felt betrayed by the deceased and perhaps wanted revenge. This evidence certainly reinforces that conclusion, does it not?"

"I believe you denied such a romance in an earlier interview, Dr. Davis," I said. "Why the change of heart? And why are we hearing about this episode in the park now, several weeks after the fact?"

Dr. Davis had her response ready. "I was trying to avoid any inferences that might cast suspicion on our medical competence. When I heard about your vitriolic exchange with Dr. Ashley earlier today, I realized that I needed to come clean. I spoke to the dean, and he concurred."

Dean Grant offered a feeble smile of affirmation. The cow dung was piling up in this conversation. Gundy lasered me with two menacing eyeballs, and I cringed into silence.

Gundy picked up the thread of conversation. "Just for a complete record, Dr. Davis, can you describe your whereabouts during Sandy's final day?" Bless this man for changing the subject without letting her off the hook.

"It was very normal. I did rounds early and had one scheduled surgery, a venous ablation. Then a quick sandwich in the cafeteria, back to the office for insurance paperwork, and setting up assignments for the following day. Finally, I was summoned for an early evening emergency, a vascular bypass surgery that proceeded well into the night. The elderly patient faced a potential foot amputation requiring surgery immediately. I left well after midnight and fell into bed only to be awakened around 4:am with the news of the murder."

"Murder? We didn't know what it was at that point. A Freudian slip perhaps?"

"Don't give me that Freudian crap. I was exhausted that night and couldn't fathom Sherman Wainwright's death as a suicide. Maybe it was wishful thinking on my part."

I thought Dean Grant might be scowling, perhaps a gas pain.

"Let me ask one final question." Gundy offered his patented bloodhound twitch. "Dr. Davis, was Prince Jeff working as your scrub nurse during either of those surgeries?"

"Mr. Laird only helped perform the night-time vascular bypass. I've already given this information to your associates. That was an excruciating surgery for us all, and no one can assist better than Mr. Laird can. A complex vascular surgery requires multiple hours of stamina with full concentration. Dr. Ashley recently had a terrible experience doing one. Mr. Laird is a marvelous young man whom I've encouraged to join our program as a med student."

She paused. "Why do you ask about him?"

Gundy wasn't letting up. "Prince Jeff has hung around Sandy quite a bit and perhaps had some jealousy issues of his own."

Dr. Davis looked shocked.

"Detective Gunderson," she said, "I can assure you that Mr. Laird (or Prince Jeff as you call him) was with me until we finished, and I then saw him retire down the hall, homeward bound for a little sleep. We had an early surgery the next day. Sandy was his buddy, and, quite frankly, I doubt he had the skills or experience to access a femoral vein properly. Let's hope you have better leads to follow than that one."

"Were you at all friendly with Mr. Laird?" Gundy inquired casually. "You know, a drink after the workday, that sort of thing."

"I don't see the relevance of this questioning. Now you're getting as obnoxious as your partner. Mr. Laird is a diligent employee and very respected by the staff. In my opinion, he's shown a good deal more professionalism than either Sherman Wainwright or Dr. Ashley Dillon. There seems to be a contagion afflicting clinical students on the Upper West Side. Maybe we need to call in the CDC."

"Maybe we should," I retorted, "yet so far, no perplexing deaths have been reported in *our* bailiwick." I smiled benignly while seething inside. "One more question, Dr. Davis," I stared her down with my practiced touch of condescension.

"Dean Grant, would you care to leave the room for a moment?" I asked out of respect for her privacy.

"There's nothing for me to hide!"

"As you wish, Dr. Davis. Do you want to tell us what you and the Prince were doing together at DomXX about a week or so ago?"

"What?! Who told you that?" she sputtered.

"Didn't need a source, Dr. Davis. My partner and I spotted you both there."

"OK, so what's the difference? Mr. Laird suggested it. I'm a grown woman. You going to arrest me for having a mid-day beer after a very tough morning?"

"No. Just curious to see you frequenting a rather vulgar sex club with an employee, your handbook guidelines and all."

"Gentlemen," the dean had perked up, helping to cover her tracks. "Dr. Davis has given you concrete evidence on who should be your leading suspect. Why don't you leave here and come back with something serious, like an arrest? We won't ask why *you* were frequenting the club."

If looks could kill, we'd be looking down a pair of assault rifles from Dr. Davis and her dean. He had suddenly become frozen in a hard-boiled frown. He jumped up and pointed to the door, which seemed an indication that our conversation was over.

We walked out, and Gundy whispered, "Liars, liars, pants on fire."

I cautioned him, "Stay calm. La-T expects you to be the adult one."

Gundy whipped on the siren. He was a charging bull at the wheel, and we were back in our parking lot in 10 minutes flat without more than a couple of bicycle hit-and-runs. He parked and planted a smug expression on his face.

"What are you grinning about?" I asked. He delicately produced a crumpled napkin that he'd filched from the dean's desk.

"More DNA? Are you accusing him or Dr. Davis?" We had a good laugh and worked up a joint report for the Case Management file, then headed home.

46. Barney Kazinski

Friday, early evening

When you deal with sludge all day long, it begins to infest your whole being. For years, I had been a filter siphoning out the criminal behavior to cleanse the city for the decent citizens, not to mention our bosses downtown. Becky had revived and inspired me anew. Having no evening plans, I decided to detour back to campus. I grabbed another stomach-churner for an early dinner at the meat truck and prepared to interview the biggest smart-ass of them all, the ubiquitous Ralph Gruber.

Thus far, he had displayed an attitude that our quest for justice was primarily live entertainment for his enjoyment, no cover charge necessary. He had us all figured out right from the get-go, a genius proclaiming his ability to do the Times' daily crossword puzzle in under three minutes,

I walked into the dorm past the security guard, who seemed alert for a change. He nodded as I flashed my badge and headed up to apartment 2F.

Ralph was expecting me. He eagerly opened the door with his patronizing grin already plastered in place. How convenient that being housed in 2F, he was situated right next door to Rosemarie Li, Sandy's girlfriend who had dumped him.

I pictured Ralph with his ear scratching the wall, listening to the two of them going at it. Maybe he'd heard some pillow talk that could shed light on the case.

Or maybe now he intended to try supplanting Sandy as a participant rather than as a voyeur.

"Hello, detective. I heard your bosses are not too pleased with the delays in this case."

"Hello, Mr. Gruber. If you don't mind, I'll ask the questions."

"OK, but I think I've already told you; I have an air-tight alibi."

"Yes, I know you were at the hockey rink earlier in the night of Sandy's death."

"Yup, detective. I was there with my guys."

"You weren't *exactly* one of Sandy's team, Ralph, were you?"

"I don't know what you mean? The guys in their orgy pad were my bros."

"Only in your dreams. Do you think if I asked the roommates, that they would agree about their brotherly love?"

Ralph started to back off. "Well, I don't know. I'm not a mind reader."

"You knew you weren't like them, didn't you? Not exactly the popular type. You probably stumbled into their lives like a piece of driftwood. How did it feel watching Sandy getting all the girls?"

"No need to be sarcastic, detective. Sometimes I joined hockey games. Sometimes we went drinking. Why do you care about my social life anyway? He didn't have anything over me."

"That's a strange thing to say, kid. You had a rivalry for your neighbor's affection? A little jealousy, perhaps? It's okay buddy. You weren't the only one."

"Jealous of whom? His maidservant of a girlfriend?"

Ralph's face had sprouted crimson highlights like a clown. I was glad to have gotten under his skin.

"You befriended Rosemarie Li. Did she confide in you?"

"He treated her like dog meat," Ralph said with a sudden burst of indignance. "She used to come over after one of Sandy's quick hits, and she'd complain about his slam-bam attitude. I was her confidante; she trusted me to keep my mouth shut."

"How did you console her?"

"I told her to get rid of the creep. He was the type who wouldn't care about you tomorrow. He never wanted to stay the night. No doubt re-loading the gun for someone else." The disgust on Ralph's face bespoke more jealousy than morality.

"Let me put it out there, Ralph. Did you ever have a macho fantasy of helping Rosemarie get rid of the boy?"

"Yes, I hated him. And I had every right to revenge. He treated me like gum on the bottom of his shoe. I'm not the only one. He played everyone, all the time, the selfish bastard!"

"Ralph. Your venom is unsettling. Calm down." Ralph stood there rattled, knowing that his big mouth had betrayed him. I pressed on. "You hated Sandy, that's clear. Did you hate him enough to kill him?"

“What? I didn’t kill anyone!” Ralph was literally shuddering. He looked like a little kid trying to stand up to his daddy. I felt sorry for him.

“Did you dream of killing the young student, Ralph?” I leaned in, face-to-face, practically diving head-first into his lap.

“No!! I didn’t kill him. I swear, detective. You’re right. I’m not popular. I’ve been a nerd my whole life. If anything, I wanted to *be* him. The best way to get close was through the wall.”

“Okay, Ralph. I’m not going to delve into your motives, and I’m sorry that you feel so lost. You are one of the lucky ones in our society going to an exclusive med school. Most people can’t even dream of applying, so buck up.”

“Detective, those roommates had parties all the time that excluded me. Who can explain why the most popular students hung out with scrub nurses and weirdos?”

A reasonable question that I ignored. “The final night, around midnight on Thursday, were there any audible signs of Sandy in Rosemarie’s room? Screaming? Cursing? Bouncing off walls? Anything violent between them?”

“Funny you should mention it. I don’t think he was around that last night. I thought I heard the British chap, the nurse trying to calm her down, but maybe it was a film. She liked those depressing gaslight films: women manipulated to think they’re nuts. That was always his tactic with her.”

“Let’s skip the movie nights. When did you get back to the dorm?”

“After hockey, detective, I went to my room to study. At around 11 p.m. or so, I got into my chat room.”

"Chat room?"

"Candy. She always models lingerie for me. We talk. She loves opera like I do."

"Jesus, Ralph. A doctor-in-training, fishing for female companionship on the internet? Hey buddy, you need a flesh-and-blood girlfriend."

"I like my Candy, but it's good advice. I'd prefer the real deal, gotta work on it. Maybe I hoped Rosemarie would come to her senses. I was there first."

"Any further thoughts that might help us? It's creepy, your listening through the wall, yet you probably knew as much about Sandy's secret life as anyone."

"It wasn't quite like a one-way mirror. He wasn't much for conversation, before, during, or after. Sometimes he'd come down for lunch, and I couldn't hear what they were saying. They might get into an argument, mostly about his hanging out lately with the British dude. Rosemarie had felt the so-called 'Prince' was inciting his worst instincts."

"So how would they resolve their arguments? Any violence?"

"Depends on what you call violence. She'd get him worked up defending his Prince friend, and then he would leave in a huff. Or, I had to pull away from the wall because sometimes they would be slamming into each other, prying the plaster loose *on my side*! Believe it or not, that quiet woman could protect herself. She liked to use her farm muscles. Then they'd go at it like two animals.

Ralph seemed very proud, projecting himself into a rapturous zone. I had to drag him back to my mundane questions.

"Let's get back on course here," I said. "Was he free to pop in and out whenever he felt like it? How would he get into her apartment?"

"Oh, he had a key. Around here, doors are frequently left unlocked. It's a casual atmosphere. With all those white coats in the closet, the dress code was loose."

"So, you never saw or heard other visitors or other voices that night indicating someone had an interest in stalking him for any reason?"

"Not really. Now and then, one of his roomies would come down and talk to her. Ross, Ross Parker, was a familiar face, the stuck-up one from Princeton. They would play loud music, mostly modern electronic stuff. I'd bang on the wall to have them lower the volume. I knew the little dipshit Ross was positioning himself for a sympathy fuck. Move over, man, I told him. I was already in line. Sandy showed up one night and practically threw Ross into the hall."

"I take it he didn't appreciate the competition. All right Buddy, you're off the hook. Please understand that I may want to question you again."

"Okay, detective. Whatever you need." He was meeker now, less obnoxious, and yet still an insecure guy. I didn't think he had the killer instinct, yet sometimes I felt he could be the type that enjoyed slicing up and wrapping his victims in tin foil for the freezer."

This kid was almost schizophrenic, a wise ass who turned into a pussy with one push. I still didn't fancy him, as the Brits would say. I felt sorry for the feckless bastard.

There he was, all alone, getting his kicks through the plaster and waiting for his 'date' with Candy. I did not want to watch when he logged in.

I scooted out, time for another visit to the roommates.

47. Barney Kazinski

Friday, later that evening

The day kept getting longer. Lack of progress, in this case, was not all my fault. Our impromptu army of investigators had narrowed the list of possible culprits without a clear, viable suspect. From all the interviews, I could not shake the feeling that all those closest to Sandy had been violating the truth, so whom could we trust?

Meanwhile, the relentless Gundy had taken a new tack to break the password code on Sandy's cell phone. The forensic I.T. specialists had given up, but our persistent gumshoe had retrieved the phone from the evidence locker.

Over the years, Gundy had developed several neat pieces of hackers' software. I doubted that his bosses would approve if they knew about it. Extracting data from the dark web and sleazy social media sources, he had built a matrix of Sandy's key personal data.

Then he cross-hatched all the data on a digital spreadsheet. He knew that even the shrewdest criminals have a habit of relying on personal markers for their passwords. While he was at it, I also asked Gundy to help me do a deep dive of internet sleuthing on Prince Jeff, whose name kept turning up.

Taking a break, I punched in my daughter's phone on West Coast time. The call flipped immediately to voice mail. I left a brief message and promised to call again soon.

There was no response in the roomies' pad, 5G. I considered busting in the door when Hector Lopez opened it, looking like his mind was fighting to perk up while his ample body seemed drained. His eyes were rimmed with a reddish tinge, no doubt from an allergic reaction to hitting the books recently. I suspected that Pil had been dispensing amphetamines to keep the motors running for his mates.

"Not looking too good, Hector," I said. "Where are your buddies?"

"What do you want, man? The roomies are working at the hospital. That includes Prince Jeff who's practically a roommate. We've got a big exam on Monday. Hey, why am I defending myself when it's way past working hours? I've got to study all weekend. What a bummer." He paused and then continued. "Detective, you need to enjoy your free time. A little botulinum toxin will relax the neuromuscular junction in your forehead."

This guy was a sweet talker. "I can see you're well prepared for the exam questions on medicinal poisons," I said. "I appreciate the offer to mix one batch in my cocktail tonight. Meanwhile, if you don't mind, I'd like to review your roomie's fatal night once more."

Hector favored me with a big yawn without moving from the doorway, so I pushed by him, and we sat down awkwardly in the middle of the living room.

"We know Ross Parker lied about his whereabouts," I said, "though he still seems to have a decent alibi. He got in around eleven and found the body before midnight after a brief rest."

Hector indulged in a slight nod accompanied by a blank stare. His temporary flight on Pil's energy medication was plunging into a rough landing.

I continued. "The two of you claimed that you went upstairs after coming home separately. No drinking, no talking, no video games, no late-night snack with your popular roommate? Sandy's door was not quite closed, and no one checked up on him. Is that correct?"

Hector shrugged, as he was almost glassy by now, like a boxer who'd taken too many shots to the head. He needed to sleep badly. I hoped to squeeze one last clue out of him.

"Hector, one thing that doesn't make sense. Why would Ross Parker have checked up on Sandy while you didn't?"

"If I answer this question," Hector perked up, "will you leave me alone? I'm out of it, man."

"Depends on the answer. I'm tired myself of playing guessing games with you guys."

"Okay, here goes. It is very simple. Ross and I arrived home at separate times by a few minutes. I knew Sandy was alive because there were distinct sounds coming from his room. Some kind of discussion was competing with very loud music. This was after eleven, although I didn't check the clock to the minute."

"Were there any sounds of sex?"

"Not sure. I could hear Sandy. He was in a manic state and did not seem rational. Maybe drugged up a bit. There were snatches of incoherent conversation and then murmurs. Hard to tell the gender of the other party, but I'd guess female."

Do you think it might have been one of his favorite females in the nightly romance categories?"

Hector tried to respond, but he was gasping and sounded like he was about to take *his* last breath, "I don't know, man.

He loved to pick up the stray ones, male or female, for companionship, usually for late-night Chinese. He never wanted to eat alone. It was almost entirely his voice that I could hear. You know the bro code – ask not, and you shall learn not."

"How convenient. We, the hearty men in blue, have a bro code too. See no evil, hear no evil, speak no evil, and enjoy your perp walk."

"Hey, that's a good one. Doesn't a Miranda warning come first?"

"You know Hector, as I've said before, once you flunk out of med school, you'll be a great defense lawyer."

"Thanks, I take that as a compliment."

"Were you around when the Chinese food arrived?

"No, I guess Ross and I had gone upstairs when the food came shortly afterwards. You could smell it through the whole house in the morning, along with all the death odors."

Hector was fading fast again, so I knew it was time to let him go.

"I need to crash for a few before hitting the books. I want to be a doctor, that's my life's mission." Hector gave me a conspiratorial smile, almost relieved as if he had just graced his roomie group with acceptable alibis.

"Let's call it a day. Get some rest and try to avoid Pil for a night."

I walked out the apartment door and headed down five flights. On a whim, I pulled up the picture of Ashley Dillon, which I'd been keeping in my wallet. It was one of Gundy's fine portraits. She looked eager and forthcoming, almost as if she were about to tell us a secret.

I arrived in the lobby and walked up to the security guard. His tag said his name was Lorenzo. I suddenly remembered. He'd been the late-night guy on a car wash-up in Harlem and had some police training doing undercover work for a precinct close to the G.W. Bridge. I knew the car wash closed around 9 or 10 p.m. since I used to be a regular customer when I did frequent overtime.

Lorenzo needed some extra cash, presumably. Maybe he was still undercover. It did not matter right now.

I handed him the picture. "Do you recognize her?"

"Oh yes, boss, you don't forget that face or that body."

"It's only a headshot, Lorenzo."

"I know boss. I filled in the rest." He made an obscene semi-circular motion with his hands.

"Well, since your memory is so good," I said, "maybe you can fill in a few blanks and tell me when she'd show up."

"She's been here a few times, kinda nervous, you know, sneaking into the building."

"What time did she usually come over?"

"It was usually right after I come on duty, around 9:30 or 10 p.m. when the car wash closed late. You couldn't miss her; la *Chica Rubia*, hot blond chick whose friend liked ordering Mandarin, just around the corner. The delivery guy would come about a half-hour after she arrived. I'd doubt it was a study date, but lucky guy, huh?"

“I think his luck ran out—he’s dead, Lorenzo. You’re better off washing cars.”

“Dead? I wondered where he’s been. Sad for the young cabrón. And where will the woman find another cowboy? I’m available, you tell her, just broke up with my girlfriend.”

“He was murdered last Friday in the early hours, somewhere before midnight. You don’t recall if the woman, first name Dr. Ashley, was around?”

“Nope, I’m not sure. I would go home around midnight, sometimes a little earlier, if things are slow. Maybe I missed her.”

His vague memory was getting on my nerves. “Try to concentrate, Lorenzo. This is a murder investigation.”

“Yeah, no wonder. I’d seen her lately and not with the cowboy. Last time was a few days ago with the tall greasy one, a British accent. I thought he was one of the roomies and started hanging with the chick. How do these jokers keep their eyes on the books?”

“Lorenzo, you’ve got me confused. You’re sure you saw the broad in the picture with the Brit a few days ago?”

“Yeah, Boss, her, and the Brit, they were together, no Chinese this time. Maybe the middle of the week, Tuesday or Wednesday.”

“Lorenzo, you can be more specific. Are you sure the blonde girl and the Brit were together? There was a carton of Mandarin discovered in the kitchen waste basket.”

“I don’t know, man, I left a little early. With exams coming up, everyone is studying in their room.

"Thanks pal, I have one last question. Who hired you?"

"Someone in the dean's office about six months ago. They wanted me to keep a log, but I don't have time. Lotta traffic, deliveries that time of night."

"Keep an eye out, Lorenzo, especially the hot white chick. Here is my card. If your memory improves, you can call at any hour. You've gone UC for us. You know the drill."

"Thanks, boss, I'll think about it. Hey, here's an idea, might help with the memory. Christmas is coming. Maybe you put in a good word for the bonus. Kinda cheap over there with Dean Grant."

48. Dr. Ashley Dillon

Friday, close to midnight

I was awakened by a quiet rapping on my apartment door. I thought I was dreaming, but then the sound came again, more insistent.

"Who's there?"

"It's me, Wendy." It was a familiar voice.

"I'm coming. I'm coming."

I had figured out who it was. Why was she here? Did she know that Prince Jeff, her presumed boyfriend, was on the prowl? I stopped in my tracks, unsure of whether to let her in. She had crossed over into enemy territory, maybe a snitch for the police, and I didn't trust her.

A defiant inner force pulled me toward the door. I opened it to what seemed like a mirage. There was a new Wendy: long shiny black hair cascading down over her shoulders, sparkling morning blue eyes, delicate eye shadow, a touch of blush. Her tailored dress had subtle geometric shapes, plenty of thigh exposed, but in an overall refined way of a more matronly woman who was transforming herself into adulthood.

"Wendy? Is that really you? You look so… so adult and in control at this hour."

"Yes, Ashley," she said, hugging me. Her cheek against mine felt maternal.

"Wendy, what are you doing here? I thought our friendship was vamoose."

"Ashley, our lives pass by so quickly. Sometimes there are misunderstandings."

"Wendy I'm still the same."

"No, you're not, Ash. We're both different. One man's death has changed us all."

"Possibly true. Do you understand how much pain I've been in? I believed that I had found peace with him."

"I understand that, and I admit, I had a momentary thing for him too." She stopped speaking, awaiting a negative reaction. "A very dangerous man. He could make you forget everything around you."

"Say that again." I was still wondering why she was here at this crazy hour.

"Sandy's gone, but I wanted to share the good news," Wendy said, practically bursting out of her dress with joy. "Jeff and I have gotten very close, very fast. He could be the one. Shocking, isn't it? Look at me. I never thought I'd leave the high seas and come into port. He's loving and caring, quite different now that his playmate Sandy is gone. Jeff warned me Sandy was dynamite until it blew up in your face, and all our faces."

She was still 'Queen Hypocrite.' Wendy, playing sweet, cozy lover with a man who had stepped right into the deceased's shoes. Her man Prince wasn't a doctor for God's sake. It was my fault for bringing them together. I kept my mouth shut, possibly hoping for our reconciliation despite everything.

"I played it safe my whole life, Wendy. Sandy was so magical..."

"Magical, alright. Look at where his magic took both of you into almost being expelled before he died. You must have remorse."

"Wendy, you don't think I was involved in this… his awful death, do you?"

She paused for a long time – too long. I needed her to confirm my innocence as much as I needed to confirm it to myself.

"No, Ashley. I know you. I realize you're troubled. You must have hated that bastard for being a manipulative ass. It doesn't strike me you'd murder him."

"Thank you, Wendy, that means a lot to me." Not an overwhelming vote of confidence. But I continued to hold my counsel.

"I've been lucky that Jeff is the voice of reason," Wendy said. He can be prissy in that haughty British way. Damn all the egos these guys have. At least my Prince has a big heart too and he's come out of the shadows now that he's liberated to be his own man."

I could feel my lack of sleep dulling my responses and invoking the early warnings of depression. Wendy was so deliriously upbeat; she had suddenly figured things out while I was still struggling to make sense of it all. Or maybe she was just another Pil groupie on a cocaine high.

In truth, I felt envious and resentful. What had happened to my friend, the wild child? She was playing a grown-up game now and condescending to me for not abiding by her new rules and new life.

I wondered how Prince Jeff, the perpetual flirt, drug purveyor, and my savior a few days earlier, had managed to implant himself back in her life so quickly. Yet, I did not want to lose her at this point. She was still my alibi for the night of the murder. If Wendy Jamison wanted to be holier than thou, so be it.

"I need you back in my life dearie."

"I'm here, gotta go now. Tomorrow's agenda is an early clinic with the little ones."

"Maybe just a few more minutes, Wendy. I'm feeling all alone."

"Buck up girl. Everything will turn out fine."

The door opened, and I could hear her wooden heels clicking away swiftly from the apartment.

49. Barney

Friday, the last tick before midnight

The phone rang very late, which was never a good sign.

"Hey dad, I got your message. I thought I'd call you back."

I looked at the clock and tried to overcome my fatigue. "It's almost midnight here; this must be urgent," I griped, then quieted to hear what my daughter had to say.

"Sorry, dad, I couldn't think about sleep yet, only nine here. Got lots on my mind."

"What is it, sweetie? I'm always glad to hear from you… when I'm awake."

"Well, it's about Tim. My fiancée. I'm having some doubts."

"Let me splash cold water on my face and call you back."

A few minutes later, we were back on the line. I picked up the thread.

"Now where were we, oh yes, your fiancée Tim. He sounded like a solid guy, a cop and all. I checked him out with the LAPD."

"I know all that, Dad. Maybe he's just not the right guy for me. Mom keeps warning me living with a cop can be hell."

For a moment, I could feel the anger spreading over my neck and back. Every muscle tensed. It felt like a replay of my arguments with her mother Jill before we divorced. I tried to calm down: this was my daughter; I kept my mouth shut as my anger receded and rotated into guilt.

"Listen babe, your mom and I had issues, but that doesn't mean you will. For better or worse, there's a lot of cop DNA in your blood."

"I know, Dad, that's just it. Look at your life. For years you barely had time for us, maybe a brief visit at Christmas or a birthday present here and there. Mom often said we barely knew if you were still alive."

She had thrown a rabbit punch. Maybe it was the hour, maybe it was my wasted life passing before me. How do you explain to your daughter that so many of your family roles were never worthy of being admired, and yet you hoped she would accept your rightful place as a father anyhow?

"Hey Dad, are you still there? I can call back tomorrow."

"No, no, no, babes. I've got a hundred things I want to say to you, and right now, none of them come to mind. I'm not very good after I turn into a pumpkin. You must realize that your situation is about you and Tim, not your mom and me. If you both truly love each other, it can work. Let's forget the past, although I'd give anything to have it over again and start back with you in the delivery room."

"Hey, we're starting over now. LOL. You know what that means?"

"Laugh out loud. I'm chill. I'd also like to think in our case it means lots of love."

"Yeah, Dad, it seems so odd to *talk* to someone on the phone. Everyone is texting now. All the emotions are conveyed by emojis. Like right now, I'd be sending you a big smile, or maybe a small, sad face, but always a huge heart. Make that 'I love you' with a couple of hearts."

I felt glad we weren't on a Zoom. Who wanted to see an old, unkempt guy in wrinkled pajamas quietly sobbing like the thunderstorm icon?

"I gotta go Sar." I was half-whispering, half-whimpering. "I'll call soon so that we can continue the conversation. Maybe we can plan a trip, father-daughter. Flying somewhere, nice scenery, a lake, hiking or fishing, or someplace where we can talk."

"Dad, I'd like that a lot. Don't forget."

She broke the connection.

Saturday, Day Nine

50. Barney Kazinski

Saturday morning

I tossed and turned much of the night, and finally, the alarm sounded. Thankfully, time for work. I could barely remember what day it was. La-Tanya had prodded us into going seven days a week, screw any regulations. In the shower, I was feeling exhausted and still shaken by the conversation with my daughter.

At our headquarters, La-Tanya had laid out bagels with salmon and cream cheese, plus some sides, a full spread in recognition that we were working overtime to break the case. After we dispatched breakfast, her ulterior motive became clear. La-T was pressing us for a decision on our first person of interest.

Suddenly, it felt like a jury preparing to reach a verdict.

"I have one request before we make a final decision," I said quickly, knowing that the boss lady was getting impatient. "Just to be sure of our next moves, Gundy and I need to wrap up some loose ends with the so-called Prince Geoffrey."

No one seemed thrilled by this delay, so I ignored the reaction and continued. "The Prince seems to have learned some lessons from his dead friend. Reading Becky's reports, it feels like he has a reputation for being a skirt-chaser in his own right, a kind of mini-Sandy, and we need to know where his affections fit into the picture."

"I thought we were coming down to an arrest decision," La-T griped. She felt betrayed by my intervention and hated to back down.

"You're dithering, Barney," Becky cut in, also annoyed at being derailed at this point.

"Trust me," I said, acting much calmer than I felt. "If we jump too soon, Dr. Ashley Dillon will claim that she's innocent while her lawyer will mock us in the media to save her reputation and her career. There's still a lot of circumstantial evidence floating around in what Becky has presented thus far. I'm hoping Prince Jeff can clarify."

"Barney, give it up. Prince Jeff is one of the supreme bullshitters of all time." Gundy's face tightened into an angry knot. He had gone over to the other side.

A surprising ally rushed in to mediate the situation. "Maybe I've been pressing you all too hard," La-Tanya conceded. "Barney's right. We shouldn't rush to judgment. Gundy, Becky, let's be fair and conclusive in our evidence, so there's no backlash or hung jury later."

Why had La-T suddenly assumed the role of skeptic? Maybe she had one eye focused downtown for closure, while her other eye knew that a high-profile arrest could rebound against us if we weren't prepared with the unquestionable goods for a conviction.

Becky tried to object, but La-T held up her hands like a traffic cop. "We've got a few suspects here, and we know Prince Jeff was involved with all of them. We also know Sandy definitively broke off his relationship with Dr. Ashley. For proof of motive and pre-meditation, I'd like to know her state of mind, and I have a feeling the Prince might provide our answer."

Without another word, Gundy and I rose in unison and headed over to Park Avenue. There was no queasy dorm for British royalty. This was a classy building. At first glance, the lobby sparkled with more rose-colored marble than the nearby, gaudy Trump Tower atrium. From the elevator it was clear Prince Jeff must be using trust fund money to live in an appropriate style.

"Modest place for a scrub nurse," Gundy muttered as we rode up in the gold-plated lift. Jeff's apartment door was opened by a haggard looking cleaning lady, cradling a mop. We could see her nimble hands had been at work polishing every metallic surface into a glossy sheen.

We moved into a large sitting room and sat on a velvet couch amidst a crowded array of furniture. At a ninety-degree angle to the sofa was a large, ornate desk backed up by a fully stocked, open bar cabinet. Facing the desk, on a wall across the room, was a triptych of large glass-plated mirrors that produced a horror fun-house distortion. In the glass, Gundy's rubbery face was twisting into warped images. Mine looked choppy and bloated, an accurate reflection of my mood.

We sank into the couch and waited. I realized that we were experiencing the ultimate narcissist's view of virtual reality. The three mirrors fanned out so that our subject at his desk could see himself in multiple reflections, presumably without distortion. Dark curtains added an ominous effect by repressing the sunlight that might diminish his visibility.

Prince Jeff waltzed in shortly thereafter, wearing sweatpants and a tight workout shirt that accentuated his formidable pecs. "Coffee, I presume?" he said. Without a response, he poured us each a cup from a small sideboard. The coffee's pungent odor made me wonder what toxic ingredients might have been provided by Pil.

Nonetheless, I sipped the coffee quickly as I needed a jolt of adrenaline for this dreary conversation. "My shift starts at one," Geoffrey said, settling himself into the prime box seat behind his desk. "Fire away gentlemen. I'm presuming I don't need a lawyer for this conversation."

Gundy managed to cantilever his body up from the couch and was starting his photographic routine. "Hope you don't mind?" he said. The Brit seemed taken aback. "Working for Arch Digest are we?" he said in a mildly irritable tone.

I wondered if this would be considered a consensual search.

"Mr. Laird, we need a little background on your relationship with the deceased," I said.

"Hasn't this been covered, detective? We were close mates. Sandy was like an all-consuming inferno. He radiated energy, and we virtually threw ourselves into his fire."

"Did you resent him then?" I inquired, trying to maintain a neutral, off-handed tone.

He bristled immediately. “Of course not. I’m rather good at gadding about with the lasses on my own.” The mirrors happily reflected his smug, dandyish look. I wondered if I smashed his jaw, would the mirrored glass fracture as well? *“Hey there, dude,” I could hear La-Tanya’s voice, “put away those nasty fantasies and chill.”*

I focused swiftly and kept up the pressure. “Your mate Sandy was well known for his prowess in the romance department. You seem to have been a partner in some of the DomXX forays.”

“Sit back and enjoy the ride, as you blokes in America like to say. It’s all those young birds fluttering around us who are looking to be fed. What can we do?”

Ah, the surge of British pride. His face had assumed a raw, knotted sneer, multiply projected on the big screens.

“Let’s get to the flight patterns of these birds, Mr. Laird. You hung out with the deceased at strip joints, so you knew his predatory tendencies. Would you think that one of his jilted lovers might be responsible for his death?”

“Absolutely not. Pure rubbish. He made no pretense of lifelong commitments. These ‘scorned women’ are such arseholes. Let’s face the truth: med school is boring. Sandy knew that. He needed some diversion. So did everyone else. The students, the nurses, the randy old maids, the steamy Resident staff, they all lined up for a piece of him willfully and on his terms.”

He paused for effect, with another star-turn of preening for the mirrors. Something about the way he mentioned the ‘steamy resident staff’ rumbled through my attentive ear.

"I presume we're discussing Dr. Ashley as one of those waiting in line?"

"Brilliant deduction. I would say she packaged herself physically for a little tumble, wouldn't you?"

I ignored his comment for the moment. "Are you speaking from personal experience, Mr. Laird? Have you had any relationship with her? Perhaps you were hoping to take your pal's place in the queue. Prince Jeff shrugged. "He could be a handful, wouldn't you agree? Needed a friendly bloke to break the ice." A prideful, toothy smile sprung forth that would have given an animal's pointed dentures a good run for the money.

Then he suddenly paused and looked around. "Where did your partner go? Aren't there any protections of privacy in this country?" He jumped up, navigated the furniture, and tore down the hall. A few moments later, he reappeared with Gundy, practically dragging him by his camera cord. Gundy flashed a foolish look of getting caught in the cookie jar, yet there was a subtle twinkle of triumph in his eyes.

I continued, pretending that nothing had happened. "Mr. Laird, let's run through Thursday, a week ago, the last day of Sandy's life…"

"Mr. Detective Barney, I've done this drill numerous times. So, this will have to be the final word. In short form, that awful day, I spent a bit of a relaxed morning with the girlfriend Wendy over here, ran some errands, and then reported cross-town to Dr. Davis for her surgery starting around 6 p.m. This was an emergency procedure, so I had rushed to help.

"We started on time dealing with the surgery: a circulatory obstruction causing an afflicted foot. Gangrene was seeping into the bones. Dr. Davis will tell you I was there until well past midnight. A bit before 11 p.m., I went outside for a quick break to grab a grinder at the supper wagon. I saw Dr. Ashley sneak across the street to the student dorm. She didn't see me. She might have been taking a break and heading for Sandy's room, per usual unsupervised. Dr. Davis rarely preferred her presence in the O.R. and tried to ignore her altogether."

"Did you call out to her?"

"No, I knew Dr. Davis wanted me back quickly. As I've said, we finished well after midnight. I was back with Wendy at the apartment after 1 a.m. She'll confirm."

"So, you had no further contact with Dr. Ashley on that evening?"

"We've known around the hospital that our resident has been off her feed for some time. I tried on a couple of occasions to console her with a friendly word that her love had moved on."

"And you were prepared to step in and comfort her more romantically, no doubt? Would you say she was ready to adopt you as her new soulmate?"

No response. Prince Jeff was suddenly impatient for us to leave. He scowled for the mirrors. So did I. We would have made a perfect top-of-card promo for World Wrestling Entertainment.

Like a referee breaking up a fight, Gundy intervened for one last question.

"Mr. Laird, I regret that I had to take a leak, but I noticed there was a copy in the bathroom of a very thick medical text involving thoracic pathology. This covers diseases of the heart and lung. Seems a bit advanced for a scrub nurse?"

"That's Wendy's. She's a pediatrics resident, hoping to move into an adult specialty like the heart. All the circulation and plumbing. Imagine reading this garbage all day long. You can't even take a proper dump without thinking about it. I must be daft to apply for earning a medical degree."

Gundy did his patented eyebrow lift-off, indicating it was time to go. We pushed up from the couch and headed toward the door.

"Please don't touch the handles. I'll open it." The cleaning lady suddenly appeared, polishing rag in hand, protecting her handiwork. I looked back. The Prince sat regally in his chair, admiring the reflections of his royal presence.

"How did that go? We didn't learn much," I said to Gundy when we were downstairs.

"Well, there you have it," he added. "Sandy and Jeff, two trust fund kids screwing up their lives and the lives of others. Perhaps that explains their bizarre friendship. The jealousy angle is a definite possibility. We'll need to make sure Wendy verifies the alibi and maybe check their late-night doorman."

"It would be lovely to think that this case got solved thanks to your taking a leak," I observed to Gundy. "Does this mean we have to add Wendy to the persons of interest?"

"I'd say she's a loose cannon." Gundy nodded. "She may have been ready to fire away."

51. Barney Kazinski

Later Saturday morning,

These days, it took more than one coffee to rouse me into an active stage. I now saw this case as a personal tipping point for the onset of middle age. We used to knock off these types of murders in the first few days. Here the puzzle wasn't sorting itself out. Even Gundy looked stumped.

We stopped at Starbucks, needing a respite before returning to our Command Post. I felt suspended in limbo, yet Gundy was pressing to get back. He had a sly grin on his face, which usually popped up when he had uncovered an important clue.

I was stuck with the same lingering insecurity: were the cases getting harder or my faculties getting softer? Back at our desks, Gundy continued to act strangely.

He was rooting around in his desk and dug up a small parcel. "Maybe this will be your lucky day after all," he said. Sitting in front of him was a plastic evidence bag with the name "Sandy Wainwright" in large letters taped on the side. Gundy extracted a cell phone with a glove and clicked on the power. He punched in a code and handed the phone to me, accompanied by a photo. It showed the dry whiteboard we'd seen outside the roommates' apartment, right near the entrance. The board portrayed the credo: "4G-ORGY."

I knew Gundy's mind. He wasn't showing off his photographic skills. Of course: 4G-ORGY translated into a cell passcode, 44-67-49.

Gundy smiled and said, "How lucky our golden boy had a sense of humor."

I put on my gloves and picked up the phone, scrolling through the most recent texts. Gundy directed me to a conversation recorded at 11:03 p.m. on the murder night. Dr. Ashley had initiated a brief cell conversation with growing desperation. Sandy's responses were slurred, as if he had been drinking or taking drugs.

Ashley: Darling, wake up.

Sandy: Not interested, babe; you're making me grumpy.

Ashley: Sandy, please get up. You're in no condition to make a decision right now. Take a cold shower. I have a terrible premonition of what might happen next."

Sandy: "I told you, woman, ours was just an interlude for me. I'm going back to sleep."

That was it, and oddly, Gundy said, there were no other relevant exchanges with females recorded on the cell, unless you counted a single voicemail from his mother worrying about her son as if he were a toddler. The rest of the phone messages were small details about med-school schedules or picking up his cleaning. It felt like he had wiped the slate clean.

Or someone else had.

I decided to check up on the DNA tests. I called the M.E.'s office.

"Peter?"

"Oh yes, Detective. Hello. I was just about to call you. I have confirmation."

"Let's have it."

"We have a re-confirmed, clean DNA match for both samples you sent us, Ms. Rosemarie Li and Dr. Ashley Dillon. They match the swabs taken by Jen in the few hours after his death. There's no question. It's those two women, one hundred percent, as far as the DNA goes.

"And what about any other suspect? I take it there was no matching evidence of the third sample we sent?"

"You mean the lady from the sex bar? Negative on any DNA present. Superman might even have failed going for a trifecta in one day. Unless of course, someone cleaned up further evidence."

I thanked Peter and clicked off.

On a preliminary basis, we could rule out Miss Shannon and Maura Davis as longshots among the women. I could not see Dr. Davis violating her own rules and regulations. And if Miss Shannon was headed for a law career, I doubted she would want to help murder her boyfriend.

Dr. Wendy Jamison could be a possibility. Perhaps she had been involved in a sleepover a day earlier. She was still a prominent person of interest since she was Prince Jeff's alibi, so we needed clearer confirmation of her whereabouts on the night in question.

Among the DNA duo, I would place my bet on Ashley as the instigator among the culprits. My theory was they had slept together and then he dismissed her. In the process, she might have tired him out so that an accomplice could move in. From that point on, my logic was fuzzy. How the final deed was accomplished and by whom, that was still a mystery which perhaps Gundy could help resolve. Would

Rosemarie Li, our ex-farm girl, have been capable of being the willing partner in a heinous crime?

I didn't trust myself, especially now, more than ever. I realized my suspicions were jumbled and possibly off-track. La-Tanya was right in being cautious. We had to be careful about rushing to conclusions, as we still had no direct proof that jealousy or revenge or any other motive was the key to the murder. If I was right about an accomplice, how broad was the conspiracy?

I couldn't help wondering again, feeding my insecurity, whether this case was about finding a killer or testing my faculties of deduction in middle age?

The motto of the NYPD had always been *Fidelis ad mortem*, Faithful unto Death. For more than two decades, the pride and duty represented by the shield had driven me to overcome any emotional bumps in my life.

Was I capable of passing an honest judgment on Dr. Ashley Dillon as the facts unfolded to implicate her?

Captain La-T was not one to play therapist or get diverted from the crisis at hand. She had assembled our "core" team tasked with winding up this case. Now that we had met with Prince Jeff, La-Tanya had reverted to wanting closure on a faster timetable.

When we entered the conference room, La-T's outward demeanor suggested she was wound up as tightly as a luxury hotel robe. That meant, 'set a course of action and don't trifle with her mood.'

"Let's get to it," she said. "We're in the ninth day and counting. Maybe one of you *elite* detectives would like to give us an official update."

There were no immediate volunteers. Gundy and I were silent while the unflappable Becky Muller looked prepared to deliver a final judgment, blistering Sandy, and his playmates.

Working as a prosecutor in the Manhattan DA's sex crimes unit will tend to erode your appreciation of macho behavior. My respect for Becky was growing. She had been an omnivorous collector of evidence while riding her investigators to squeeze every drop of relevant facts out of the hospital community. The bulging plastic files of evidence supported the details which she'd accumulated. No doubt her hard drive was filled with relevant data. But to what conclusion?

Everyone in the room looked at me to provide an update, so I figured I'd better jump into the quicksand. "We've got pretty strong evidence that Ashley Dillon is our main suspect, but much of the evidence is circumstantial," I acknowledged. "She's lied to us on several counts, although she may have been covering up on behalf of her career since, like all residents, she was forbidden to get intimate with a younger student."

"I'd say she's lied to us on virtually every major point," Gundy corrected me.

"Of course, deceit does not always mean pre-meditated guilt in capital crimes," I responded lamely.

I tried to explain the significance of Ashley's last-minute phone call to Sandy. But Gundy wasn't backing down. My amiable partner was more pumped up than usual. His arms were flailing, and his face was bathed in crimson.

He angrily itemized the litany of evidence. “Ashley lied about having a romantic relationship with Sandy in the first place. She lied about having refused sleeping with him on his final day, a lie which is confirmed by our DNA swatches.

Ashley claimed to have a quick meal with Dr. Wendy Jamison, yet her whereabouts in the late evening hour were contradicted by Prince Jeff’s sighting of Ashley crossing the street sometime around 11 p.m. From the later cell phone message, it appeared that her wounds were raw, most likely as he had once again dumped her after sleeping with her. While the night-time security guard did not identify her, Barney said he was a bit flaky. He might have arrived late or left his post early.”

Gundy’s voice softened as he moved into the grayer evidence terrain. “By the roommates’ chronology, including Ross Parker, there were sounds, most likely female, coming from downstairs somewhere close to or after 11 p.m. Ashley might be the logical dinner partner, although dinner didn’t arrive until around 11:30 p.m. when she would have most likely been back at the hospital placing her frantic call to Sandy. In that case, I’d name Prince Jeff as the second most likely dinner partner, but he claimed only to have seen her crossing the street without any interaction. Another lie?”

The others in the room nodded. From long experience, they respected Gundy for sorting out facts in a major investigation. He continued like a prosecutor summing up a tenuous case: “Bottom line, we have the uncertain motive of revenge, a chronology that doesn’t give anyone the clear opportunity for murder. As to the murder weapon, how can we find the incriminating syringe in a surgery wing? Good luck.”

I thought Gundy was getting ready to throw in the towel, and then he surprised me. "Here's the good news. We know Dr. Ashley had the skill to deploy a syringe. Her sexual charms could have wooed a drunk Sandy or drugged him into trusting her to give an injection. But if that was the case, why call rather than race back afterward to try and persuade him to wake up and re-connect?"

Becky offered a more nuanced view despite her distaste for the suspects and the victim. "There's no question that Sandy had quite a few enemies, many of them at close range," she reasoned. "You know the old line about keeping your enemies close and your friends closer. Sandy did that very well. We only lack one final piece of evidence…"

"What's that?" I jumped in.

Becky took her time in response, building our attention as the defense attorney would do for the jurors at trial. "There were quite a few potential revenge seekers; we need to be positive that Ashley was the only one in position to deal the final blow," she said. "Our evidence has to stand up in court given that the defense will have no problem casting doubt with the multitude of possible women seeking revenge."

"How does his reputation as a womanizer affect your thinking that the murderer was a woman scorned?" I asked. "A lot of people had motive and opportunity: the surgical boss, the scrub nurse, the sex club owner, the roommates, the jealous neighbor Ralph listening through the walls, the reigning girlfriend, Rosemarie Li."

"All we need is Colonel Mustard with a lead pipe in the library. Barney has a legitimate concern," La-Tanya said, "yet it's time for action."

"It's hard to hate someone who is dead, but in this case, I hate those lying and cheating party boys who take pleasure in treating their women like dartboards," Becky said. "No question, the boy might have deserved to die, but we've still got to be sure we have the right culprit."

"So, whose side are you on, Becky?" La-T queried, her frustration growing.

"I'm not on anybody's side. I'm trying to imagine how defense counsel will whittle away our lack of direct evidence by questioning a circumstantial case. There is no weapon. There's no definitive proof as to who saw him last. Yes, Ashley was wrathful. Yes, she fantasized to others about killing him, especially if she'd just learned she was part of the second game in a lovefest double-header. Nonetheless, there is some contrary evidence that we would have to disclose."

"What's that?" La-T asked in a suspicious tone.

"I've been reviewing the reports from the field that are still coming in," Becky said with a confident sense of knowing she was the most well-informed person in the room.

"There's a lot of support in surgery for Dr. Ashley as a teacher and as a model of professionalism. The deceased casually irritated a lot of people with impertinence and arrogance. Ashley's dedicated her life to medicine and has mentored numerous students. She's sensitive to the female staff and nurse-practitioners who follow up the major medical procedures. The male surgeons like to leave the dirty dishes for the nurses to clean up."

"You're going off course," Gundy snapped. "We're heading into what a great feminist she was. Are we going to upgrade Dr. Ashley as Joan of Arc, or is she a cold-blooded killer? Some of it may be circumstantial, but there's a big heap of conclusive evidence on her plate."

Gundy turned pensive for a moment. "I've got an idea," he said. "Maybe we need to see if we can have Sandy's cell phone analyzed further by forensics now that we've gotten the code. It seems odd that there are so few texts or calls from other women besides his mother and Dr. Ashley. That might shed fresh light if they can recover some of the deletions."

La-T was showing signs of unrest, watching us turn our discussion into a quest for further information. She felt clearly vexed now by our continuing delay in making an arrest.

"How many times do I tell you we need closure on this case?" she glowered, mostly at me. "I've defended your skepticism Barney," she said. "I will give you one more day, then we've *got* to clarify enough evidence to make an arrest. Tell the forensics team they're not going to church tomorrow. We need answers now."

No one was about to challenge the look on her face as she started pounding the table. "It's the old Sherlock Holmes formula. When you eliminate all the other suspects, you're left with only Ashley Dillon or Rosemarie Li having confirmed via DNA as the best prospects. We will interrogate them again and rip out the truth."

La-T paused and panned around the room. Her eyes were deep dark pools, and her jaw was pressed outward like the prow of a ship steaming ahead without a landing site. Her manner said, "no case is perfect, but we need to make our bet and our arrest."

"Let me give you all one final warning," Becky said, displaying her own exasperation.

Perhaps she anticipated stepping into the media spotlight if an arrest occurred and the case would now pass to the DA, where her prosecutor's background would make her a natural spokesperson. "I think we should review the exculpatory factors for each suspect just to sharpen our conclusions. We need to knock out as many suspects as possible."

"Alright let's hear it," La-T agreed with a reluctant sigh.

Becky stopped for a moment, her argument pinpointing the finale when the criminal prosecutor must scale the jury's last-minute rampart of skepticism. "Remember, at trial, the defense doesn't have to prove anything. The burden is on the prosecution. That is why you need to nail down a single perpetrator. I don't see any two female suspects working together here."

"Yes," I pursued Becky with a predatory delight, as if I was the defense counsel in an actual trial. "Wouldn't you say, Detective Muller, that Dr. Dillon's being intimate with Sandy Wainwright might be considered an indication that they had reconciled, thus stripping away the motive for the crime? Perhaps we have it backward, and Ms. Li was the injured party who was seeking revenge."

I looked up very innocently at La-Tanya, who was not charmed one bit by our mock trial. She glared at both of us.

"Perhaps Gundy can help us with this one," Becky said coyly as if she was looking for a life preserver on a badly leaking boat. I had a nagging feeling that I was the one about to drown.

Gundy cleared his throat, flustered by being caught in a divided loyalty situation and unwilling to choose sides.

"I think we can counter the idea that Dr. Ashley and her paramour had reconciled," he said pointedly. "I attended the autopsy, and the evidence was clear that someone had created and nursed a deep-rooted clot up from the thigh and eventually into the lungs."

"On target," La-T took back the controls. "Maybe Ashley had realized that her lover was also playing piggie-in-a- blanket with Ms. Li. So much for reconciliation."

La-T looked at me with boiling eyes that conveyed the message: 'You struck out, Now let's move on."

I refused to back down. "Are you sure? We're going to put the girl behind bars with some holes that might embarrass us later."

"Clam it, Barney. You of all people know how much pressure we're under to make an arrest, and we've got motive, proximity, competency with a murder weapon, a history of lying, and as if that wasn't enough, we have DNA spilling from his body. How much better can you do?"

"Except the DNA is only one-half valid, it's covering one of two potential partners."

"Prepare to make the arrest, Barney. That's an order."

"All right," I knew when to concede. "I'll call Doctor Ashley and tell her to be at home early tomorrow."

I suddenly felt nauseous as my stomach grappled with my conscience. Let Gundy make the arrest.

Sunday, the Tenth Day

52. Dr. Ashley Dillon

Sunday morning

The cops found me in my apartment, waiting for their arrival per Barney's instructions. I had assumed this was to be a short interview, so I had dressed in scrubs, prepared to go to work afterward. Imagine my chagrin that Detective Kazinski had sent his associate, Detective Gundy, along with a second unknown detective who was in my apartment reading me my Miranda rights.

For some reason, I had thought deep down, despite our recent flare-up, that Detective Kazinski 'got' me and was on my side. So much for that.

They hauled me down to a basement holding tank in midtown, where I was being held for further transport.

A fierce male officer appeared and forced my hands behind my back, affixing the stainless-steel handcuffs to my wrists. Tighter and tighter, he clicked until I could not feel my hands anymore. I screamed in pain.

"Oh my God! What are you people doing? I didn't kill anyone! I can't even kill a spider!" I protested.

"Shut up, lady, if you know what's good for you," the officer responded, handing me off to a female cop to frisk me. She patted me up and down as if my green scrubs contained a hidden weapon.

"Where are your clothes?" she asked blankly, devoid of emotion.

"What do you mean?" I replied. "These *are* my clothes. Haven't you ever seen a doctor before?" I was growing more enraged by the police treatment. "It wouldn't hurt if you could find a sweater or jacket in this frigid place."

She ignored me, pretending she hadn't heard my complaint.

In the eyes of the police, I was a murderess. They expected to see blood dripping down from the cuffs. What was happening? Hadn't I tried to prevent Sandy's death? At this moment, I was suddenly unsure. I was hallucinating, maybe withdrawing from Pil's traveling medicine show.

"Those strings need to go," the female officer stated bluntly, swiftly cutting the ties off my scrubs.

"Wait! You can't! I have nothing…" but it was too late. She had cut my scrub pants, and my lazy wash-and-go routine was suddenly exposed to the world. I had been so time-pressured that my slim panties were the only cover over my birthday suit.

I recoiled as everyone present started laughing. Without the use of my hands, I waited, shaking, as the female officer leisurely pulled up my bottoms and re-tied them tightly to my scrub top.

"Put her in a holding tank," the officer said, freeing my wrists and handing me off to another female cop who shoved me into a cold cement room with a single wooden bed and exposed toilet. I was alone. She looked at me with a touch of sympathy and started to walk away.

"Officer, wait. I need a private bathroom! And what about food and water? I'm entitled to at least some basic things."

I sat down, tears filling my eyes. My face tightened while warm urine trickled down my legs. I had soiled myself. What had become of my life? And where was it going? My second year of Residency was eight months away, yet my lust for a younger man had left me in an ugly trap.

"Excuse me!" I railed. "Can I have my phone call, please? I'm sure I get a phone call."

The female officer re-entered the holding cell and silently handed me a phone.

"Make it quick," she said.

Embarrassed to call my parents, I awkwardly tried to dial the only person I felt I could trust at this point, Prince Jeff. My left hand was shaking with anxiety. No one picked up.

"Okay! That's enough." The officer firmly pulled the phone away.

Several hours passed by. I sat huddled in the corner of the cell, wrapping my arm around my legs for warmth, my body trembling from the cold. I was given a tasteless dinner on a tray and a blanket, plus a small Dopp kit with hygiene accessories.

The next morning, I found myself cuffed in a line with eight other prisoners. I had gone from trying to save lives to being a faceless member of a chain gang. We were being transported to NYC's Detention Complex, affectionately dubbed 'The Tombs,' where I could expect an added stay before appearing in front of a judge.

I was now facing an endless line to nowhere, like hogs headed to the slaughterhouse. The Tombs was a cold, dreary crypt, with pink insulation poking through its broken-down walls and chipped yellow paint. The dank corridors reeked of urine and unwashed bodies.

After a long wait, a light flashed on my face as an anonymous officer took photographs. I had already experienced the humiliation of having my mug shots captured at the precinct. Why the hell did they need more photos? No explanation was offered. Shortly thereafter, I was shoved back into the line.

"Stay to the right!" The commanding officer ordered. "Don't even think about moving an inch to the left!" Was there an electric fence? This was neither the time nor the place for my irreverent inner monologue, but a part of me couldn't help noticing the absurdity of this whole experience.

At the Tombs, the women and men were segregated, and I soon found myself in a massive holding cell filled with about fifty other women. We were given moth-eaten gym mats for comfort and moldy cheese sandwiches for nourishment. I had probably only been there for six hours or so, as time ceased to exist, the dead clock on the wall setting a pace of going nowhere.

After another long stretch of time, I waited in an endless line to use the payphone. I was too spoiled to want to try to make this easy on anyone. The rumor had spread that I was in for murder, and the women in line for lesser crimes managed to judge me with disdain.

I longed for the love/hate relationship I had with my parents. Any human connection. What I would not give right now for the meat wagon or my mom's crazy recipes. I had not heard a word from my family. I needed a lawyer to get me released on bond.

Then suddenly, a flashlight peeked through the bars of the holding cell.

"Dr. Dillon?!" A new female warden swung her flashlight around her cell. "Dr. Dillon?"

Startled, I pushed forward out of the crowd and stood at attention.

"Come with me," she said, holding the cell door open.

Monday, the Eleventh Day

53. Barney Kazinski

Monday morning

I awoke in a daze from a wretched dream after thrashing through the night like a child learning to swim. My concern about our limited evidence against Dr. Ashley had unleashed itself in troubled slumber. I was drenched in a sweat that stemmed from an embedded sense of guilt.

I lurched awake and into dutiful cop mode, hurriedly dressing and dashing over to our Command. The office was buzzing in tumult like a bee colony stirred by a nasty intruder.

Captain LaToya sat in her office, serene and detached, with only a touch of the old fire in her eyes. Her door was open.

"What's going on?" I asked. "Something feels out of whack."

"New evidence," she said in a monotone, a voice of self-defeat. "Go down to Forensics."

I raced down the stairs into the central Forensics' atrium. A series of Gundy's photos was being projected on a large screen. There were several identical panoramas of what looked like a living room. Then I realized Becky Muller was clicking through the images, bearing the same resigned look as our boss.

It appeared our case was blowing up.

"You're looking at the living room and dining nook of Rosemarie Li," Becky said. She dragged her red dot pointer across the photos arranged along one wall. "I've been studying Gundy's unique photo collection. While many of the hospital interviews cited Dr. Ashley's overt rage at Sandy, a few classmates had emphasized that Rosemarie Li was nursing her own concealed streak of anger while trying to grieve and return to her normal life."

"So, the current girlfriend was upset," I interjected. "What else is new?" It suddenly dawned on me that Becky was on my side trying to be a white knight who rescued the truth.

"What inspired you to keep digging, Becky?" I asked, in a restrained told-you-so voice.

"I never stopped, Barney. Something did not feel right. If you look carefully," she observed calmly, waving her red dot at the screen. "You'll notice that, in one panorama, Rosemarie's wall has a solid arc of photos. These were taken after your first visit following the murder."

I nodded and waited for her to spring a trap the way that prosecutors love to do.

Becky maneuvered her red dot. "Now, let's look at an identical panorama shot during your second visit to Ms. Li on Friday, day eight of our investigation."

"Looks like a row of lovely white frames to me," I said, not quite getting the message yet. Gundy glared at my attempted humor.

"Your eyes may need one of Pil's stimulants so you can wake up," Becky said, and she wasn't smiling.

"Let's not argue over who was asleep at the switch," I murmured just loud enough for her ears. She ignored me.

"Look more carefully at the second batch of photos." She slowly panned the line of frames with the pointer and then stopped abruptly. "What do you see, gentlemen?"

There was a blank space where a picture frame had clearly been removed. The space had a dark rim, but inside, it was lighter than the surrounding wall.

"OK," I get it. Do we have any idea what was removed?"

"We do," Becky replied. Gundy sat quietly, his face alert to her follow-up.

"Here is what we're looking for—the missing frame," Becky said. She clicked and projected a framed photo of a young man and a young woman sitting in front of an old car, probably a second-hand Chevy parked behind them. They had a dusty but happy look, their arms around each other. Somehow, we had missed this photo on our first visit.

"The young woman is Rosemarie," I observed. "I can't tell the male."

"Our very own Prince Jeff," Gundy said. "This was probably taken in front of a modest apartment building where Ms. Li had been lodging over the summer while she awaited her scholarship to kick in. There is some kind of graffiti near the door behind where they are sitting. They look comfortable, like longtime friends. Or they could have been lovers."

"A very nice piece of deduction," I said. "Is this conclusive? They became pals. He came to see her. She hadn't met Sandy yet. They were both outsiders, a potential romance…"

"He was working as a research assistant for Dr. Maura Davis over the summer," Becky said. "She was doing research for the dean's office. They could have well been thrown together."

Then she added: "Got one more photo," and clicked again. "This is a picture of a textbook that was on the table next to Rosemarie Li's desk. Gundy found this one buried in his photos. I don't know how he managed to recall the shot."

"This is the same textbook that I recently saw in the bathroom of Prince Jeff's apartment," Gundy jumped in. "My photo clearly shows the text involved 'Thoracic Pathology.' which describes diseases of and cures for the lung and heart. Prince Jeff told us the textbook belonged to Wendy, but that could be a false alibi."

Becky now had our full attention. "Presuming that Jeff needed some expertise in blocking the pulmonary system, he originally had turned to Rosemarie to help him understand the factors involved in a lung clot," she said. "There was a study guide to the textbook in her pile of books that Gundy originally photographed. She might have worried why Jeff was so interested in lung clots and backed off. She knew that Sandy was having clot issues as his father had been sidelined by them from pursuing an athletic career. And this textbook was complex and aimed at doctors and older students. Thus, why was Prince Jeff so interested in the subject?"

Gundy picked up the discussion. "Jeff had then turned to Dr. Jamison, a pediatric physician who was studying at an advanced level in order to switch specialties. She could help Jeff, although it's likely she thought his interest in clots was legitimate, part of his studies and not based on murderous intent."

Gundy continued, "All we know is Jeff was logically the only person who had transported the actual textbook from Rosemarie's to his own apartment. That was prior to Sandy's death. We'll have to ask Wendy for details of the chronology and get some guidance on the content."

"What do you think Barney?" Gundy rarely consulted with me unless he had concerns about the evidence.

"This all seems pretty circumstantial to me," I said. "We have no actual proof of Prince Jeff's intent, nor do we know what role the women might have played in helping him, or whether they knew what he was planning."

I looked at Gundy, who had that devilish look when he felt he had nailed the final piece of evidence necessary to prevail.

"You're right Barney," he said, reading my mind. "There's one more piece to this puzzle. Becky, please jump in." The two of them had suddenly become a tightly knit duo and as lead detective, I felt a bit left out.

Becky was unruffled and eagerly pursuing their chain of logic. "We now know that Jeff had been involved in helping Dr. Davis over the summer. I went back and checked the Morbidity cases that she might have been involved in and it turned out there was one in the fall where a deep vein clot had formed and traveled into the lung, resulting in the death of a woman who seemed to have a Yoga neck issue. The case was originally reported as a nicked artery that had bled out, but an autopsy showed a clot had formed and forced the entire circulatory system to close down. Good so far?"

I nodded,

"Let me continue," she said. "Jeff hadn't been at the surgery but from Maura Davis's description, he knew if he could re-create the clot, he would be able to execute a murder that would be hard to pin on him since he didn't perform surgery and there would be someone else handling the logistics. He'd also have Dr. Davis vouching that he was involved in her surgery well after midnight. The one thing we don't know is who helped him as he would not have had time or experience to do this terrible deed by himself. That brings us back to the women, and we need to figure out who was the other person having dinner with Sandy on the night of his death."

"For starters," Gundy said, "we have a warrant to search Jeff's apartment, and Wendy's if necessary. We can go pick up the textbook if you like. We'll see if there are any markings inside that might indicate he was the one using it."

"Let's head back to the Prince's palace." Gundy was pushing us to move swiftly as if we were fishermen reeling in a suspect before he could slip the hook.

"Agreed," I replied. "Where does Dr. Ashley fit in? You clearly realize we may have made a false arrest. Come on, please join us, Becky."

We arrived over on Park Avenue in twenty minutes, sirens blazing, Gundy swerving, bystanders scampering to safety. Blowing past the doorman, our shields raised as if they were weapons, we stormed the elevator and rode up to the Prince's aerie.

A flustered Dr. Wendy Jamison responded to our pounding on the door. "Oh hi, detectives. Three of you? Are you looking for Geoffrey? He isn't home."

"Well, yes. We are looking for…"

"Hey, Barney, Becky! Check this out over here." It was Gundy walking toward us with the red Thoracic textbook in tow. He'd remembered to put on gloves.

"Dr. Wendy Jamison. Your boyfriend mentioned that this textbook is yours. Can you confirm that for us?"

"Um, no. This book's not mine. Geoffrey was using it for reference of some sort for his upcoming med boards. Why would he say it's mine?" Gundy opened the book and held up Wendy's name etched in blue ink.

"Dr. Jamison, are you sure you didn't pass this textbook to Prince Jeff, and he, in turn, might have shared it with Ms. Rosemarie Li before bringing it back here?" I asked.

"I, I… no, I mean. I had no idea," she responded, now sensing something was up and searching to distance herself. "That's not my handwriting," she declared.

"You did presumably know that Ms. Li and your pal Jeff had a brief fling going back when they first arrived in New York?"

"I vaguely knew they were friends before Sandy became involved with her."

"What else might you have known, doctor?" I provoked her. "Where was Prince Jeff on the night of the murder?"

"He was at the hospital in surgery with Dr. Davis! He returned here long after midnight. I think that's been well established with your colleagues." Wendy's face was flushed.

"Look what we've got here." Gundy was flipping through the textbook, landing on a heavily highlighted chapter.

"What is it?" Becky was closely observing every part of this drama.

"Looks like a possible blueprint. There's a chapter on pulmonary embolisms, with a sidebar on how air can cause them in legitimate surgical situations. There's plenty of yellow highlighting and even a schematic of a male thigh where a deep tissue embolism might form and break off and travel in veins northward. It's here drawn to scale and prominently displays the underlying circulatory vessels."

Wendy turned and ran to the bathroom and slammed the door. I walked over to the door and heard what sounded like a mixture of retching and crying.

"You okay, doctor?" I knocked gently. Did this woman have any idea who her bedmate was? Or was she a co-conspirator?

She emerged from the bathroom, mascara running down her face, legs wavering, unsteady balance. She seemed on the verge of collapse. Gundy grabbed her arm. "Come on, Dr. Jamison. Let's bring you down to the station, where you can provide a few more details. Meanwhile, we'll find Prince

Geoffrey Laird and Ms. Rosemary Li and figure out who was doing what to whom."

Gundy looked at me with a touch of sadness. "Maybe it's truly over."

"Wait a sec, hold your horses." Wendy had regained her composure. "I told you Prince Jeff was with me well into the night. I don't know why he was using the book. It was probably in the bathroom for his entrance exams."

"All right, Dr. Jamison." Gundy's face showed the usual skepticism when watching witnesses alter their stories. "You've got a few questions to clear up. I'll read your rights."

54. Dr. Ashley Dillon

Later Monday morning

I was sitting in a waiting area, not quite sure what was happening.

I could not try to contemplate my terrifying future, which might include jail time as an accomplice to murder. I hoped for mercy since I hadn't plunged the syringe into his body. However, my innocence only went so far. I had left Sandy on the fateful night, tired and sedated, while his door was open for the real killer.

I hated life. I hated my parents. I hated myself. Ultimately, I hated Sandy for making me a reluctant accomplice to murder.

The devil was in the details, as they say. The irony was that I had started to enjoy my medical career if only the doctors would be as empathetic to me as they pretended to be to their patients. I cared about their treatments. I wanted to do no harm and cure them. Why hadn't I maintained an uncomplicated life without being drawn into Sandy's vortex?

Suddenly, a tall figure in a trench coat appeared like a mirage in the desert.

"Detective?" I asked, squinting to make sure my eyes weren't deceiving me.

"Yes, Dr. Ashley. It's me, Detective Kazinski."

"What are you doing here?"

"I'm here to take you home," he said softly. It was the first civil exchange that I'd had with the police in days.

"What is this? Am I living in an afterlife?" The beginnings of a panic attack took hold. I wanted to pinch my skin to be sure I wasn't dreaming, although my hands and wrists were blistered.

"No, Dr. Ashley. You're not dead. There's been a mistake. You're free, or at least free for now." The detective sounded less than decisive.

"Free? No trial? No lawyers? I'm confused." I did not trust what was happening.

"Come on. Let's go. There will be some legal proceedings later. For now, on the prosecutor's say-so, you've been cleared by the court to wear an ankle monitor. The police and the Manhattan DA's office will be watching you, but at least you're out of this shithole."

The CO had brought a tray of personal effects and my suitcase. He affixed the monitor tightly around my ankle. I signed some release forms and prepared to leave with one stipulation.

"Wait! I mean, yes, let me out of here, but why on earth would I go *anywhere* with *you*?"

"Save it for the car, doctor." He told me to follow, and I walked robotically with him outside. The sun was blinding me. I got into his car without a further word.

"You want to tell me where I'm going to take you?" he asked.

"Just about two blocks north of Hillside, same street, back to my apartment."

I remained quiet, trying to make sense of what was transpiring. Finally, I broke my silence.

"So, do you want to tell me what this is all about?"

"We haven't concluded this case, and you're still not completely off the hook. We've found some loose ends requiring investigation," he said. "In fact, we may have more questions for you."

"Questions?! For me? So, you lock up an innocent woman, demolish her life, and you still have more questions? No thank you, detective."

"No more questioning today, but please be careful with your words. I'm still a cop, and you're still a person of interest."

"Tell me what really happened. You screwed up, picked the wrong horse," I said.

"Look, I understand that you are upset Ashley, but at least you are out of there now."

"Dr. Dillon is my official name. I was completely free before you came along. Now, what am I supposed to do? I've lost my job, my family, my friends, my reputation! How am I going to pay my rent? You have an answer for that, detective?"

We rode silently until we arrived at our destination. Barney stopped and pulled a couple of twenty-dollar bills out of his wallet and handed them to me.

"What is this for?"

"Consider it the down payment for the price of freedom. Go get yourself something to eat at your favorite meat wagon. You're skin and bones, Doctor. We may have overreacted, but you are still culpable, especially when it came to telling the truth."

Suddenly, I felt anger and sadness mixing so deeply that no tears could wash them away. "Let me assure you, Sandy did not deserve to die, and even if he did, I was certainly not the one who wanted to end his life."

Barney walked around the car to open the door.

"I'm going to need time to digest all of this. Thanks for the ride," I said. "You can keep your cash." I threw the money back through the open door as I got out of the car.

I walked hesitantly, almost blindly, towards the foreign-looking structure that I suddenly realized was my apartment building.

A few months later

55. Rebecca (Becky) Muller

Sorting out the case

I should have listened to my own advice and realized that we still didn't have sufficient evidence to convict the perpetrators of Sandy's murder. Furthermore, at the District Attorney's urging, I volunteered to put on my prosecutorial hat and go back in the ring.

There is an old courthouse adage that lawyers "have a fool for a client" when representing themselves with direct emotional involvement in a case.

That warning applied to me in many ways. While I prided myself on objectivity as a prosecutor, somehow this set of defendants had rattled my emotional balance. My colleagues were also thrown off guard. Our collective pride in hastily dispatching controversial cases proved to be our downfall. Given the pressure from the downtown bosses, amplified by Captain Lawson, we were "encouraged" to assemble the evidence without proper preparation, and things blew up in our faces.

Miscalculation number one: after all the focus on the women in Sandy's life, it had dawned on us that much of the criminal intent was inspired by Prince Geoffrey. Thus, we decided to begin by targeting him as the linchpin of our case, putting off the actions of the women for subsequent prosecution. We believed that in their fury, all three might have wanted to throw him under the bus to save their own necks. That proved to be a mistake, as we should have realized in our investigation. Our error became evident in the first phase of discovery.

Prince Jeff had carefully wooed Ashley, Rosemarie, and Wendy. They had no intention of becoming snitches. Their very skillful defense lawyer knew they had us if they stuck together in their alibis. Without their support and testimony, we had no one to place Jeff in Sandy's room, and as a surgical nurse, it was dubious that working alone while assisting Dr. Davis in her surgery, he could have administered the lethal dosage of air that killed Sandy.

Miscalculation number two: we thought that regardless of the open questions, there was sufficient evidence of Geoffrey resenting Sandy and seeking to replace him as the romantic leader of the pack. This would provide motive even without the murder weapon or the psychological evidence of intent to commit murder. We were too impressed with all the hard work we'd done, and blind to the holes in our logic.

Finally, miscalculation number three: we failed to anticipate just how committed—and persuasive—Dr. Maura Davis would be while defending nurse Jeff.. Her love and respect for the defendant turned out to provide a powerful, personal endorsement of his character that had some of the jurors dabbing their eyes. Geoffrey, for her, was like an only child that she would never have on her own. Her emotional defense helped convince the jury to let him slide out of our net.

Enough excuses except for the final and totally unexpected blow.

From day one, the grieving Wainwright family was concerned that the prosecution's conspiratorial theory of revenge would permanently sully "their" boy's reputation and throw mud on their philanthropic activities. Starting with the autopsy, they had tried to snatch the body and bury him in California as an "innocent child" who bore no responsibility for his death.

This desire for secrecy surfaced during our final prep for Prince Geoffrey's trial and became a huge roadblock going forward. While they wanted the perpetrators brought to justice, the Wainwright family now sought to have the case handled discreetly, which meant preferably a plea bargain that could be sealed. Sandy's parents knew the media hysteria meant that a Manhattan trial would become a public spectacle. His sexual reputation and penchant for alcohol and drugs would be the bedrock of the defense's case, showing that Sandy's wild behavior had enticed the others, especially the women he rejected, into criminality.

To make matters worse, the family confirmed it was planning to erect a Sherman "Sandy" Wainwright hospital at Hillside devoted to childhood diseases. The donors wanted Wendy Jamison to be the director of this new institution due to her ongoing, empathetic experience with their son.

I knew we were in trouble, starting with Doctor Jamison, who already had a very solid case for innocence. She was living with Geoffrey and supported Maura Davis's assertion that he was in surgery long past the time of the crime and didn't return home until well past midnight.

That left us with Ashley and Rosemarie. We believed Jeff had initially targeted them to help him, choosing the two women he felt were most resentful and jealous of Sandy's duplicity. Jeff also had pursued the earlier summer relationship with Rosemarie. However, both women were still in love with the victim and had sex with him on what was, in Jeff's plan, to be Sandy's last day.

The two women had decided out of an inexplicable loyalty not to go through with the final plan. We were left with the barebones argument that Prince Geoffrey was still out of his mind with jealousy towards Sandy and had decided to go it alone, using Wendy only as an unsuspecting prop by his use of a textbook. However, Jeff's consulting with a "textbook" seemed logical to the jury as preparation for exams, not as a manual for murder.

Dr. Post was another lost cause. His scans and autopsy reinforced the likelihood that there might have been foul play, including possible assisted suicide via clot formation. The family again persevered that this was very speculative concerning the way he died. Meanwhile, the city leaders who had been so anxious for a conviction now reversed course and argued we should not jeopardize the children's facility named in Sandy's honor, which the family was prepared to fund and build.

We tried a gentle prosecution, but the three women came across as victims of the pressures of med school. Rosemarie denied any complicity in Sandy's death. Ashley denied it, and Wendy denied it. Their allegiance was now to Geoffrey, and they stuck to their collective alibis. Sandy's roommates did the same thing.

In the end, we decided to withdraw charges and promised further investigation for the benefit of saving face with Police Plaza downtown. The TV legal analysts weren't buying our excuses and used their "Breaking News" segments to expose our incompetence.

At that point, I, Becky Muller, considered handing in my resignation.

Case closed. It was lost.

Or was it? Out of frustration and stubbornly refusing to accept defeat, I followed La-Tanya's advice and took a break before one final re-winding of the entire investigation. Reviewing the possible suspects who might have been guilty of the murder, I went through a process of elimination. The roommates had managed to present strong alibis; Ross Parker was covered by his roommate Hector. Why would he have called in the death when he could have claimed he went to sleep? There was Pil, but he was doing business in the wee hours at a nearby bar on the fateful night, according to several witnesses. The ever-annoying Ralph had been time-stamped in the chat room with Candy from eleven to after 1:30 a.m. He could have run up to Sandy's room, but how would he have known when his hated rival was semi-conscious?

Thus, it looked as if we had reached a dead end. I still wasn't totally ready to give up, and only stubborn perseverance reaped an unexpected reward. I walked over to the Mandarin restaurant to talk to the deliveryman as part of re-tracing all possible steps. The owner checked his records of who was making the final shift deliveries on the night of the murder. Yes, his delivery boy, his son Kai, had taken over the dinner before midnight, and two gentlemen were getting ready to eat when he left.

But there was an error in the delivery. The Chicken Lo Mein, Sandy's favorite side dish, had been omitted. Kai promised to go back and get it after he completed two other deliveries. When he returned and walked in, having found the door unlocked, one of the gentlemen, now in a blue scrub outfit, was administering a needle to his customer 'Mr. Sandy,' to help him sleep. "He call it sedative," the owner Mr. Wu reported.

And why hadn't this information been given to the police? "We afraid to get involved with the police, hurt our business," the owner explained. I knew this was a code for an immigrant without papers.

I didn't care about illegal immigration right now.

What bothered me was who the second diner, most likely a male, might be. Since Prince Geoffrey was tied up in surgery, I wanted to review all possibilities one last time.

I laid out Gundy's photos of as many people as possible who might have been a co-conspirator.

Kai, the deliveryman, spent an agonizing amount of time looking at the portfolio spread before him. I feared he was not going to be able to confirm the second instigator. After studying the photos until I was ready to give up, he picked up one of Gundy's black-and-white prints and, nodding slowly, handed it to me.

Suddenly, everything clicked into place. Gundy and I left the premises knowing what we should have realized all along.

The Final Piece

56. Barney Kazinski & Becky Muller

Of course, we should have known.

It was decided that Becky and I would make the final arrest. After months of frustration, we yearned for closure. I picked her up at our Command Center and drove to the hospital, finding a parking spot near the student dorm. An arrest was standard procedure in my line of work, and yet I felt a sense of nostalgia as we walked past security and took the elevator up to the 5th floor for what would be the last time. We had called ahead and asked the roommates to assemble in their living room, but only Ross Parker was sitting there looking very glum.

"Read me my rights," he said sadly, holding out his wrists to be handcuffed.

"How did you know?" I asked.

"When I heard that Detective Muller was questioning the owner of the restaurant, I knew it wouldn't be long."

Confronted with this confession, Prince Geoffrey tried to claim that he was helping his friend Sandy take a sedative and he didn't have the training to administer it by injection.

But Ross had wisely decided to take a plea and testify on our side; he had a flawless memory that unraveled the whole plot. In retrospect, Ross had been the weakest link in the roommates' chain of evidence all along. On his roomie Hector's advice, he had lied about going bowling and then lied again about his actions after 11 p.m. To save his ass, and secure a milder sentence, he told the truth for once. He had injected the air into Sandy's body. But he argued persuasively that Prince Geoffrey had been at the center of the conspiracy. Furthermore, given Sandy's family history of clots, the instant susceptibility to a Pulmonary Embolism might not have been completely Ross's fault.

We now had leverage on our British Prince. Dr. Davis be damned. I threatened Geoffrey's lawyer that he could face a trial now and possibly a charge of murder in the first degree. On the advice of counsel, Prince Geoffrey Laird decided to take a lower manslaughter plea (including brief prison time) and Ross would plead to a reduced charge of practicing medicine without a proper license.

None of these 'plea bargains' pleased the media, nor our police bosses. But as usual, money talks, and, in this case, civic philanthropic money talked even louder.

The Wainwright family was pleased and relieved by the avoidance of a trial and made generous pledges to the hospital endowment to sponsor post-doctoral research facilities for arcane adult diseases.

Thus, we had a partial victory snatched from the embarrassment of defeat! The family shipped their son home, and the New York City Mayor got front-page coverage celebrating the funding for the Sherman Wainwright Children's Hospital.

The police department and local officials chimed in about the "excellent addition" to the city's health arsenal. All the pressure for vengeance had finally subsided, as the media recognized what the new state-of-the-art hospital would mean for parents and children alike.

La-Tanya Lawson and her team got special recognition and a beautiful medallion at a dinner attended by the family, city officials, and all the brass from One Police Plaza.

As for Ashley, her life and career were badly tarnished, at least in the short term. She was dismissed by Maura Davis for her role in violating Hillside's rules by "intimate association" with a med student, and she struggled to get another position domestically.

Ashley discovered there was a need for surgeons in Guatemala. At the dean's request, Dr. Davis recommended her for a job there and promised to consider bringing her back in two years. Rosemarie got more favorable treatment; as a medical student, her only failing had been falling in love. She would take a gap year back on the farm in Iowa. Meanwhile, Wendy would complete her advanced education in pediatrics while awaiting her new position once the Wainwright Hospital was constructed.

Conclusion

57. Barney Kazinski

What might have been…

Dr. Ashley Dillion had departed quickly for Central America with a terse goodbye to her parents. Incredibly, within a few days, I received an oversized postcard, stamped from Guatemala, displaying a backdrop of recently discovered Mayan ruins. The card said simply, "Yearning for a meat pie. Any chance you could deliver one down here?"

It was signed with a flowery "A." I began immediately starting to book tickets to the Caribbean. Still, I had a few other items to take care of, including an eternity's worth of overdue follow-ups for cases that I had ignored and needed to transfer to others. Gundy was very helpful in sharing more of the caseload.

As I sat in my office, entering my notes, I reflected on the conundrum of Sandy's death: what *might* have been and what *should* have been.

He had a golden life laid out ahead of him, and yet he had boozed, drugged, and womanized it away. He was probably a very decent young man, with a fatal flaw of always thinking the grass was greener elsewhere and thus stringing women and roommates along to the point of anger and revenge.

Rosemarie and Ashley loved too much without seeing the warning signs of a man unwilling to settle down. Their desperation could have turned heartbreak into further tragedy. But luckily for them, there was no evidence or inclination to force them to trial per the family's wishes.

As for Ralph Gruber, he was probably still watching 'his' Candy and hoping he could find a human being who would reciprocate real love in the flesh.

La-Tanya had settled back in as Captain of our crew and made peace with One Police Plaza. After Becky's success in concluding the case, we celebrated at the bar down the block, where Mickey poured his most expensive champagne gratis in our honor.

Miss Liz Shannon was heading for her law degree and managed to find an intern's job with the Manhattan D.A.'s office. I am sure a lot of her former clients were popping valiums these days.

As for me, I had purchased my plane tickets for a vacation, and maybe a new life could open up. I could sure use it. I had the postcard from Guatemala posted on my bathroom mirror.

Barney Kazinski: Epilogue

I hopped aboard the flight and watched a couple of movies so that I wouldn't have to think about my personal litany of regrets. You do not get a mulligan in life, a replay of an errant shot, the way you do in golf. Now in metaphorical terms, I wanted to strike the ball properly the first time.

We landed in bright blue sunshine, which I hoped would be an omen that love was at hand. This was the moment I had craved, and yet I wandered almost dizzily through the airport down to the baggage claim.

Then she came into view, a red-haired angel amidst a crowd of fuzzy faces. How could I rise to the moment after so many years of neglect?

We both rushed towards each other and pressed together in a heart-stopping hug. "Dad," she said softly, "welcome to LA. It's been a while." Finally, we broke free. I dug out a wrinkled flight envelope from my pocket. "Hand me your suitcase, Sarah, and we're good to go, headed for the Costa Grande of Guerrero in Mexico. I hear the fishing is pretty good with plenty of time for hanging out real nice and slow. We've got a lot to catch up on."

THE END

Acknowledgements

The old adage is so true: "It takes a village." In my 60+ years involved in print or digital publishing, I've been very fortunate to work with so many talented writers and colleagues. My sweet spot has always been in the mystery or thriller vein, going back as a child to the Hardy Boys.

And in the 1980s, our company (Warner Books) entered a partnership with Otto Penzler, whose Mysterious Press has been legendary for aspiring and established writers. We had a number of successes together, most memorably involving the Demon Dog of American literature, James Ellroy, whose body of work including "L.A. Confidential" was a definite highlight in our careers.

It was inevitable that having worked with and published so many fine authors I'd have to try, as I turn 80, taking a shot (so to speak) at a mystery novel. At the risk of selecting a few special adult suspense novelists, I'd name Nelson DeMille, James Patterson, David Baldacci, Michael Connelly, Brad Meltzer, Sandra Brown, Donald Westlake, and Scott Turow as personal favorites because we worked on multiple titles together.

I won the lottery for the greatest boss ever in William "Bill" Sarnoff, our chairman from a storied communications family. Bill always had our back, in good times and less good times. To say he's a mensch is a gross understatement. By coincidence, our birthdays are fifteen years and one day apart. I'll be 80 in 2024, he'll be 95 and he's still got his fastball and always grabs the check at our lunches! He's also a very generous contributor to causes for those in need.

When it comes to important business clients and friends, I'd put Nicholas Delbanco and his spouse, Elena at the top of the list. He's a man who gets up every day and writes brilliantly, with a discipline that I haven't quite mastered. He's also a very good literary guide since he built the University of Michigan MFA program in prose and poetry, aided in great part by the generosity of the late Sam Zell and his widow, Helen.

Nick's spouse, Elena is also a writer and scholar who cares deeply about the state of our world, along with her two daughters and five female grandchildren! (The sons-in-law don't seem to be complaining about all this feminine talent in their midst.)

I've also spent many glorious and informative breakfasts with Wayne Kabak and his wife, Marsha Berkowitz at Barney Greengrass, the iconic home-style Jewish restaurant. I first met Wayne when he was an agent and lawyer who read and fought (gently) almost every bloody clause in our author contract, but now we can just be friends. Marsha, like her husband, loves theater and the Yankees, so we have much to talk about since I'm a native Chicagoan for whom the Yankees were the villains when I grew up.

Another thoughtful friend is Roger Cooper, a veteran publisher who loves to argue about politics. We know how to have spirited discussion starting at breakfast and continuing through the day by text, all of which I relish.

I would also cite Steve Potash, the head of Overdrive, a company that has been a pioneer and leader in bringing digital education and entertainment to our world. He's been a close advisor and friend.

I must thank several people who have been important in completing the book. For the medical parts, I was lucky to have Dr. Rachel Wellner, an oncologist, as an early partner. Her creative imagination was responsible for some of the medical plot points and character development in this book.

Dr. Mark Klein, a Washington D.C. radiologist and author was very helpful in showing me X-rays of the heart/lung relationship. He's also been a counselor in the art of taking the broader aerial view in life, which can calm my tempestuous nature.

There are three books that contributed to my limited medical knowledge: "Medusa's Clot: The Ill-Humor of Pulmonary Embolism" by Dr. Michael D. Helzner; "Cardiac Failure Explained" by Dr. Warrick Bishop; and "What the Dead Know" by Barbara Butcher, the leading medico-legal investigator over 23 years for the New York City Medical Examiner's office.

On the police front, I was aided by two retired detectives who happen to be married. David Fitzpatrick and his wife Virginia made a number of helpful editorial suggestions.

I must give credit to a few longtime colleagues. At Time-Warner Books, Maureen Egen was our President and editorial director who plucked books off agents' shelves (such as "The Bridges of Madison County") and turned them into bestsellers. Mel Parker was a brilliant paperback director who helped find and developed many hardcover authors such as Jim Patterson and gave their titles new life in paperback.

Jamie Raab had great female intuition as a publisher and senior editor, including the nurturing of Nicholas Sparks and his huge bestseller, "The Notebook." And the late, great Rick Wolff was a sports and business guru who discovered "Rich Dad, Poor Dad," a financial classic. He was also a fun partner for sporting events. His daughter Samantha has carried on the sports tradition as a true maize-and-blue Michigan fan!

On the business side, one of our best executives was Tom Maciag, the finance director who countered, with great sensitivity, our enthusiasm for buying books deploying the painful reality of the P&L spread sheet.

I've also been fortunate to have some great assistants who have kept me on track. They include Letty Ferrando, Donna Nolan, and Judi Cuervo.

I have a few social network friends, mostly for their inspiration and, for the daily joy of on-line friendship. Among them are my former roommates in Ann Arbor, Tom Weinberg, James Reinish, and Jack Meyer, and an ex-fraternity brother named James Klein.

Two former partners in the literary agenting field, Meg Thompson and Susanna Einstein taught me a great deal about how to find and cultivate talented authors.

I have enjoyed numerous meals and discussions over the years with a lot of very smart and helpful friends from the publishing or related creative industries, including Bill Shinker, Bob Miller, Jane Dystel, Victoria Skurnick, Kelly Leonard, Sharon Washington, Victoria Eastmond, Linda Duggins, Kathy Johnson, Kate Bohner, Karen Torres, Martha Otis,.Cathy Redlich, Carol Ross, Vinita Bhatia, Karen Kelly, Carol Van Den Hende, Zibby Owens, Aaron

Priest, Kathy Eldon, Jeff Rosen, Daniel Rosen, Andrew Rosen, Jon Fine, Dr. Sherman Silber and his wife Joan and their brilliant son Joe Silber, Dennis Krieger and Steve Hoffman. I'm also very indebted to my main physician (and best literary reader) Dr. Richard Stern and his wife Joan. And I must pay homage to the 'nutritional' support from the #1 hot dog purveyor in Manhattan, Billy at 93rd and Central Park West.

I want to thank John Ingram and Phil Ollila of the Ingram Book Company for their support over the years and introducing me to Jeff Bezos and Jeff Belle of Amazon.com who were very important in the early years of introducing our company to the world of digital publishing.

I also have great nostalgic fondness for David Naggar at Amazon who was our baby-sitter and employee for a few years before becoming a publishing star.

Finally, I must do a call-out for my longest relationship (over 25 years) with an author, Mona Golabek. Her book, "The Children of Willesden Lane," has become a classic in the Holocaust field which has reached millions of students and teachers with the inspiring story of her 14-year-old mother, Lisa, becoming a concert pianist in London while bombs were bursting overhead.

Let me emphasize that none of the people above is responsible for errors of facts or interpretations on my part. This is a work of fiction, and all of the fictional situations and characters are totally made up with no reference to actual persons, living or dead, or to the hospital or medical examiner's office that is described in the novel.

This is NOT a procedural detective novel in the meticulous way that many experts write detective fiction.

This is primarily a work of imagination and hopefully the reader will view it in that way.

This is a self-published work. I turned the manuscript over to a talented team at "Base Camp" in Houston called the Amazon Publishing Agency which is not part of Amazon.com. Our project manager, Solomon Elias has been in constant communication to make sure we get a satisfactory publishing experience. This group is responsible for formatting this book and helping to distribute it in digital and printed markets.

We have a dynamic two-woman team in the marketing and publicity arena. Sarah Hill and Renske Dilven of Bobi Media in Manhattan are our Social Network gurus. I'm very grateful to my friend and publishing expert Michael Friedman for bringing the women of Bobi Media to my attention. Hopefully, many of our targeted readers will view videos and other promotions and be the earliest reviewers of **Death in a White Coat** starting in mid-May, 2024 when we launch.

And last, the final words which are truly first in importance. This novel has been a multi-year undertaking. My impatient family—from my spouse to children to grandchildren—has repeatedly wondered if this book was actually going to emerge after more than a dozen drafts. The answer is yes at last, and I hope everyone feels it's been worth the effort. For me it’s been a true labor of love.

I am grateful to you all for your concern and suggestions. I have come to appreciate over 80 years that family is everything. I first met my spouse, Barbara as a freshman at the University of Michigan during a parents’ weekend in 1962. When we first saw this gorgeous redhead in a camel’s hair coat dashing across a restaurant where we were sitting, my mother said, "That's the girl you should marry." Fortunately, we had mutual friends and I tracked Barbara down. No question: mama knew best!

I hope you enjoy this book. Now I understand how all our authors over the years have felt about releasing their babies into the world. Our readers are the judges and juries in the end.

Larry Kirshbaum

May, 2024

About the Author

Larry Kirshbaum has had a long, successful career with the printed (and now digital) word.

Starting in high school in Chicago as editor of the Francis Parker weekly newspaper, he then majored in English at the University of Michigan, graduating in 1966.

As a senior, he became Managing Editor of *The Michigan Daily,* a student newspaper published six times a week.

He married a former classmate, Barbara Feder in 1967 and started a journalistic career at Newsweek Magazine. He co-wrote a book on student protest with Roger Rapoport called, *"Is the Library Burning?"* published in 1970 by Random House. Thereafter, he migrated into book publishing and spent more than 30 years at the Time Warner Book Group, becoming CEO in 1997.

He and Barbara live in Manhattan with their children and grandchildren nearby. They will celebrate 57 years of marriage and their 80th birthdays in 2024.

Printed in the USA
CPSIA information can be obtained
at www.ICGtesting.com
CBHW031307300824
13925CB00028B/100

9 781917 281416